LAST RAYS
OF
DAYLIGHT

a Paul Dodge Novel

LAST RAYS
OF
DAYLIGHT

a Paul Dodge Novel

CHRISTOPHER FLORY

Light Messages
Torchflame Books

Durham, NC

Copyright © 2022 Christopher Flory

Last Rays of Daylight: a Paul Dodge Novel
Christopher Flory
christopherflorybooks.com
cmflory@christopherflorybooks.com

Published 2022, by Torchflame Books
an Imprint of Light Messages
www.lightmessages.com
Durham, NC 27713 USA
SAN: 920-9298

Paperback ISBN: 978-1-61153-459-7
E-book ISBN: 978-1-61153-460-3
Library of Congress Control Number: 2021925584

For Bob,
a kind, generous man,
willing to help anyone
in time of need.

Thank you for always being there for me.
I miss you most of all.

CHAPTER 1

THE TEMPERATURE ROSE to over a hundred degrees. Moisture drained from her petite body, ounce by ounce, and her mouth felt like it was stuffed with a wad of cotton. With little room for movement inside the crate, she turned her head from side to side and moved her arms up, down, left, right. Pressed her hands against the top of the container, her wrists bending back until reaching their physical limits.

It was no use. She wasn't strong enough, or the lid was too heavy. Or both.

As her head cleared, she realized she needed to do all she could to keep her muscles from cramping.

She tried to recall how she got into the crate, dimly remembering crying out as rough hands squeezed her arms, pressing them to her sides. And another, clamped against her mouth, muffling any noise trying to escape. Next, the sharp pain of a needle stabbing into her thigh. Time seemed to stop. She had no way of knowing how long she had been out. Hours could have passed. Days, even.

She noticed the men had taken her phone and her watch. They stole her jewelry, school ID, even her shoes. The pain in her leg was unbearable, despite the drugs. She passed out again.

When she awoke the second time, her head pounded and ears rang. Her vision was blurry, and her body had just enough energy to hold her head up and peek through the air hole. Water splashed in through the hole as soon as her face was an inch away, wetting her eye enough to clear her vision for a few minutes.

She realized her ears weren't ringing. It was the sound of wind gusting over the container. The noise reminded her of a freight train that used to pass by her house. It vibrated the crate, pushing and pulling, shifting her from side to side, while water continued to splash in through the small air hole.

The noise and shaking stopped. A faint light penetrated the darkness through the air hole and lit her face. It was eerily silent outside except for a groaning sound from above her, where she couldn't see. The noise sounded like old metal hinges. Or a teeter-totter as its riders rocked, one side up, then down, over and over until deafening scraping replaced that sound.

Metal on metal.

Something heavy slipped, or was pushed, off something else made of metal.

Seconds passed. The light from the air hole extinguished as she felt the top of the container crash in on her. The pressure was unbearable. She couldn't move. Tears ran down her cheeks as her lungs sucked in one last gasp of air before her body went limp and her eyes closed for the last time.

———

As the sun sank into the horizon, it cast a shadow over the starboard bow of *Kelly's Dream*. The last rays of tropical sunlight danced, sparkling like blue diamonds on the tops of the waves.

Dodge leaned against the stern railing as the boat gently rocked in Long Bay's waters just outside Charlotte Amalie in the US Virgin Islands. He held a lime margarita on the rocks, and his free hand was raised above his brow to shade the Caribbean sun from burning his retinas.

The last three months, he'd spent most days fishing from the side of *Kelly's Dream*, a forty-five-foot sailboat. He ate what he caught and sampled different tropical drinks native to his new island home. The days were long and hot, but the breeze at night kept it cool enough to sleep.

Dodge didn't mind the heat. He had spent many a winter in the Northeast. He preferred sweating shirtless, over snow shoveling while bundled in a heavy winter coat and insulated rubber boots. Snow was something he could live without forever. He heard people, over the years, say they missed the seasons after years in a tropical climate. Many people longed for fall and its vibrant colors. Others missed the spring transformation into new life. The Caribbean had two seasons. Hot and very hot. He preferred the former and tolerated the latter.

With Anna—a woman he rescued from a dirty cop who was holding her hostage and fell hard for last year—Dodge had left the US mainland over seven months ago. The trip had started with no destination in mind. Just raise the sail and keep the sun on your left in the morning, on your right in the afternoon, and the shoreline in sight. Sailing was new to him, and he figured if anything bad were to happen, the closer to shore the better.

After three weeks of slow going, *Kelly's Dream* pulled into port at Key Largo, the first of several inhabited islands that make up the Florida Keys. The boat dropped anchor, and the couple used a dinghy to get ashore at one of the marinas on the island. They had lunch at an outdoor bar which sat next to the hotel used to film the movie *Key Largo*, starring Humphrey Bogart and Lauren Bacall. The movie was a favorite of Dodge's. Anna had never heard of the film, but said she knew of the actors' names. The revelation made him feel old. They were fifteen years apart and didn't share many interests. But the evening ended like every other: after a few drinks, the two retired to the cabin and made love. He always felt closer to her after sex, causing the doubts to fade for a few days, or a week.

The next stop was over fifty miles west of Key Largo, to the tourist mecca of Key West, which was one of those places where a person could be whatever they wanted. From scuba divers to drag queens, Key West had it all. It was a smaller version of New Orleans. Duval Street served as the epicenter of the island and was the closest thing to Bourbon Street, outside of New Orleans. Most bars and restaurants sat on, or within, a few blocks of the primary thoroughfare.

Resorts and marinas surrounded the island, with the continental United States' southernmost point one block west of Duval, on Whitehead. Vast crowds gathered every night at Mallory Square to watch street performers and view the sunset over the Gulf of Mexico. Dodge and Anna preferred watching from the deck of *Kelly's Dream*. The couple spent three nights there before deciding to move on from the US mainland.

After a week at sea, *Kelly's Dream* docked in San Juan, Puerto Rico. Dodge had planned to spend a week on the island, but the reoccurring sound of gunfire at night echoing across the water reminded him of why he left home. But it scared Anna and made her miss home.

Anna's changing attitude became more apparent the longer the pair stayed. Still, he said nothing. He feared rejection, and part of him was scared to be alone with the ocean's vastness as his only company.

Two more days passed before Anna decided it was time for her leave.

"I miss my friends, and I had a good life," she said. "I know it wasn't perfect, but I liked it."

Dodge didn't know what to say to that. He missed some people back home as well, but he didn't have the emotional attachments that others had to people. A flaw that always held him back in relationships.

He knew Anna loved him, but theirs was a relationship built on lust and personal loss, which isn't an excellent combination for success outside the bedroom. She needed more, and Dodge imagined he did as well.

"Why don't you go home for a few weeks," he said. "When you're ready, I'll get you a plane ticket, and you can come back down, stay for a while, and go back when you get restless."

A last-ditch, half-hearted effort to change her mind.

The couple spent one more night together in a hotel in Old San Juan, each one knowing it was over, but trying to cling to something lost with every ounce of their being. There was passion and even tears before they both fell asleep. In the morning, a cab came to pick her up for a flight back to the mainland. He had decided not to ride with her to the airport. Anna gathered the few belongings she had acquired, and Dodge watched as the cab pulled away, until its yellow silhouette disappeared down the street.

As he sat on the boat, drinking a bourbon, Dodge watched as flights departed overhead from San Juan Airport, wondering if each plane was the one Anna was on. Was she looking out the small oval window toward the open water, regretting her choice to leave? Would he ever see her again?

Dodge wasn't sure if he wanted to return to his old life as a parole agent, and he guessed his final destination, St. Thomas, would be the perfect place to help him make up his mind.

He pulled the anchor and set a sail for the largest of the three islands that made up the US territory in the Caribbean Sea. The sun was high in the sky, but a massive storm was brewing off in the distance. A once-in-a-lifetime type of storm—one hundred-twenty-knot winds and fifty-foot seas.

Dodge needed to reach the relative safety of the harbor at Charlotte Amalie before the seas turned deadly. It was about a day's sail from Puerto Rico, and the storm was only a few days away. The ocean was already beginning to stir, but the added wind would help speed his journey.

CHAPTER 2

THE MORNING WAS THE SAME as every other morning on Kelly's Dream, though the impending danger added some urgency to his actions. Dodge sat on the port side, balancing a plate of eggs and toast on his lap, while coffee sloshed in a cup on the deck beside him as he watched the sunrise over the mountains to the north. The morning was warm and the sun shone bright, but clouds were beginning to pour in from the east, and the Coast Guard was warning pleasure crafts to stay in the harbor until the storm passed.

The thought of staying in paradise bounced around in his head—a decision for another day. For now, he needed food stores, as well as general use items such as toilet paper. He checked the weather report before venturing into town to pick up the supplies on his list.

The area of low pressure that had formed five hundred miles to the East of St. Thomas was now just days from making landfall. He needed to prepare Kelly's Dream by anchoring her in the deeper waters of the harbor.

The harbor provided excellent protection from the unpredictable open seas. Still, hurricane winds of a hundred miles per hour could break a vessel free from its moorings, smashing it against rocks or piers. Past storms had reaped havoc on the island and the live-aboard population maintaining residences in the natural harbor. Dodge wanted to be prepared, which included making sure he had a room reserved somewhere in Charlotte Amalie to ride out the storm.

The news was not good. The National Weather Center upgraded the depression to a Level One hurricane. Predictive models showed the storm gaining strength and speed, with the US Virgin Islands falling well within the five-day cone of uncertainty.

Five days could change everything. The storm could lose strength and fizzle out. Or it could change directions and miss the islands. Or worst-case scenario, the storm's power increases and it slams into the tiny Caribbean island as a Category Three or Four hurricane. A Category Three or higher meant he could do little except wait and pick up the pieces alongside everyone else on the island.

Since arriving on St. Thomas, Dodge had made use of a private pier to tie off his dinghy. He paid $120 per month for unlimited use of the dock. In return, the pier owner filled up the gas tank of his dinghy each time it was tied up to the pier.

The pier manager, Sebastian, walked toward Dodge with a three-gallon, red gas can as he tied the anchor rope to a cleat fastened to the dock.

"Good morning, Mister Dodge."

"Good morning, Sebastian."

"Can I fill you up today? A storm is coming, and running out of fuel will make the days after harder to get by. Gas will be difficult to get for a few weeks after the storm because of power outages."

"How long can power outage last?"

Sebastian bent over with an outstretched hand to assist Dodge from the dinghy, onto the pier.

"No telling," he replied. "Sometimes it lasts for two or three days. Other times, no power for a week or more."

Being without power for a week or longer didn't resonate well with Dodge. He checked the fuel tank on the dinghy, though he knew it was full. The inflatable boat was utilized so often, the tank never fell below three-quarters full over the past week. Sebastian made sure of that.

"What about the generator for the boat?" said the pier manager.

Dodge followed Sebastian's gaze across the bay, toward *Kelly's Dream*. He remembered topping off the generator's fuel tank in Puerto Rico, a month ago. The tank held twenty gallons of diesel fuel and burned a gallon every two hours of use. The cool breeze blowing in off the ocean helped support a natural form of air conditioning inside the boat's cabin, which kept the generator from running all night.

Not wanting to tempt fate, he asked Sebastian if he could have two three-gallon fuel containers to take back to *Kelly's Dream*.

"I'll bring the gas cans back tomorrow morning."

"No problem, Mister Dodge. I'll put the fuel in the dinghy before you return from the market."

Dodge nodded and began the short walk across the pier, toward downtown Charlotte Amalie and its open-air markets.

At the end of the pier, Dodge made a left at Veterans Drive, which was the major road running parallel to the harbor's shores around Charlotte Amalie. The fresh-fish market was a ten-minute walk, covering three-and-a-half blocks from the pier.

Buying his dinner from the morning's catch was a source of enjoyment. He had become an expert at cooking fish on the small grill mounted to the deck of *Kelly's Dream*. No spices or marinades needed. Fresh-caught fish had a unique flavor—a flavor lost during freezing and shipping—and that was one of the first things Dodge had learned in his life at sea.

After stopping to buy a coffee from one of the local street vendors, Dodge remembered he needed to visit the ATM to get cash. He had handed over his last twenty to Sebastian. A bank was located one block before the fish market, with an ATM inside the lobby. Dodge used the branch to wire money to and from other accounts when paying the bills related to his house back in the States. He figured that if the coming storm knocked out power, cash would be the only way to make purchases until they fixed the electrical grid. Being an outsider with no money, needing to rely on others' charity, was not how he envisioned the days following a storm.

The bank operated on island time and didn't open until 10:00 a.m. A line had formed, waiting for the doors to open, and stretched twenty feet from the entrance.

Once inside the bank, Dodge noticed an out-of-order sign taped to the ATM's screen, which forced him to find a line to wait for an available teller. After a five-minute wait, he walked up to the teller who had motioned him to the service window.

"How can I assist you today?"

The teller was a tall woman by the island's standards. She wore a blue dress, with her hair tied back into a ponytail. Her skin was coppery and smooth, not the leathery texture many islanders skin regresses to after prolonged exposure to equatorial sunlight. Dodge found the woman attractive, and she appeared to be close to his age.

"I came in to use the ATM, but it seems to be out of order."

"I'm sorry for the inconvenience, sir. We lost Internet service this morning, and everything is on the fritz. If you need money, I can help you withdraw from your account."

"I don't have an account at this bank, but I have used your services to wire money between banks back home."

"Well, if you have used our wire transfer services before, your other bank accounts are on record. I can have the manager make a call, and we can get your money to you shortly. Will that be OK?"

Top-notch service so far.

"That would be great."

"I'll just need an Id."

Dodge handed over his passport, then watched as her long ponytail swayed side to side as the slim figure retreated to a small office, where a short, fat man sat behind a desk. The man looked at Dodge and shook his head at something the teller said. Then she returned to the customer service window.

"The manager authorized a withdrawal of up to five-hundred dollars from our reserves. We can put the transfer in tomorrow when the Internet is up and running again. Would that be sufficient for you, Mister Dodge?"

"You can just call me Dodge."

"Dodge, I hope to be of service to you in the future."

The teller counted out five hundred dollars in tens and twenties, then placed the bills in an envelope and handed it through the slot between the window and the countertop. Dodge smiled as he took the money, and the teller returned his smile. He liked her, but noticed she was not wearing a name tag. He wanted to return so he could get her name, but not today. He had a plan for today, and flirtatious banter was not on the list of pre-storm chores.

It felt good to have a plan again. Dodge left the bank and walked the block to the fish market to buy a piece of whitefish and some fresh vegetables for dinner. He needed to make sure the bilge pumps were working, check the fuel lines, and secure the sail around the mast to keep it from getting damaged in the storm's wind. Unless the advisory grew worse, he planned to eat dinner and lock himself in the cabin to ride out the weather.

CHAPTER 3

THE STORM PICKED UP SPEED as it entered the warm waters surrounding the one-thousand-mile stretch of the Caribbean islands extending from the Gulf of Mexico to the Caribbean Sea. It swept south through less densely populated islands, before changing direction and tearing a path through the ocean channel between Puerto Rico and St. Thomas. The Category Four hurricane raced past with wind gusts up to 125 miles per hour, causing massive damage to the east side of Puerto Rico and the western half of St. Thomas.

Charlotte Amalie, with its large natural harbor, absorbed much of the flood surge, protecting the boats anchored in its waters from being washed out to sea, and the businesses along the shore from being submerged in five feet of water. Electrical power was nonexistent for anyone without generator, and food shortages would surely become an issue if the local power company was not able to restore service within a few days, for the markets and restaurants.

The damage to Charlotte Amalie could not have been worse, like at the airport and its western communities, where the winds tore the roofs off buildings and tossed light aircraft across the tarmac. Entire swaths of the Airport District were now the equivalent of a war zone—pure devastation.

The Federal Emergency Management Agency (FEMA), was on the ground within hours after the storm passed. The National Guard cleared the main runway at the airport so food, water, and other supplies could be brought in from the mainland US, and so medical personnel could evacuate the severely injured.

Dodge was tired after being up all night. At one point, as the heaviest rain band pounded the boat with several inches of rain in a less than a half-hour, he had to use a cooking pot to remove water that had gotten into the cabin, as the bilge pumps could not keep up with the deluge.

After a quick nap Dodge ventured into town to assess the damage to the local area. Though *Kelly's Dream* had survived the event, the small sail, or head sail, had a tear on one of its edges. In his haste to get the two sails stowed and protected from the storm's powerful winds, Dodge hadn't secured the leading edge properly. The constant pressure exerted on the loose fabric by the prevailing winds was more than the stitching could take, causing the double-folded edge to fail. But the error should be reasonably cheap to repair.

Overall, the first-time sailor was lucky. He had avoided any serious damage, and his supplies had weathered the storm.

"Count your blessings," he said to himself.

As Dodge approached the pier, he noticed that Sebastian was not waiting in the yellow plastic chair with a red gas can, ready to top off the dinghy's small tank. In fact, the chair was floating under the dock, tangled in fish netting washed ashore by the storm surge.

He hoped his friend had not been sitting in the chair when it tipped over into the ocean. Sebastian would not have lasted long, as waves relentlessly smashed him against the pier's wooden posts.

A person would survive two to three minutes, max, in those conditions.

As Dodge tied the dinghy to the dock, a glance of the area under the pier for his friend turned up nothing. He decided against pulling on the fishnet because finding a floater tangled in the net's webbing was not an appealing outcome. Nor was waiting for local authorities beside a bloated and decaying body of someone you knew. The police were no doubt busy dealing with the chaos after the storm, and it could be hours before they arrived.

Dodge believed his friend was still alive.

The pier sustained no visible damage from the crashing waves and strong winds of the storm. The deck's horizontal slats were in good shape, and none appeared to be missing. Seaweed and random bits of garbage the storm carried on its journey across the ocean, littered the shore and the streets. Residents walked the shoreline, picking up debris, and stacked trash bags stretched to capacity, next to the curb for pickup. Dodge imagined the locals believed that keeping the tourist areas clean would keep the economy running, as the tourists were the island's lifeblood.

He took a left on Veterans Drive, heading for the fish market and most of the tourist shops. The bank where he'd met the tall, copper-skinned teller happened to be in the same direction. Dodge had thought of her a great deal over the past few days and wanted to know her name, maybe even go out for a drink or dinner.

He had succumbed to the realization that his relationship with Anna was likely over. He missed her. Sometimes, on his outings to the islands, he would catch a glimpse of a woman walking away, her long, dark hair blowing in the Caribbean breeze, and he would think of Anna.

Just that morning, while the salty air hung heavy in the cabin from the storm, his nose picked up the slightest hint of her perfume, causing his mind to wander. Then reality creeped back in, forcing him to face the truth. He knew they would never be together again in that way. It was time to move on, making the idea of not leaving the island more of a possibility for him.

But he was unsure how to broach the subject, or even how to approach the teller. But once he knew her name, it would be more comfortable. He might ask if she could show him the sights, where the best restaurants might be, and invite her to join him for a meal and a bottle of wine. Having a plan was good.

As he meandered on the sidewalk, a black four-door, late-model Ford pulled up beside him, its driver's side window rolled down. The car's occupants wore black suits over white shirts and black ties. Both men donned black sunglasses. Dodge could see the grip of a black Beretta 92F protruding from a shoulder holster under the driver's jacket.

Why don't they just wear a sign around their necks that says, Federal Agents.

The driver said, "Excuse me. Are you, Agent Paul Dodge?"

"Depends on who's asking."

The passenger said, "That's him."

Dodge leaned over for a better view of the car's interior. The man in the passenger appeared to be in charge, and he was holding a photo of Dodge, which he quickly folded and stuck in his pocket.

"I'm at a disadvantage here," Dodge said. "I don't have a picture of you. So why don't you tell me who you are and what you want."

The driver glanced at the passenger, who nodded.

"My name is Special Agent McCaffrey," said the driver. "And this is my supervisor, Agent Williams."

"That's the name part," Dodge said. "Now how about what you want."

He had guessed right about the passenger being in charge. Agent Williams took over speaking for the pair.

"We are part of a joint task force which includes the FBI, DEA, and US Attorney's Office here in the Virgin Islands. The task force has been tracking a group of Trey-Deuce members for the past seven months. They mostly traffic in drugs and low-level stolen property."

"That doesn't sound like a case that would interest the federal government," Dodge said. "Why not leave that to the locals? They would have more knowledge of the players than you, and they're more familiar with the city and surrounding countryside."

"That's right, Agent Dodge," said Williams. "Normally the FBI would not be interested in petty drugs and stolen TVs."

"So, what turned the feds on to this case? And while I'm asking questions, how did you get my name? And how did you find me?"

"We...I mean, I...sent out a nationwide message for assistance in a case the task force recently picked up," Agent Williams said. "We received hundreds of replies. Most were weeded out as attempts to get overtime or use the opportunity as a vacation to the sunny Caribbean. Then one day, my phone rang. The caller identified himself as a police officer from Virginia. He said he knew the exact person we needed to help us with our case. As luck would have it, that man was vacationing on our very own island."

He reached into the back seat to grab a file and shook it as he talked.

"This is all the information I could gather on Paul Dodge. The file was impressive. War hero and local legend."

"You're too nice," Dodge said.

"Yes, I am. The file also contains some disturbing facts. A lack of discipline. A tendency to go rogue, and an unhealthy disrespect for authority and chain of command."

"Don't believe everything you read."

"This file reads like a Stephen King novel. But the one common theme through all the chaos is this. You are the best at working the type of case I have."

A stiffening back forced Dodge to rise. He stretched, then leaned over to see into the car again.

"What kind of case do you have?"

"I can't read you in until you agree to help us out, Agent Dodge."

"You have to show me the candy before I get into the van, fellas."

"What the hell does that mean?" Agent McCaffrey said.

"It means you need me, but I don't need you. Either give me some details, or I walk. I'm late for lunch."

15

The two agents stared at each other. Dodge stood and began walking away toward the fish market.

"Have a pleasant day!"

Agent Williams jumped out of the car and yelled at him to stop. When Dodge ignored him and continued walking, Agent Williams gave chase and grabbed his arm.

"Don't do that." Dodge glanced at the hand wrapped around his forearm.

Agent Williams released his grip. "What do you want to know?"

"You have to tell me everything. If I like what I hear, I'll consider helping you out. If I choose not to assist, I won't share what we talk about with anyone. You have my word."

"We can't talk here in the open."

"I know a place."

"How far is it? We can drive if you get in."

Dodge got into the back seat of the black Crown Vic. "Head to the pier."

"What's at the pier?" Agent McCaffrey said.

"My home."

———

Dodge and the two FBI agents settled in on the deck of *Kelly's Dream*. Dodge sat in the captain's seat, behind the helm, and the agents each squeezed into small camping chairs their host had retrieved from the cabin. Waves lapped against the side of the boat as the last remnants of the storm's rough seas made their way into the harbor.

The lead agent began discussing the Bureau's involvement with the Trey-Deuces, letting it slip that Detective Renquest was the person who had recommended Dodge. According to Agent Williams, when Renquest saw the message on the teletype, he immediately thought of Dodge, knowing he was on extended leave and had plans to dock in St. Thomas for a while.

Dodge could almost hear him say, *"Why not send a couple suits his way for a chance to earn some money while on vacation?"*

Dodge was interested, and the money would be nice, but a longing for the thrill of the hunt was what swayed him. He excelled at his job, and he secretly feared he might lose his edge if his talents went unused for an extended period.

Agent Williams wanted Dodge to serve in an advisory role as a consultant. Dodge shot the idea down before they could finish explaining what a consultant role entailed, saying he would only work if he was deputized and given a weapon. The agents argued against the demand, saying the Agency bureaucrats in DC would never approve. The liability alone could break the Department of Justice if a contractor shot a civilian or wrecked a government vehicle.

Dodge floated the idea of signing a waiver, taking responsibility for his actions and releasing the FBI from legal liability. The two agents discussed the idea, and eventually gave in to the demand.

He guessed the FBI would have expected his request. Sending the agents to talk to him without the authority to negotiate would have been a waste of time and resources.

The agents came prepared with a contract, credentials, and a weapon, all locked in the trunk of the black sedan. The contract guaranteed Dodge $5,000 for two weeks of consultation, which he gladly signed. More funds could be approved if the case lasted longer.

Good deal.

"Now that I'm on board," he said, "let's start from the beginning."

Agent Williams replied, "As I said earlier, the task force has been following a local street gang for a few months."

"You said the locals are small-time drug dealers. What piqued the Bureau's interest?"

"We received a tip about a Mexican cartel operative trying to move some cargo to the US from Mexico City. He couldn't use the highway or waterway systems because the cargo was perishable, and the trip would take too long."

"So, we aren't talking about drugs here."

"No, but we didn't know what the cargo was. Intelligence chatter put the shipment on the island the day before yesterday. The container was at the port in the inspections area, and we were working with customs to inspect it for contraband."

"And then the storm hit," Dodge said.

"That's right. We sent an agent to the port to check on the cargo container after the storm passed. While searching, he came across something else. Something worse." Agent Williams dropped his head and looked at the ground.

"So, this has nothing to do with the Mexican cartel shipment you all were monitoring?"

"No, it doesn't."

"What did he find?" Dodge said.

Agent Williams nodded to McCaffrey, who produced a stack of photos from a black leather briefcase. He handed the pictures to Agent Williams, who passed them to Dodge.

The first picture, taken from about ten feet away, showed a stack of metal containers that had fallen into a pile from the storm wind's sheer force. The photo revealed twisted steel and shards of broken wood, rendering it impossible to make any deductions about how the containers were arranged before the storm.

The second picture showed the scene from twenty feet away, after the top half of the containers had been removed by a crane. Containers at the bottom of the pile were considerably more deformed due to the amount of weight pushing down on them. The crate on the very bottom had initially been about one-quarter of the size of a standard shipping container. It was now the size of a refrigerator.

"Is there a closer picture of the container at the bottom of the pile?" Dodge said.

Agent McCaffrey motioned toward the stack of pictures Agent Williams had handed Dodge a moment ago. There was a picture taken from only a few feet away. He could make out a hole in the side of the container. The parole agent ran his fingers though his short brown hair as he stared at the photo.

He guessed the hole was originally placed in the middle of the container's side but was now positioned near the top due to the crushing effect from the weight that had landed on top of it.

"What is this hole for?" Dodge moved his long, thin finger to point to the spot in the picture. "I'm no engineer, but I believe the main objective of shipping crate design is to keep the contents dry, by keeping water and debris on the outside."

But before either agent could answer, he saw what looked like faded and smeared reddish-brown paint on one side of the container.

"Please tell me that's paint." His finger still hovered over the photo.

"The substance was dry by the time we uncovered the box from the pile," Agent Williams said. "The techs also mistook it for paint, but a closer examination proved the substance was, in fact, blood."

"Human?"

"The answer to that question is why we came to you."

"There was a person in that container." Dodge shook his head.

Williams nodded. "Yes."

"Was it a child?"

"Yes."

"Is she dead?"

"Yes. And who said it's a woman?"

"It's always a woman. Do we have an ID on the victim?"

"The body is at the medical examiner's office. We had a Bureau doctor flown in this morning from Puerto Rico to assist with the autopsy. DC didn't want to leave this one in the hands of the locals. Dead kids in a custom holding area aren't what the bosses on the sixth floor want to see on the evening news."

Dodge understood how bureaucracy worked. A dead kid made for good headlines, but unfortunate news cycles for the heads of agencies.

"Any findings released yet?"

"The ME pinned the cause of death on asphyxiation. A lack

of oxygen once the other containers collapsed on top of her."

"What about the blood?"

"The girl, who looked to be around fifteen, had a compound fracture in her left femur. Not fatal, but enough to force her into shock. Add the lack of oxygen to the fracture, and she lived for maybe two to three hours, max. The doc said her death would have been excruciating."

"I'll need to see the body."

"As soon as the medical examiner finishes the autopsy. You could just read the report."

"That is not how this works. I start with the body, then go to the crime scene. Investigations are a process, and I might see something the ME missed."

"That's why we brought in our examiner. To clean up any mistakes by the locals."

"And who cleans up your mistakes?"

"That's why I brought you in, Agent Dodge."

There was something about Agent Williams that Dodge liked.

"Get me copies of everything you have so far, including all the background material on the cartel member identified in the communications, and as much as you can dig up on the Trey-Deuce leaders. I'll take tonight to look over all the evidence, and we can hit the morgue first thing in the morning."

"Tell me what you need, Agent Dodge. I have a daughter about the same age as our victim. We need to find out who she is and how she got here."

"I agree. Get me the information, and I'll meet you first thing in the morning."

Dodge and the two agents traveled back to shore in the inflatable. Sebastian was waiting on the dock for him with the small red gas can.

"Filler up," Dodge said.

"Yes, sir, Mr. Dodge."

He handed Sebastian a hundred-dollar bill, but the supervisor waived his hands out in front of his body, determined to refuse the gesture. The man couldn't have much, so if he lost anything, the impact on him and his family could be devastating. Besides, Dodge just received a five-thousand-dollar cash infusion from the FBI. He wouldn't miss the money.

After a few minutes of protesting, Sebastian finally gave in and slipped the bill from out of Dodge's hand and shoved it into the front pocket of his cutoff jean shorts. He smiled at Dodge. Dodge returned the smile and patted his friend on the shoulder, then strolled back to the dinghy to head back to *Kelly's Dream*.

CHAPTER 4

THE FBI CASE MATERIAL ARRIVED at the pier at 7:00 p.m. Agent Williams delivered three file boxes, an official FBI identity card, and a brand-new, still-in-the-box Glock 23. Agent Williams made sure Dodge signed the waiver, releasing the Bureau from any liability if he got injured or killed while conducting his duties.

A burst of adrenaline released through Dodge's veins at the thought of working a case again. It was always the same for him. New cases were to Dodge like skydiving or base jumping are to an adrenaline junkie.

Agent Williams said he would send a car to pick him up tomorrow morning, at 9:00 a.m.

"Get some sleep. It's going to be a long day." Agent Williams got into the black Crown Vic and headed east on Veterans Drive.

Dodge smiled at the comment, knowing sleep was not a remote possibility. He had too much material to read. Short naps might be all he would get over the next thirty-six hours, but it would be enough.

Sebastian helped load the file boxes on the dinghy, and Dodge headed back toward *Kelly's Dream*. The five-minute trip gave him enough time to plan how he was going to attack the pages of information the file boxes contained.

He would start with all the pictures of the crime scene. Using the photos as a jumping off point allowed Dodge to imitate arriving at the crime scene with no advance knowledge of what had happened. He had asked for details concerning the case during his meeting with Agents Williams and McCaffrey but did his best to push the pre-existing knowledge aside. It was important not to approach a crime scene with any bias. Bias kills investigations by giving the investigator tunnel vision, forcing self-fulfilled prophecies to appear valid—a sort of misguided Manifest Destiny.

Next, Dodge would read the medical examiner's report. The autopsy results should match what the responding agent found at the scene. With that information, Dodge would have time and manner of death.

The last part of the process would begin tomorrow, during an examination of the body and a trip to the crime scene. Dodge was a man of rules. Rules were important and kept him alive. They also drove his investigative mind.

He took two hours examining all the photographs. He spread the pictures across the table, like a puzzle, to help him better understand the crime scene. Having photos or video of the crime scene was the next best thing to being there in person.

The customs area where the container was stored sat at the south end of the airport property, near a location known locally as Red Point. According to Internet maps, the only way to access the US Customs staging lot was via Airport Road, which ran the terminal's length at Cyril E. King Airport, providing access to several hotels and restaurants. The airport rested on one side, and Lindbergh Bay on the other. A ten-foot wire fence topped with razor wire surrounded the customs staging lot. No one unapproved was getting in without cutting through the fence, which appeared to be electrified.

The security of the property gave Dodge the confidence that the lot was secure and no one had broken in and planted the body or corrupted the crime scene.

Dodge then compared the container photos with the coroner's initial findings. The report stated the young woman died from asphyxiation. Her chest had been compressed by the container material, putting pressure on her ribs as it crushed under the weight of the containers falling on top of it.

"What a terrible way to go," he said to himself.

Next, he focused on the section of the medical examiner's report describing a broken femur the victim had suffered. The medical examiner noted there was no bruising or pressure marks near the contusion, a compound fracture. The femur bone had protruded about a half-inch through the skin. This type of wound would have caused immense pain for anyone.

Dodge had seen grown men cry over the same injury on the battlefield. He couldn't imagine anyone, especially a teenager, being able to tolerate the pain from the broken leg and the fear as the container collapsed around them. The question was: How, and when, was the leg broken? Did that play into her death? If she suffered a broken leg before being placed in the shipping crate, what had happened?

He hoped seeing the body and the shipping crate in person would help answer his questions.

The time was well past 3:00 a.m., and Dodge felt his body succumbing to sleep deprivation. There wasn't much more he could do until he had a look at the body and the crime scene. But two questions the medical examiner's report didn't answer kept him awake. First, why did the medical examiner's report not mention results from a rape kit? The girl in the container was not over fifteen years old. If the plan were to sell her for sex trafficking, her captors had certainly sampled the merchandise first. A human trafficking victim was no longer a person. She was a piece of property to be discarded when they were finished.

Second, there was no mention of the toxicology test results. It bears to reason that the girl's abductors would have used drugs to subdue her into a nearly unconscious state during the trip.

Dodge placed the pictures and documents back into the boxes. The boat's work area doubled as the dinette. He thought it best to try to get a few hours of sleep before starting work tomorrow.

Dodge had worked with the Bureau in the past, and agents liked to hold back vital information to test a new task force member's knowledge on a particular subject. It was bush league, but you learned to play by their rules if you wanted in the game. Besides, Dodge already knew Agent Williams had withheld information from the coroner's report. But Dodge's advance work with the files ensured he would not look like a fool on the first day.

The night air was cool, and moonlight shimmered across the bay. Dodge slept on deck under the stars. It was peaceful, and the waves lapping against the side of *Kelly's Dream* made a sleep-inducing sound. Much the way, the hum and click of windshield wipers can lull night drivers into a state of semi-consciousness.

Dodge closed his eyes, letting the night air and the sea's sounds push him off to sleep. He dreamed about Kelly and Anna, the three of them sailing on *Kelly's Dream*, across a vast sea of blue. The three of them laughing and enjoying the day. Then the water turned black and the skies red. He was sailing into a storm. Dodge looked around, but Kelly and Anna had disappeared. The girl from the bank replaced the two women. She stood on the bow of the boat, pointing off toward something in the distance. The bank teller's lips moved, but no sound came out. She continued pointing into the blackness, yelling in silence at him. The waves became more significant and lashed the boat. He could feel the warm water hit his face as the waves lashed over the deck. Then a bright light became visible. As it got closer and became more brilliant, Dodge was unable to keep his eyes open any longer.

CHAPTER 5

THE LIGHT FROM THE MORNING'S SUN forced Dodge to shade his face with his hand as he tried to open his eyes. He sat up and removed the beach towel he had used as a blanket during the night. The sun rose over the mountains to the east and cast its rays across the bay. He noticed the men in long deep-bowed boats leaving shore, and the early morning sun provided the island's fishermen with enough light to guide them to the traditional fishing spots a few miles offshore. A quick check of his watch showed the time as 5:30. He needed to shower, eat breakfast, and grab a coffee before meeting the FBI driver sent to take him to the medical examiner's office.

Dodge stripped off all his clothes except his boxers, as he wasn't about public nudity, and dove into the bay's warm blue water. Two laps around the boat got his blood pumping. The more blood flowing to the brain, the better he would do with cognitive tasks.

After a few laps around the boat, he climbed aboard Kelly's Dream for a quick shower and shave. Might as well look good for the FBI. Without a suit on board, he would make do with a pair of brown cargo pants and a light-blue button-up shirt.

Five minutes after showering, Dodge was fully dressed, donning the Glock 23 in the small of his back, and the extra magazine in his left front pocket. He had loaded the pistol and the spare magazine with .40-caliber hollow points. DOC issued .40-caliber weapons for parole agents, meaning he always had some extra ammo lying around. Even on his boat.

It was now 6:00 a.m. As the side of the dinghy made contact with the wood pilings holding the pier in place, the rubber squeaked while rocking with the waves as Dodge used the anchor rope to tie off to the pier's cleat. It was too early for Sebastian to be waiting in the yellow chair, so he left a note telling Sebastian, no fuel needed today. He then walked the half-mile trek to a local coffee shop and ordered a large coffee with two creams and two sugars. The extra sugar wouldn't hurt, considering the long day Dodge expected to have. After paying cash for the coffee, he walked back to the dock to wait for the black Crown Vic to pick him up.

After downing the last swallow of his coffee, Dodge pondered getting another cup, when the sound of car tires turning off the pavement and into the gravel parking lot caught his attention. He turned to see the black Ford from the previous night slow to a stop, and Agent Williams exited from the driver's side.

The boss came himself. Meaning, I must rate high on the importance list.

"Good morning, Agent Dodge," said Williams.

"You're early. I was just contemplating getting another cup of coffee when you showed up. And just call me Dodge."

"Come on and get in the car. There's a place to get food along the way."

"We aren't going to the medical examiner's office first?"

"This is Saint Thomas. The medical examiner's office doesn't open until after ten in the morning. Everything is a little slower down here, even in government work."

The slow pace of the Caribbean way of life was fine, only as a tourist. He felt it reeked of unprofessionalism. Time is the most important factor in a death investigation, and you can't get it back.

"So why are you so early?" Dodge said.

"Insomnia. So, I came into town to get some breakfast before the office opened. Then I thought, why not swing by the docks to see if you were up?"

"I didn't sleep much last night either," Dodge said. "There was so much information in the files I wanted to go over before today."

"You see? It wasn't a wasted trip," Agent Williams said. "Would you care to join me for some breakfast?"

Dodge ate a bowl of fresh fruit before coming to shore, but he had a habit of never turning down food when working. Things happen in homicide cases. Things you need to run with, usually around dinner time.

"Where do you have in mind?" he replied.

Agent Williams unlocked the passenger's side door.

"Get in. I know just the place for a plebe to the island."

Dodge always liked Navy folks. The Navy had the best chow, and the service branch was his second choice behind the Air Force.

He opened the door and climbed in. "Your island, your treat."

The two men headed north from the pier, through the tourist shops and boutiques that lined the narrow city streets. Once past the waterfront downtown area, Agent Williams traveled on Commandant Gade Northeast for about three miles, then turned north on Mafolie Road. The men stayed on Mafolie for a mile before coming to a restaurant on a hill. The car pulled into the parking lot, and the two men got out. Dodge had to go to the bathroom by the time they arrived at the restaurant. A by-product of drinking strong coffee in the morning. Agent Williams said he would order while Dodge tended to his needs.

Dodge could smell the food cooking as he turned the corner from the bathrooms located in a separate building behind the hilltop restaurant. As he approached the customer order window, he noticed Agent Williams sitting at a picnic table overlooking the town and the ocean. The table had a multi-colored umbrella tilted to the east to help shade diners from the morning sun. A six-pack cardboard container, its alcohol contents replaced with different hot sauces, salsa, and ketchup, sat in the table's middle.

Dodge sat down across from Agent Williams.

"That's quite a view."

"I used to come here three times a week before I became special agent in charge," Williams said. "As an agent down here, your schedule is flexible. Do your work, and they'll leave you alone. As the agent in charge, I have to be the first one in the office and the last one to leave. The paperwork never ends. I'm more of an administrator now. I point people in the direction I, or the Bureau, needs them to go."

Dodge's boss, Chief Johnson, had often made the same complaint. The constant griping was one of the principal reasons Dodge hadn't been promoted to a supervisory position. The salary didn't seem to be worth the headaches.

"Somebody has to be in charge," he said, because he didn't know what else to say.

Agent Williams pointed south. "If you look hard, you can see your boat anchored in the bay."

Dodge squinted and saw the tiny white dot, among many white dots, contrasting against the turquoise-blue water. It was weird—his entire life just a white dot on the ocean. The whole thing made him feel insignificant. Small. In his world back home, he was a big fish in a small pond. But here, he was just another tourist.

Now, he wasn't sure how he felt about the situation he had put himself in—coming to the island with no plan. Just a man and a boat.

The waiter brought the food Agent Williams had ordered. The plate was family style and had different fare from the waters around the island. In the middle was a whole broiled rockfish, which Dodge thought weird for breakfast. Clams, shrimp, and conk surrounded the fish, all fried golden brown. At the ends of the platter were arrangements of bananas, grapes, mangoes, and papaya. Dodge had eaten fruit earlier that morning, so he figured some protein would be good for him. The fish was terrific. The skin was crispy, while the fleshy, white meat was firm and juicy. A taste of the ocean in each bite.

Agent Williams doused everything with a green hot sauce from the cardboard container before putting each forkful into his mouth. The men finished the meal without saying a word, just staring out over the ocean.

By the time they had eaten breakfast and driven the five miles back to town, the FBI office was open. The daily briefing on the case was provided by the FBI agents and customs officials. Local police were left out of the investigation because the girl was not from the island and was found on federal property. Dodge agreed and didn't believe keeping the local police force at arm's length was a problem. Besides, the task force could always choose to clear a local detective if they later found themselves in need of the island's police force. For now, playing your cards close to the vest was the best way to proceed, until they knew more. It wasn't uncommon for local gangs to have a source inside the police department.

When the briefing was finished, Agent Williams opened the room up to questions. Dodge looked around at the other faces at the table, and no one else appeared to have any.

"What about a toxicology report?" he said. "I read the medical examiner's report you sent over, but there were no results from drug tests or chemical analysis."

Agent Williams looked at Agent McCaffrey, who opened a folder and slid a paper across the table to Dodge. The report showed elevated levels of barbiturates, and several painkillers, present in the girl's blood. The kidnappers drugged her for the trip, but Dodge still wondered about the broken leg.

"As you can see," McCaffrey said, "there were copious amounts of opiates in her system. We believe the abductors drugged her before abducting and hiding her in the shipping container. We found no water or food in the container, so we assume her captors intended on a quick trip."

Dodge nodded, saving the question about her leg for later.

"Anything else, Agent Dodge?" said Williams.

"One more thing. Why was a rape kit not completed? I would think it would have been first on the list to secure any

DNA evidence present on the girl's body. And you can call me Dodge. We are all friends here."

The question appeared to catch Agent Williams off guard. Then he nodded to the others in the room. Everyone stood and left, except for Dodge, McCaffrey, and Williams. Once the door closed, Agent Williams sat in the chair at the conference table's head, closed his folder, and gave the new guy the once-over.

Passed test two.

"That is why you are here," Williams said. "I need someone with more than a simple knowledge of child abductions. The knowledge needed in this case is more psychological in nature. We know the groups involved, but we need to know why. A profile, if you will." He glanced at Agent McCaffrey. "Show Dodge the rest of the file."

"Are you sure, boss?"

"Yes. He moved the timeline up a little quicker than I had planned to reveal the details, but he asked all the right questions. Give it to him."

Agent McCaffrey slid another manilla file across the table to Dodge.

Agent Williams continued. "What you have in front of you is everything we know about the victim. Her name is Maria Delgado. She is fifteen years old, and a citizen of Colombia. Her father is Jesús Martinez Delgado."

Dodge was not an expert in the drug trafficking world, but he knew that name. Jesús Martinez Delgado was one of the biggest drug dealers in the world. The DEA guessed he had ordered hundreds of murders in the United States, and likely thousands more south of the border. Delgado was a dangerous man who had eyes and ears on every continent. There was not a part of the world that his drug trade didn't touch.

Skimming the files, Dodge saw the results from a rape kit the medical examiner had completed. It came back positive for sexual assault. Agent Williams decided not to include that information in the packets for entities outside of the FBI. There were bruises on her thighs, and the medical examiner found semen on her legs and underwear.

The following section in the report provided details about the broken femur. The report stated the femur break occurred before they placed her in the container.

Dodge could feel the anger building inside his chest. Maria Delgado had been drugged and placed in a shipping container headed for St. Thomas to smuggle her out of Colombia, right under the nose of law enforcement. Either this was a well-thought-out plan, or a spur-of-the-moment reaction to a bad situation. Dodge wasn't sure which applied here. He needed to see the crime scene before drawing any conclusions.

"Why not tell the rest of the team about what's in this file?" he said.

"The Bureau is not sure where this investigation will lead," Williams said. "I put in a call to DOJ to see if any open operations are running on Delgado at present. HQ assured me there are not."

"But you don't believe them?"

"I don't know what to believe right now. All I know is I have a dead fifteen-year-old girl found on US Government property, assaulted, and maybe tortured. I need you to help me fill in the details from the sexual assault angle. I'll deal with drugs and vandalism to federal property down here. Child trafficking and rape are well out of my area of expertise."

Dodge stood from his chair. "We need to start at the beginning. I need to see the crime scene in person. From that point, we can put the puzzle of Maria Delgado together."

Agent Williams nodded, and the three men walked to the parking lot and rode in silence the entire trip to the airport.

CHAPTER 6

AGENT MCCAFFREY PARKED THE BLACK CROWN VIC in a gravel lot north of the US Customs lot. The three men strode the scant distance to the customs office and used their IDs to access the facility. Agent Williams told Dodge and McCaffrey to check out the crime scene while he met with the supervisory customs official on duty. He wanted to secure any video footage of the lot before customs locked the system down because of the public relations nightmare that was sure to follow. Control of all the information was crucial for the Bureau.

Dodge walked the perimeter of the scene where the girl's body was found, staying outside the yellow caution tape, to get a broad vision of what lay in front of him. Rescuers had stacked containers to gain access to the body of Maria Delgado. To help him visualize what the scene looked like when it was discovered, he recalled the pictures from the photos in the boxes on *Kelly's Dream* the night before, flipping through them in his mind, one by one. The entire lot was still a mess. The storm had knocked out power to the airport, so no containers were being loaded or unloaded. Debris washed in from the bay, and wind damage to the trees and the surrounding buildings made concentrating more difficult. It was hard to picture something that no longer existed.

"Did you bring any of the photos?" Dodge said.

"I left all the files at the office," McCaffrey said. "I figured we were at the site, so why bring the files. Do you want me to go back to the office and get them?"

Dodge considered asking the junior agent to do just that. It was a rookie mistake, and one he was sure Agent Williams would not have made. Having the images on-hand at the crime scene was important for several reasons. First, the crime scene was three days older. Things had changed because of the damage the storm caused, and the constant heat from the Caribbean sun beating down on the area. Second, the pictures preserved the scene as it was on the day of discovery. Workers had to remove the pile of containers to gain access to the container with the red substance oozing down the side, which led to the discovery of Maria Delgado's crumpled body. The containers couldn't be put back the way they were, making it difficult to see the effects of immense weight on the box Maria had been trapped in.

But most importantly, always be prepared. It didn't matter if the notes were needed. Bring them, anyway.

"No," Dodge replied. "There's no need to drive back to town. Just get your phone out and take pictures of the crime scene now. Containers have been moved, and we need to document the changes."

"Sure thing, Agent Dodge."

Agent Williams joined the two men after interviewing the customs supervisor on duty.

"Was customs able to provide any video footage from the day of the storm?" Dodge said.

"No. The supervisor said the video system hasn't worked for at least three months."

"Three months, and no surveillance cameras. Only the US government could get away with that level of incompetence. I thought after nine-eleven CBP, ICE, and CIS had a free grab at the purse strings?"

"Apparently, this island is not a very popular destination for illegal drugs or terrorists attempting to get into the US," Williams said. "No threat, no money. I imagine most of the funds went to New York, LA, and Miami to pay off the mob longshoremen for cooperation."

"That's why I believe they picked this place," Dodge said.

"Low security and inattentive staff. The entire place has the makings of a low-budget horror movie."

Agent McCaffrey returned from documenting the scene and asked if there was anything else Dodge needed.

"Where is the container Maria Delgado was in?" Dodge said.

"The medical examiner had the entire container wrapped and taken to the morgue," McCaffrey said. "He wanted to be sure not to damage the girl's body during the extrication process."

Agent Williams turned to Dodge. "Unless you have something else, we can head to the medical examiner's office. Doctor Jerrel should be at work by now."

Dodge took one last look around and nodded to Agent Williams.

"Let's go see the body."

The coroner's office was located in the Department of Health complex near the restaurant where he and Agent Williams ate breakfast that morning. The drive took about fifteen minutes, during which, there were few cars on the road—mainly emergency vehicles and city clean-up crews removing debris from the streets left over from the havoc the storm's high winds reaped on the trees and vegetation.

Dodge asked about Maria Delgado's broken leg. Agent Williams believed the broken leg had happened before placing her in the container. Agent McCaffrey and Dodge both agreed. Dodge would go with the easiest solution until proven wrong. Occam's Razor states that the easiest theory is usually the correct one, and Dodge had often found that to be true. But he still wanted to know how her leg had been broken, and why Maria's abductors had stuck her in a shipping crate? Why not kill her in Colombia and toss her body in the jungle or off a cliff? The extra steps needed to move a person—an injured girl—across borders only increased the chances of being caught.

Nothing made sense. There were too many unknowns to develop a theory. He hoped Dr. Jerrel could provide clarity with his complete examination.

The three men stood around the clean stainless-steel table

holding the body of Maria Delgado. Dr. Jerrel had completed the autopsy, and the body had the usual incisions stitched closed: a Y-shape cut from the waist to each armpit to remove and examine all the organs. A small puncture wound in the lower right side of the abdomen, made by inserting a thermometer into the liver to gauge the time of death. Last, a row of stitches just under the scalp's hairline for removing the top of the skull and examining the victim's brain.

Dodge hated the idea of cutting into a dead body. He understood the need for answers, but sometimes thought, *Just let the dead be.* Secretly, he hoped that when he died, they would never find his body, depriving the hacks a chance to dice him up and reduce his life to the weight of his organs.

Agent Williams said, "Well, Doc, what else did you find out?"

Dr. Jerrel picked up the chart off the table and put on his reading glasses.

"Do you want a recap of the preliminary findings, or just the recent stuff?"

Agent Williams looked over at Dodge, deferring to his decision.

"The new findings should be good enough," Dodge said.

"Fine," Dr. Jerrel said. "If you need to ask questions, just stop me by speaking up." He looked down at the chart. "So, the time of death is hard to place. The water from the storm and humidity makes it hard to determine the exact time. The amount of blood on the scene confirms the girl was alive when the box collapsed around her. We know the storm winds hit their highest point at 10:15 p.m., and they found the body around 8:30 the next morning. That gives us a window of eleven hours for the time of death. I am sorry I can't be more precise."

After visiting the scene, Dodge guessed as much. The critical takeaway was that Maria Delgado was alive when she went into the crate. Whoever put her in that crate probably didn't expect her to die in it.

"That's fine, Doc," he replied. "What did you find out about the broken leg?"

Dr. Jerrel flipped through a few more pages on his chart.

"The femur broke five centimeters below the hip joint. The bone broke through the skin and caused massive bleeding. The wound had a makeshift bandage, made from what appears to be a cotton shirt, tied around it at the protrusion point. Agent Williams, your forensic tech sent the bandage to the lab for analysis. You can coordinate with him for the timing of the results."

"Anything else, Doc?" Dodge said.

"That's about it. The rest is up to the Bureau's lab. I'll keep the body for ninety days, or until someone claims it. Then the FBI can take it, or we will bury her on Pauper Hill."

None of the men spoke. The thought of Maria Delgado interned in an unmarked grave on an island she didn't live seemed unfair. They knew who her father was but weren't sure how to do the notification. Ultimately, a fat, old white bureaucrat would make that decision. Dodge hated politics, and he sensed Agent Williams felt the same.

The information gained from Dr. Jerrel's briefing gave him confidence that they would solve Maria Delgado's death.

Lunchtime had come and gone while the three men were in the medical examiner's office getting the autopsy results, but the men were no longer hungry. Dead kids had a way of ruining appetites.

Dodge suggested they get coffee and discuss what they knew so far. Agent Williams offered to use the coffee truck near the pier. It was close to Dodge's boat, and when finished, they all should go home and rest. Each man had seen enough for one day. They would get an early start the next day.

Agent Williams handed Dodge a check before leaving. The Bureau agreed to the five-grand fee and authorized another twenty-five hundred in expenses.

Dodge needed to go to the bank to cash the check before going home. It gave him an excuse to see the teller again. She hadn't escaped his mind completely.

CHAPTER 7

JESÚS MARTINEZ DELGADO was a man of gigantic stature. He stood six-foot-seven, with bulging muscles, and looked as if he worked out daily. He forged a belief in physical fitness at an early age out of necessity, not for recreation. Jesús came from a single-parent home in the mountains surrounding Bogotá, Colombia. His mother was a maid at the hotel where the family lived. And his father was killed by a rival cartel during the cocaine wars in the late 90s.

Jesús's mother worked long hours to support her family, but there was never enough money. She tried to make sure the children went to school, stayed off the streets, and didn't make the same mistakes their father had made. The result of all that hard work was one civil servant, one doctor, and one narco trafficker and mass murderer.

Jesús started in the drug trade as a runner for the same cartel that had killed his father. The cocaine labs were located deep within the jungle-covered mountains. The cartels needed people to deliver the finished product to the local towns and villages where middlemen would pick up the packages for the long journey to distant countries, like the United States. Running drugs in a backpack up and down mountains was strenuous labor, and the cartel assigned only the fittest boys this task. Jesús was faster than most, and able to carry twice as much product through the jungle trails, which earned him the nickname *El Gato de la Jungla,* or the Jungle Cat.

Young Jesús quickly made his way into the inner circle of the cartel leadership. When he turned eighteen, upper management forced him to prove his loyalty before trusting him with their most guarded secrets. Jesús's brother was his first target. Jesús completed the task with such brutality, bringing his brother's severed head back to the compound as proof of the deed.

Cartel leaders feared his ruthlessness, and rightly so: he had plans to assume command and consolidate the cartel's power into one man—himself.

In less than a year, Jesús Martinez Delgado had killed or silenced the opposition on his way to the top. He rewarded the men below him for continued loyalty, using cartel money to shore up his support in the local villages and towns. The network Jesús put together kept him up to date on strangers and government soldiers searching for him or his compound. He had spies everywhere, including in the US government.

On his rise up the cartel ladder, he met a woman in a Bogotá nightclub. Her name was Maria Fuentes, and Jesús fell in love with her at once. She had large brown eyes capable of capturing a suitor with one glance, and straight hair, as if it had been ironed, that flowed down her back and ended just above her waistline. She was stunning.

People spotted the couple all over Colombia, vacationing at wineries and other well-known tourist destinations. Their relationship became so intense that young Maria Fuentes became pregnant. The news thrilled Jesús. He had always wanted to be the father he barely remembered having. He swore to raise the child right, taking care of its every need.

Maria Fuentes and Jesús married at the jungle compound in a small family gathering. As time went on, her pregnancy became complicated, and Jesús had to take her to the hospital three months before the child's due date. Here, things went astray.

Jesús had paid off the hospital staff to keep his wife's admittance a secret. The last thing he wanted was a rival cartel member—or worse, a government soldier—to find out he was vulnerable and attack his family. One nurse at the hospital recognized Maria from an earlier ER visit and felt compelled to confirm her identity. The nurse found the old records and discovered that Maria was a member of the Colombia National Police—an agent in the Narco Trafficking Division.

The nurse, overcome with greed, knowing the drug kingpin father-to-be had already paid one bribe to the hospital staff to keep his family safe, contacted Jesús, with whom she traded the information on his lover for a few thousand dollars. This betrayal incensed Jesús. The love of his life was all based on a lie. How much information had she passed on to the police?

His rage grew, and he began putting a plan in motion to get the undercover snitch out of the hospital, to a place where the baby could be born in relative safety. Once his child was out of the betrayer's body, he would kill her.

Jesús recruited the nurse to help. They planned to roll Maria right out the front door, with no paperwork left behind to show she was ever at the hospital. He posted guards at the door of her hospital room and told her it was for her and the baby's own wellbeing. He paid janitors to keep him appraised of anything unusual happening at the hospital.

Janitors were everywhere, cleaning up messes and taking trash out of rooms, and doctors and staff talked freely in front of them. The perfect spies. He just needed a few weeks to set up a safe house, and then he could carry out his plan.

The baby came prematurely, and the nurse delivered the child in a hotel room bathtub. Once the nurse deemed the child healthy, Jesús shot Maria Fuentes in the face. She cleaned the baby and wrapped it in a hotel towel before handing her off to Jesús. The nurse then took a bullet to the head. No loose ends is a rule Jesús Martinez Delgado takes seriously.

Over the first few years, money was passed out to those willing, or able, to keep a secret. Others were eliminated as an example, and the young girl grew up.

Fifteen years later, a plane touched down on an abandoned airfield in the San Lorenzo Mountain region of Puerto Rico, seventy miles west of Charlotte Amalie. Delgado stepped off the plane, where his top lieutenant, the man in charge of drug distribution in the Caribbean-based US territories, waited for him with a truck.

"*El Gato*, welcome to beautiful Puerto Rico," said Top Lieutenant José Melendez.

Jesús was not on the island for pleasure. "Did you find her?"

"We did, sir. She is at the medical examiner's office on Saint Thomas."

"Do we have anyone that will help get her back?"

"We do. I put in a call this morning. Our contact will meet us at Black Point, which is just north of the airport. The boat will anchor offshore, and will have three armed guards scanning for unwanted visitors." José Melendez paused. "Maria looks pretty bad, sir. Are you sure you want to see her like this? I could arrange to send her home privately, and our doctor could make her more presentable before you see her."

Jesús held back his rage. "I want to see my baby girl."

"Yes, sir. Come on and get in the truck. We have to meet the boat in less than an hour."

"Have you found out who did this to her?"

"Not yet, boss. No one is talking, but the FBI is involved. And if that's true, we will know something soon."

"Remember, I want the son of a bitch brought to me alive. He'll die at my hands. Nobody else is to lay a finger on him."

"Understood, boss."

The two men rode in silence the rest of the way to the rendezvous point. Once on the boat, Jesús paid the captain and the armed guards for their help. The men were more than happy to get their money in advance. In a typical business transaction, the men had to force a customer to pay once they completed the job. The payment time didn't matter to Delgado. None of the men would live long enough to spend their cash.

The trip to St. Thomas from Puerto Rico would take about four hours. The captain had planned the route to avoid swaths of open water that the Coast Guard regularly patrolled. No need to be the cause of your customer's detainment or having your boat confiscated by the US government.

The crew raised a US flag for added security. A ship bearing US colors was less likely to be searched if stopped. The Coast Guard was looking for drugs and foreigners from the Middle East. A group of dark-skinned men out for a day cruise shouldn't rise to the level of boarding and search.

Once in the bay, off Black Point, Jesús, José, and one man from the boat took the dinghy ashore to a blue BMW waiting just beyond the tree line. The motor was running, with a driver sitting behind the steering wheel, waiting for orders. The three men hurried inside the vehicle, and the driver pushed on the accelerator. Sand and gravel flew from under the wheels, and a cloud of dust formed where the car had sat just a few seconds prior.

CHAPTER 8

DODGE HAD ABOUT TWO HOURS to walk to the bank and cash the check Agent Williams had given him earlier in the day. He had to admit, working for the feds had its perks. No one at DOC ever handed him a check for twenty-five hundred dollars for expenses. The experiences over the past ten years while working for DOC had been more like a dental procedure when trying to get money back. The procedure was rarely worth the pain and had become so convoluted over the past five years, he stopped submitting expense reports at all, choosing instead to file the loss on his taxes each year. This was what the state bean counters hoped would happen, and he was complicit in the fraud by ignoring it, but he didn't have the energy to deal with it anymore.

The bank was almost void of customers when Dodge arrived. He scanned the teller windows for the tall woman he met the last time. She was working behind the third window, and as luck would have it, she was the only teller with a customer.

A shallow voice called from somewhere behind the row of customer windows.

"Excuse me, sir. Can I help you?"

In an effort to buy some time until the man in the tall teller's window finished his deposit, or whatever he was taking forever to do, Dodge pretended like he hadn't heard the teller.

"Excuse me, sir. I said, can I help you?"

Avoiding eye contact worked as a distraction for only so long. He was on the verge of being rude, and he didn't want the tall teller to remember him as the nasty guy who appeared to be stalking her. He caught creepers. He wasn't one.

"I'm sorry." He walked to the counter. "I wasn't paying any attention at all."

"Not a problem at all, sir. It's pretty slow in here today, so it inconvenienced no one in the slightest." Her name tag said *Mary*.

Dodge slid the check under the glass partition, hoping the US Department of Justice's official seal, stamped in the upper left hand, would help.

"Well, Mary, I need to cash a check. I don't have an account here, as I am just visiting the island. But I have used your bank for some transactions involving my bank back home. I hope that will not be a problem."

Mary's eyes opened to twice their regular size. She didn't have the authority to cash such a large check for a non-customer. Dodge interjected before she could say no.

"If it helps, I talked with that young lady at window five the other day. The manager she spoke to approved my transaction that day. Maybe she can allow this one."

"There is not a manager in now," the short teller said. "Normally, these types of requests would have to go through management first." She looked toward the tall teller. "Nikki, can you come down here when you finish with your customer?"

The tall teller's name was Nikki. Dodge only had to wait a few minutes before she could get free from the clingy customer who had been occupying all her time. He wondered if she would even remember his name.

"Mister Dodge, how can I help you today?" Nikki said. "Do you need another wire transfer?"

She remembered his name. *That is an excellent sign.*

Mary spoke up before Dodge could answer.

"Mister Dodge has a check for twenty-five hundred dollars, issued by the US government. He would like to cash the check but does not have an account with us. Without management approval, I can't cash the check."

Nikki glanced at Dodge, and he was sure she winked at him. It could have been a simple blink, but it appeared intentional.

"Everything is fine, Mary. I'll take care of him. Mister Jenkins approved a transaction for Mister Dodge earlier in the week, and I'm sure this one will be fine. Besides, a check from the United States government should pass scrutiny, don't you think?"

Mary nodded, and he followed Nikki to window five. Mary went back to counting the money in her drawer, writing the totals of each bill on a notepad.

"Thank you for helping me out again...Nikki, is it?"

She tapped the name tag on her shirt. "It is, Mister Paul Dodge?"

"Just call me Dodge."

"Well, Dodge," she smiled, "how would you like your cash?"

"Half in hundreds, and the rest in twenties should be fine."

Nikki began counting out the money, starting with the hundred-dollar bills. Her voice reminded Dodge of a military cadence as she called out the number of bills in the growing piles until five stacks of one thousand each lay on the counter in front of him. Dodge liked her even more now.

"Is there anything else I can help you with, Dodge?"

Now was as good as a time as any to find out if she was interested.

"Nikki, you and the bank here have been so accommodating to me. I have all this cash now and will probably eat dinner alone. Would you like to join me? I mean, as thanks for helping me out again."

He waited.

Nikki smiled. "I would like that very much."

A rush of adrenaline pumped through his veins. He felt like a schoolboy again and was sure she could hear his heart pounding inside his chest.

"My boat is in the bay," he said. "So just tell me when and where to meet, and I'll be there."

"I get off at five and need to go home and change into something a little less stuffy. Let's say, seven o'clock. There is a little bistro in Frenchtown. We can meet here at the bank and walk there."

"Sounds good to me." He began writing on the back of a check deposit slip. "Here is my number. If anything comes up, just text me."

As he walked away, Dodge realized he hadn't examined Maria Delgado's shipping crate after attending the autopsy. Agent Williams told him the medical examiner had the container at his office. The crate was a key piece of evidence, and it was the only part of the crime scene he had not laid eyes on in person.

He looked at his watch—4:15. That gave him plenty of time to view the box, take notes, and clean up before his dinner date.

The walk to the medical examiner's office would take too long. Dodge needed to make it before the medical examiner left and locked the building up for the night. He took a taxi and arrived at the coroner's office at 4:40. There were two cars in the parking lot—a white four-door sedan, and an official government vehicle assigned to the Department of Health. He hoped he wasn't too late and headed straight for the ME's office. He knocked on the door, and an assistant in a white lab coat ushered him into the lobby.

"How can I help you?" he said.

"My name is Paul Dodge. I was here earlier with the FBI agents, concerning the body found at the airport."

"Ah yes, I remember you. I'm afraid Doctor Jerrel left for the rest of the day. Is there anything I can help you with?"

"No. I need to see the container they found the girl in. The FBI told me they sent the crate here for body extrication."

"I can take you to see it, if you like," the assistant said.

Dodge received two text messages. The first was from Nikki. She wanted to know if they could change their dinner time to eight o'clock. She had an errand to run after work. A quick stroke of the keyboard and a reply was sent. The second message was from Agent Williams. He said there were fresh leads, and that they should meet the next day to discuss the new developments.

Nikki's delay gave Dodge the time he needed to go back to the ME's office and get a good look at that shipping crate.

Following the lab tech through the maze of offices and out the back door to the building, Dodge noticed the entire building appeared to be empty. He looked into the individual offices and saw no one working. The tiny hairs on his neck tingled. Why go outside? If the medical examiner wanted to keep the crate secure as evidence, he wouldn't leave it out in the elements, unprotected from prying eyes and civilian gawkers.

Dodge reached back and pretended to check for his wallet, searching for his weapon in the small of his back. Still there.

The assistant raised his arms to push the door at the back of the building open, and Dodge noticed the protruding grip of a handgun poking out the side of the now tight lab coat. ME assistants didn't carry weapons in any jurisdiction Dodge had ever worked.

The view through the door windows showed no outbuildings behind the principal building. No place to store the crate securely. The woo-woo hairs on his neck were in overdrive. His whole body tingled as blood rushed to his extremities. Everything was wrong. He needed to act before they were outside. No way to tell if he was walking into an ambush. Best not to wait and find out.

Dodge used his foot to force a massive blow to the small of the assistant's back. The armed man slammed into the door, forcing it to swing wildly as he fell into the parking lot behind the government building, landing on his face. The gravel tore his skin as he slid to a stop on his stomach. Dodge followed the man through the door, weapon trained on his head. The man rolled over onto his back and reached for his gun, but once he noticed the .40-caliber Glock pointed between his eyes, he dropped his hands to the side.

Dodge dragged the man to his feet and forced his hands behind his back while facing him toward the building. After reaching for the place on his belt where his handcuffs should be, Dodge remembered that he didn't have any, so he had the man drop to his knees, cross his ankles behind him, and then lean against the wall, using the top of his head to keep his balance. The position forced him off balance and slowed any sudden moves he might try to make.

"Who are you?" Dodge said.

Silence.

"Where is Doctor Jerrel?"

The man remained silent.

"You need to understand something. I'll get the answers to my questions. Answers can come easy or hard. It is entirely up to you."

The man said nothing. Dodge needed a new approach.

It wasn't until after the man's head cracked open like a ripe tomato thrown against a wall, that Dodge heard the shot. Dirt and gravel flew everywhere as he ducked behind a dumpster for cover. The man in the lab coat lay dead on the ground, his brains matted to the wall of the building.

Dodge played the scene back in his head. He counted the seconds between the man's head splitting open and the sound of the shot. About two seconds. Which meant the shot came from about two hundred meters away, most likely from the hills behind him.

He would wait a few more minutes before venturing out from his hiding spot.

CHAPTER 9

ABOUT FIVE MINUTES HAD PASSED while tucked behind the dumpster, until he heard the sound of sirens echoing off the building and down the narrow streets from two blocks away. Dodge knew the shooter would abandon his shooting perch at the first sign of police. He also assumed that it would have been easy enough to have killed him first if he were the target. The killing was about cleaning up a mess, closing all the doors. But staying behind the dumpster for another minute wouldn't hurt, either.

The first police vehicle turned into the parking lot and stopped twenty yards from the dead man in the lab coat. Dodge had his FBI ID in hand, and his weapon holstered in the small of his back when the first officers stepped out from their vehicles. The local police cleared the area and sent a tactical response team into the health department building to remove casualties and any potential threats that may still be inside. The SWAT team handed Dodge a radio, which he used to direct the air unit's helicopter to the location where he thought the shot might have originated. The chopper circled the hillside—first, in small, tight circles. Then, in larger circles. After fifteen minutes, with no signs of a shooter, the helicopter returned to its landing pad at the heliport.

Dodge called Agent Williams and informed him of what had just happened. He walked Williams through the entire scenario, from his arrival and the cars in the parking lot, to the lab assistant's headshot. Agent Williams told him to go home and get some rest. A debriefing would take place the following day at the FBI office.

Dodge looked at his watch—7:00 p.m. He wouldn't have time to go back to the boat to change before meeting Nikki in Frenchtown.

Just then, the tactical unit commander exited the building, calling the all-clear.

"Commander," Dodge said. "Did I hear you give the all-clear?"

"Yes, Agent Dodge. We have accounted for all staff. The assailants locked everyone in a cooler. They are safe and unharmed."

"What about the ME? The dead guy told me he had gone home early for personal reasons."

"We didn't find the doctor inside. I could ask the staff if he was here, or if he left early today."

"That sounds good. Also, why not send a unit to the address on file to make sure he's safe?"

"I'll send two of my men over as soon as we finish up here, sir."

Dodge said thank you, gave the commander his phone number, and walked back through the building, to the front parking lot. Fire rescue, ambulances, and local police filled the lot. He would never get a taxi to come and pick him up in this mess.

He flagged down a local sergeant and asked if any of his men were heading back toward town. The sergeant put a call out on his radio, and a patrolman on the scene said he could take Dodge into town and drop him wherever he needed to go. A cop car with lights and sirens—way better than a yellow taxi.

The drive to Frenchtown took about twenty minutes. Traffic was heavy and re-routed all over town to keep gawkers from getting a peek at the crime scene. At 7:25, the patrol officer let Dodge out at the French restaurant. Thirty-five minutes early. Plenty of time to go to the bathroom, splash water on his face, and check for any blood spatter that may have gotten on him from his would-be assailant's head wound.

A thorough checking uncovered no blood specks or skull fragments on his clothes or in his hair. He stepped out of the bathroom and spotted Nikki sitting at the bar. She was beautiful. Her hair was down, the tips brushing the tops of her shoulders. Her eyes were the color of the Caribbean waters surrounding the island, and her skin shimmered like glitter.

He took a deep breath and approached her.

"Hello, Nikki."

"Hello yourself. I see you didn't have time to change for me."

"Something came up. Didn't want to keep you waiting."

Nikki smiled. "I would have waited."

Dodge motioned for the girl at the hostess desk.

"Can we get a table for two, please?"

"Sure thing," the hostess said. "I have a table available now, if you don't mind a rooftop table."

Dodge shrugged at Nikki, who said the rooftop table would be perfect.

Once the hostess pushed in Nikki's chair, Dodge sat across from her.

"So how long have you been on the island?" he said.

"I came here five years ago, for a week's vacation. Five years later, here I am."

"Must take a lot of guts to stay in a place you're unfamiliar with, and full of people you don't know."

"I've always been adventuresome. I was smart and educated and got the job at the bank inside a week. The pay is not great, but I can afford a nice little place just off the beach. Besides, having bankers' hours in paradise means time for wine and sunsets every day."

Dodge motioned to the bartender. "Speaking of wine."

The bartender approached the table and took the couple's order—a Chardonnay for Nikki, and a bourbon on the rocks for him.

"I'll be back with those drinks shortly."

"Now that you know all about me, what about you?" Nikki said. "What brings you to paradise?"

"A hard year."

"How long you plan on staying?"

"I don't know. I just picked up some temporary work, as you saw by the check you cashed for me. The funds could extend my stay by a month or two."

The bartender brought the couple's drinks and set down wine in front of Nikki, and bourbon in front of Dodge. The two toasted by tapping their glasses, and each took a sip.

"A month or two, huh?" Nikki said.

"Give or take a week or two."

Nikki picked up her glass and swallowed the remaining wine in one fluid motion—a skill Dodge learned in the Air Force. One that other people learn in college.

A college graduate.

"Well, I guess we don't have much time, do we?" she said.

"Time is relative," he said.

"Time is finite. So, we better get started." Nikki stood from the table and grabbed her purse. "Let's go see that boat."

Dodge took a twenty out of his wallet and laid it on the table. The two waited out front for a taxi and made the quick ride to the pier. Once on the boat, Nikki walked right to the cabin door and dropped her dress to the deck at the top of the stairs. She glanced at Dodge over her shoulder.

"You coming?"

Dodge stripped off his shirt and left it on the deck next to her dress. The two made love as the waves rocked the boat back and forth.

The two laid in bed, both trying to catch their breath.

"Who is Kelly?" she said.

"What?"

"The boat's name is *Kelly's Dream*. Who is Kelly?"

"Someone not around anymore."

"Did she divorce you?"

Dodge looked away. "She died."

Nikki sighed. "I'm sorry. I didn't mean to bring up awful memories."

Dodge rolled onto his side. "Not your fault. No way you could have known."

"Still, I'm sorry about the memories. Anything I could do to make it up to you?"

She ran her hand down his chest, past his stomach. Dodge flipped her over, and they made love again. This time, it was more primal. Shorter, but better.

They lay in bed, sweating and panting.

After a few minutes, Nikki sat up and started getting dressed.

"Going somewhere?"

"I need to get home. I have to feed my fish."

"That sounds like a line to me."

"No, really. I own tropical fish, and I need to make sure they get the right amount of food each day. Being a fish parent is an enormous responsibility."

Dodge laughed. "Will I see you again?"

"You know where I work. Just stop by and say hi. Besides, sex on a boat was always a fantasy of mine."

Dodge and Nikki took the dinghy back to shore. She kissed him goodbye and squeezed his butt for good measure. He watched her walk off into the night.

He liked this girl. Even if he would possibly only get to see her for just a month or two.

Dodge got back into the dinghy and pointed it toward *Kelly's Dream*. Sleep would come quickly tonight.

CHAPTER 10

DODGE WAS AWAKE AND STANDING on the mainland by 8:00 a.m. He had a coffee cup in one hand and gripped a notebook in the other. Before falling asleep the night before, he remembered the reason for going to the health department was to see Maria Delgado's shipping crate. The shooting had prevented that, and he needed to return to examine it.

The tactical commander called and left a message late last night, saying the medical examiner was safe at his home. He had left the office early for personal reasons, just as the man impersonating an assistant had said. Dodge wondered just how much luck played into the doctor not being at his office during the shooting. He couldn't shake the feeling that everything was related to Maria Delgado. The other bodies in the building were locals who died of natural causes, most likely.

His taxi arrived at the coroner's office at 8:30. The building was open early because the local forensic team was still on sight, processing the crime scene. Dodge figured while he was at the site, he could give his fingerprints to the techs. He had been to the office twice, and undoubtedly left prints when opening doors, as well as in the medical examiner's office when viewing Maria Delgado's body.

The tech took Dodge's prints, then provided him with a pair of protective gloves to wear while on scene. Dodge asked a local officer about the shipping container and was pointed toward the lab at the building's back. Upon entering the room, Dodge found that he was not alone. The doctor was there, and so was Agent Williams.

"Good morning, Dodge," Williams said. "I thought you might be back here today."

"You did, did you?"

"Yes. At first, I tried to figure out what you would do. But I don't know you that well. So, I went with what I would have done if I was in your shoes."

"I didn't examine the shipping crate yesterday," Dodge said, "which was my sole reason for being here. Is that it?"

He circled a damaged crate in the middle of the room. Examined five of the six crushed sides—the sixth being the side contacting the floor—and found the box to be unremarkable. The hole he had noticed earlier in the photos was obviously to allow fresh air into the crate so Maria could breathe, but not big enough for any prying eyes to see inside. The ME had cut one end of the container free to reach Maria's body. The cut piece was resting on the floor next to the crate. Dodge asked the coroner for a sheet so he could slide on his back into the damaged container. He needed to experience what Maria Delgado went through as the box collapsed around her, without contaminating the scene.

Even for a girl of Maria's size, the box's space had been small before being crushed by the other containers. Dodge was a little larger than the average male—six-foot-one, two hundred pounds—and the space was tight. But the evidence team had removed all the packing material meant to keep young Maria from moving around too much, and the stocky parole agent was able to move his arms side to side, and rotate his head left to right. The confined space smelled of urine and feces—the result of the victim's bladder releasing its contents after her death.

Dodge felt sorry for the girl. As he began to inch out of what had become the girl's coffin, a speck of light crossed over his dilated brown pupils, causing him to squint and look away. He opened his eye and cocked his head to the left to keep the light from shining directly into his eyes again. Then he saw the thin stream of light coming from the small air hole, which would have provided the last rays of daylight Maria's eyes saw before being suffocated.

A chill ran down his spine. He was overwhelmed with a desire to get out of that crate.

As he slid out, he noticed scratches on the inside of the top wall of the box. It looked like writing.

"Agent Williams, do you have a flashlight?"

Williams looked at the doctor. "Not on me. Doc, do you have one handy?"

The coroner said he had one in the lab for power outages and walked across the hall to retrieve it. He returned with the flashlight and handed it to Dodge, who was still lying inside the crate. Dodge pointed the light toward what he thought were markings on the crates inside wall. He could make out four distinct letters. The first was J. The second, U, or a V. The third letter was an A, and the fourth was N. J-U-A-N. Maria had scratched the name Juan on the top wall of the crate.

Dodge crawled out of the box and stood next to Agent Williams.

"There is something etched into the inside wall of the crate," he said.

Agent Williams turned to the coroner. "Doc, can you give us a minute?"

He nodded, leaving the two men alone in the room with the crate.

"The doc doesn't know the Bureau has identified the girl," Williams said. "So, let's keep as much of this just between us for as long as we can."

Dodge agreed. The name *Juan* meant nothing to the two men now, but it was still early in the investigation.

"Is there any sign of the guys from last night who were in this room?" Dodge said.

"They were definitely in the room. The techs removed a side of the crate to get the body out. After they finished processing the evidence, the side was put back in its original position so the crime scene team could rebuild the events of that night, using the damaged crate as a starting point. When I got here this morning, the side was on the floor."

A sense of confirmation came over Dodge. That intruders were here to see the crate, linked the break-in to Maria Delgado, somehow.

"Now, if we can just identify the dead guy posing as the doctor's assistant," Dodge said, "we may be able to cut the list of possibles in half."

"The Bureau is working on that. I hope to hear something from his fingerprint comparison and DNA sample by the end of the day."

The Bureau moves a hell of a lot faster than the state.

The same tests would take weeks, or even months, to process through state crime labs, which suffered from backlog and lack of funding.

Dodge and Agent Williams stared at the shipping crate, each thinking about the fate that befell little Maria Delgado. No one deserved to die this way. Alone, in a dark, cramped, dirty box. Dodge wanted to get justice for her.

The two men left the health department and made the fifteen-minute drive back to the FBI field office downtown. Once in the office, Agent Williams, along with Agent McCaffrey, who had been overseeing the evidence processing, debriefed Dodge on his involvement in the attack at the health department the day before. Both men were relieved he hadn't discharged his weapon. Shots fired meant lots of paperwork, and Dodge guessed if those shots came from an outside contractor, that meant even more paperwork. Likely, a trip to Miami or DC to explain the decision to provide a contractor with a weapon.

Secretly, he, too, was glad he hadn't shot anyone. That was part of the job he would never miss. Justified or not, killing a man hung around an officer's neck like a noose, tightening its grip until they couldn't breathe, and started abusing alcohol or drugs, leading many to take their own lives.

The three men sat in Agent Williams's office, discussing the recent evidence and each of their thoughts on the direction the investigation should turn. Dodge favored running down the name from inside the crate and finding the crate's origin, including airport staff that had contacted it in both countries.

Agent Williams wanted to work the Trey-Deuces angle. He felt their involvement in the death of a Colombian cartel leader's daughter was more than spurious. Finding out how the Trey-Deuces were involved might break the case wide open.

Agent McCaffrey felt scrutiny of Jesús Martinez Delgado and his close associates was warranted. Who would kidnap a drug lord's child? If that is in fact what happened, who did Delgado trust to be close enough to the girl to take her without raising red flags?

All three men wanted to know who had broken into the ME's office. They decided to divide and conquer, each man following the lead of his choice. Dodge would begin at the airport. Agent Williams would hit the local police department for information about the Trey-Deuces. Agent McCaffrey would take a flight to Bogotá, Colombia, to talk to the DEA, and his Colombian counterparts, about Jesús Martinez Delgado's criminal organization.

CHAPTER 11

DELGADO SAT ON THE BOAT'S STERN, tired and deflated from the failed attempt to retrieve his daughter's body. The plan was simple: bribe the medical examiner twice what he makes in a year to look the other way so Delgado and his henchmen could repatriate Maria's body. It should've been easy. They had brought plenty of cash to pay off the ME, plus anyone else who vowed to stay quiet.

Delgado was always cautious and had taken enough firepower if things didn't go as planned. He had hoped for the best but prepared for the worst. No sleep or food for over twenty-four hours was taking a toll on his physical and mental state.

Upon returning to the boat, he shot the remaining two hitmen. Their bodies were wrapped in plastic, taped tight, and shoved into a storage compartment to be dumped in deeper water once the boat returned to sea.

Melendez had tried to talk him out of killing the two men. But Delgado was not a man who accepted failure or left witnesses to talk to cops. He kept the boat captain alive only because they needed someone to navigate the highly patrolled waters between St. Thomas and Puerto Rico.

"So boss, do I need to find more men?"

Delgado stared out over the blue water. Two men. Three men. Hell, even twenty men didn't matter if he couldn't get the simple details correct—details like when the medical examiner would be at work, and when he would be home.

"No," Delgado replied. "We will do this ourselves. There are already too many bodies piling up. Eventually, we will have to kill someone that matters to somebody."

"What do we do now, boss?" said Melendez.

Delgado stood and walked to the cooler strapped to the boat's back seat and took out a beer.

"We need a distraction. We need to get the federals to look in another direction."

Melendez also grabbed a beer from the cooler, and swallowed half of it in one gulp.

"How do we do that, boss? I mean, we are down to you and me, and an old man. Who do we know on the island that can help us?"

Delgado had never thought about it before, but why was Maria on this island. Her captors could have sent her anywhere. They could have sent her to a rival drug cartel. She could have been dropped off a cliff, into a mountain lake. Or offshore, into one of the deep channels surrounding Colombia's coasts. But no, she ended up on this island for a reason. He had been so fraught with grief; he hadn't considered anyone outside of Colombia being involved. He just wanted to get his little girl and take her home. But her presence on St. Thomas proved his initial thinking was wrong.

Before the plan went south, he had seen the crate in which Maria had died. The shipping label was still intact, and St. Thomas was the ultimate destination. That meant someone on this island knew something about what happened. That said, he would soon know something. He would kill everyone on the island, if necessary, but he would get answers.

"Right now, we wait," Delgado replied. "We will go into town tomorrow and find out as much as we can about who runs this island. Once we have that information, I'll meet with them. If they know anything, they will tell me, or I'll dry up this island. There won't be so much as an ounce of cocaine to sell. If they still don't tell me, I'll kill their families. Eventually, someone will talk. They always do."

"What do we tell the captain?" Melendez said. "He's frightened he'll be the next one stuffed into a storage locker."

"Tell the captain he can have the other three men's shares. If that doesn't calm his nerves, shoot him in the head."

———

Dodge pulled into the parking lot across from the US Customs office at the airport. Agent Williams had provided him with one of the pool vehicles assigned to the FBI office—a dark-blue Chevy Impala. It wasn't the classic Ford sedan, but it still looked like a government vehicle, right down to the dash-mounted red and blue flashers.

He wanted a better look at the shipping documents on Maria Delgado's crate, so he headed for the duty officer's desk. If he were lucky, the bill of lading would contain a shipping address and the name *Juan* in the shipper details. He could collect his check and take Nikki out to another dinner. But deep down, he knew it wouldn't be that easy. It never was. Whoever had taken the girl had put in motion a sophisticated plan to get young Maria out of Colombia. Having a name on the shipping label that led back to the perpetrators would be a sloppy mistake. A mistake Dodge was sure they wouldn't make.

The security guard at the front door looked at Dodge's credentials and asked if he carried a weapon. The guard told Dodge to keep his gun, as the office was low on security staff because of the storm. Many locals had to spend extra time at home, fixing the damage caused by high winds and flooding. Customs figured the extra firepower in the building couldn't hurt.

Dodge waited ten minutes while the duty officer searched the records for the shipping manifest. The duty officer was old and about one-hundred pounds overweight. He moved with the steady precision of a sloth with two broken front legs.

After a thorough computer and paper file search, the old man returned to the desk.

"I can't seem to locate the paperwork for the crate you requested," he said.

"What do you mean you can't find the paperwork? The FBI seized the crate. You don't remember a crate the FBI took custody of with a dead body in it?"

"Of course, I remember. That poor girl stuck in that wooden crate for days. That is not something you forget."

The customs office's incompetence astonished Dodge.

"You remember the crate, but the paperwork is missing. Is that what you're telling me?"

"No. I am telling you that there doesn't seem to be any trace of the crate at this storage facility. Without the paperwork, the crate doesn't exist to customs."

How could an organization be so bad at its mission? First, they left the crate outside, and the storm damaged it. Then the body of Maria Delgado was found inside the container, and customs loses the paperwork? No shipping names or addresses. No identifiable information.

Customs was cleaning up its mess. Dodge guessed DC had decided to make what happened to Maria Delgado disappear, starting with the trail of paperwork placing the crate in their custody. He wanted to reach across the desk and strangle the old, fat man, but knew the decision to lose the paperwork originated way above his pay grade. He was just following orders.

Whatever had happened to the shipping manifest, it was now near impossible to track the crate from its point of origin or find the shipper. Dodge would have to find another way to get the information he needed.

As he sat in the blue sedan in the parking lot, trying to plan out his next move, he felt a vibration in his front pocket. He pulled out the phone Agent Williams had given him, but the screen was blank. Then he heard a bell chime. The message was from Nikki.

I thought we could have a drink, then dinner tonight. Around 8:00 p.m.—Nikki.

A quick stroke of the tiny keyboard and the response was sent. *Yes.*

As Dodge leaned back into the seat of the FBI pool car, he knew the story about lost paperwork was bullshit. The physical papers were shredded or burned, but the digital trail was never entirely deleted. There was always a backup or a copy saved to some random employee's desktop computer. Those documents cross the desks of ten employees from different agencies before the shipment hits open water. The same is true once it hits port. Nothing goes away forever anymore. Dodge just needed to figure out who saw the bill of lading and find out what they remembered. He hoped the computer records still existed, but he wasn't sure how to get his hands on those.

He thought about what his team knew about the shipment. They knew the country of origin and a name, and the ultimate destination. They also knew the name of the boat it sailed on, including the day it hit port. A little-known fact is, anyone can track any airplane or ship in real time, on the Internet. Some websites publish the data, and it's all free and accurate.

Dodge would look up the shipment when he got back to the FBI office. He also wanted to run background checks on all the dock employees who had access to the area Maria Delgado was found in. From the day it arrived, until the Bureau removed it from the yard. Trey-Deuce members working at the docks and airport cargo areas were a given. Uncovering the moles would be a massive break in the case.

On the other side of town, Agent Williams met with the local police gang unit, trying to figure out how a criminal street gang could tie into young Maria's death. He didn't trust the local cops any farther than he could throw them, but he needed a break, and he was willing to take the risk that the locals would tip off gang leadership.

Williams thought forcing the gangs to make an unexpected move might even help. Impulsive actions are sloppy, and often riddled with mistakes. Mistakes are good...for the cops. Mistakes provide a point of entry to apply pressure. Leverage is how a cop gets answers. Police work was not rocket science. It had nuance.

The lead officer on the gang task force told Agent Williams he was sure the Trey-Deuces were not involved in human smuggling, especially if it involved a child. They mainly dealt with narcotics and protection rackets. Agent Williams was convinced the lead agent was on the Trey-Deuces payroll. He had heard rumors for years, but never paid much attention, as the Bureau didn't use local authorities often. Besides, he knew the Trey-Deuces were somehow involved. His intelligence was firm on that fact. Almost irrefutable. Almost.

The local officer provided a name and location where they hang out and sell drugs. Agent Williams thanked the officer and assumed he made the obligatory phone call to the gang leaders before getting to his car. But Williams had a name and a place, and that was more than he had that morning.

He headed back toward the FBI office and planned to fill in Agent McCaffrey by phone, and Dodge once he returned from the airport.

CHAPTER 12

AGENT MCCAFFREY LANDED at El Dorado International Airport in Bogotá, Colombia, at 3:00 p.m. local time. After retrieving his luggage from the carousel, he walked out to the arrivals area, where he spotted the black SUV with diplomatic plates.

The local FBI office had requested the State Department send a car to pick up Agent McCaffrey. There had been random violence in the city over the past month, targeting the US Embassy and government personnel. Congress and the White House cut aid to local farmers as a retaliation for the kidnapping and murder of US citizens by cartel members in Colombia.

For decades, the US government had helped fund a worldwide program to give money to poor farmers who choose not to grow drug crops, like poppies and coca plants. Farmers took the aid money and still planted the drug crop because the drug cartels didn't offer them a choice. But the program made for a feel-good news story, and made the people back home feel like their government was trying to solve an unsolvable problem.

The embassy had a sizeable protective cement wall surrounding the perimeter of a small chunk of sovereign US soil. The FBI maintained an office at the embassy, as did the CIA, ATF, and DEA. It was easier to keep government employees safe in a building guarded by a US Marines and a Diplomatic Security Service detachment. Embassies were equipped for repelling any attack from outside their walls.

The checkpoint gate lifted as the black SUV approached, and the driver didn't even have to stop. A vehicle sitting motionless at a checkpoint would be an easy target for fringe groups and cartel hit squads. Once inside the compound walls, the black SUV stopped in front of the main entrance to the embassy, and Agent McCaffrey exited the vehicle and checked in at the security station. The security guard handed him a red visitor badge, then pointed toward the FBI's office. McCaffrey's shoes echoed down the long corridor for thirty seconds, before he stood in front of a glass door with the DOJ and FBI emblem emboldened on its translucent face. He entered and waited in a lobby chair, for the special agent in charge to meet him.

In Charlotte Amalie, Dodge and Agent Williams met at the FBI office. Dodge told Williams about his trip to the customs office, the lost paperwork, including his theory of why US Customs in DC would want to dump this case. No one in DC wanted to be the one tasked with the job of explaining, on the cable news networks, how a dead girl ended up in a secured US Customs area. It was easier to make the whole thing go away.

He also told Agent Williams that he was sure the Trey-Deuces had their people at the loading docks and in the airport baggage areas. It was the only way this entire scheme would ever work. If the FBI could root out the infiltrators at the airport and inside customs, they might flip them against whoever was behind Maria Delgado's death.

The senior FBI agent explained what he had learned from his meeting with the local police, and his concerns with their possible ties to the Trey-Deuces. He was worried about the location they gave him; the gang's clubhouse was not in a nice part of town. Even locals didn't venture into that neighborhood at night, and tourists were warned before leaving the cruise ship about the dangers in the areas surrounding downtown. It was a virtual dead zone for major retail outlets. The only businesses were a few mom-and-pop grocery stores, liquor stores, and bars. Any raid on the gang at that location would turn up little evidence, and the members would be long gone before the raid team made it to the address. There were lookouts, with cell phones, covering the entrances to the neighborhood, who would spot them before leaving the office. The whole thing was a dead end.

"Have you heard from Agent McCaffrey?" Dodge said.

"Not yet. His flight was scheduled to land in Bogotá around 3:00 p.m. local time. He had a meet-and-greet with the special agent in charge, followed by a briefing with the DEA. If he doesn't call by 6:00 tonight, I'll call him."

"Do you think he'll have any good news to report?"

"I don't know. But at this point, I'll take anything. Because right now, we have jack."

There was no arguing with Agent Williams's logic. Dodge knew it would be easier to leave the whole thing to the wolves. An enraged father and cartel leader would make a formable foe for anyone, including a small-time island gang. But too many questions needed answering before Dodge could justify walking away and allowing a revenge killing to occur. Besides, Maria Delgado was assaulted. That's one thing Dodge wouldn't let go unpunished. Holding people who hurt children responsible was why he did what he did. It was at the core of his identity. He would never allow a child rapist to walk free, even if it placed him in harm's way.

"Do you have any idea who broke into the ME's office?" Williams said.

"Nothing concrete. Just a gut feeling is all."

Williams nodded. "So, what is your gut telling you?"

Dodge paused. "My gut tells me never to reveal gut feelings, because if they turn out to be wrong, I risk looking like an idiot."

Agent Williams was silent.

"If I had to make a guess," Dodge said, "I would start by narrowing down who would benefit from anything learned from the crime scene."

Agent Williams was still silent.

"Because of what was in the ME's office, I would say it limits the pool of potential suspects to three groups. The first being local drug addicts looking for a quick score. This kind of thing happens all the time on the mainland. Junkies will break into a pharmacy or a veterinary clinic to steal the stock meds."

"People break into veterinary offices to steal animal medicine?" Williams said.

"They do. Painkillers for animals are the same kind as the ones you get from your doctor. Only, the narcotics the vet keeps are much more potent because animals have a higher tolerance than humans."

"Unbelievable!"

"Some people even hurt their pets on purpose to get the meds prescribed legally."

Agent William's face turned red. "People are jacked up, Dodge."

"They are. The second group are the ones responsible for Maria Delgado being in that crate. I assume she should not have been found in the customs yard. Therefore, they will try to get her back."

Agent Williams brow wrinkled as he squinted and shook his head. "But she was dead."

"All the more reason to get the body and hide it somewhere deep in the ocean or high on a mountain. Someplace no one would find her remains. No body, no crime."

Williams shook his head. "People are messed up."

Dodge nodded. "The third group is actually an individual."

"Jesús Martinez Delgado," said Williams.

"Exactly. A father would want to reclaim the body of his daughter. He is a drug dealer, but he's still a father."

"You think he would risk coming himself? I mean, his face has been all over the news for the past five years, and we would know about any movement he made outside of Colombia."

"You didn't know his daughter was kidnapped," Dodge said. "I'm not so sure the intelligence apparatus is functioning at full capacity on this one."

"If he was here—"

"He is here. And he'll try again."

"You seem sure," Williams said. "How can you know that?"

Dodge thought about the events just several months ago. His own actions, acting alone, had been foolish and risky, but he did it anyway.

"Because it's what I would do," he said.

Agent Williams shook his head. "I heard that about you."

"From back home?"

"Your pal, Renquest."

"He lies a lot."

Agent Williams nodded. "So, who is your money on?"

Dodge sat silently for a moment. "Well, Delgado is here."

"If that is true, we have a once-in-a-lifetime chance on our hands."

"Maybe. He'll be determined, and he has already killed one of his own men. Though, he didn't kill anyone working at the ME's office. Why, I don't know, but we won't be that lucky next time."

"You think?" Williams said.

"You said whoever broke in got a look at the shipping crate, right?"

"Yes."

"So, getting his daughter back isn't the only thing he's after. He wants to know who is responsible. I doubt his behavior will de-escalate now, especially since he didn't get what he came for."

Agent Williams frowned. "The press is all over this now. It will only be a matter of time before they identify Maria Delgado as the girl found in the crate."

"He knows that, too. He'll want to work fast and get off the island as quickly as possible."

"Commercial airlines are out of the question," Williams said.

"My guess is, he goes by boat. A commercial fishing vessel, or something else that would hide in plain sight."

"Maybe a two-seater from one of the old military landing strips on any of a hundred islands down here," Williams said.

"It's what I would do."

His dinner appointment with Nikki made Dodge end the meeting. Agent Williams said again that he would wait until 6:00 tonight to call Agent McCaffrey if he hadn't heard from him by then.

The two men would meet tomorrow morning and form a plan about how to best approach the Trey-Deuce issue. Dodge also needed time to think about Jesús Martinez Delgado. He had to find his sources on the island. They would certainly know something.

CHAPTER 13

ENDING THE MEETING WITH AGENT WILLIAMS early gave Dodge enough time to take the dinghy out to Kelly's Dream, shower, and put on clean clothes before meeting Nikki for dinner. This time, he chose a restaurant in town that Agent Williams had recommended. A small Italian place a block north of the tourist district. Williams had told him the pasta was homemade with local ingredients. But it was the Kobe beef steak that intrigued Dodge. He had never had a Kobe steak before, and he'd always wanted to try it. There were restaurants back home claiming to serve the ten-dollar-per-ounce steak, but he had always been skeptical. A TV documentary once showed how the cows were hand-fed and brushed. Every day, the animal was treated like a king, until it was killed. Could hand massaging the live animal and playing music make the meat more tender? Dodge couldn't see how, but he wanted to find out.

It was about 5:30 when Dodge finished tying up the dinghy to the pier. Sebastian was waiting in his colorful chair, sipping beer from a bottle stuffed into a brown paper bag. Dodge gave him a fifty-dollar bill and told him to keep the change.

Sebastian beamed. "I'll get right on it, boss."

The deed made Dodge feel good about himself. He liked to help Sebastian. He seemed like a good man, and life on the island had to be complicated as a local. All that tourist money coming to the island, and locals had to bite and claw for every penny to feed their families. *Life isn't fair, but I can only do so much.*

Dodge put a hand in his pocket and flipped through the edges of the folded bills like a deck of cards. *About three hundred dollars.* He walked two blocks north, then three blocks west, and arrived at the restaurant at about ten minutes to eight. Nikki was waiting for him at the bar, wearing a long white linen dress with a light blue silk top, and sandals adorned her finely pedicured feet. She turned as he approached.

"I hope I'm not late," he said.

"No, I got here early. Figured I'd have a drink before you showed up."

"Starting without me?"

Nikki smiled. "Didn't know if we would have time to eat or not."

Dodge smiled back. "I think we'll eat dinner this time. If that's okay with you?"

"I could stand for some food. You never know when you may need some quick energy."

Dodge laughed. "You want to sit at the bar, or should I get a table?"

"I already put in for a table. Hope that's all right. Wouldn't want to offend your sense of masculinity."

"You getting the table reaffirms it."

"How's that?"

"It's like back in the day, when the wife had dinner ready for her husband just as he arrived home from work."

"You don't seem like the marrying type."

"What makes you say that?"

"You exude single loner."

"A man can change, can't he?"

"Not in my experience."

He shook his head. "Mine either."

The bartender handed Dodge a drink menu and then placed a coaster in front of him before walking away to take a waitress's drink order. When the bartender came back, Dodge ordered a Blanton's on the rocks.

The two sat at a table in the corner. Nikki took the chair against the wall, leaving Dodge the chair with its back to the entry and exit. He decided not to say anything and took a long pull off his bourbon.

"So how was the bank today?"

"It's a bank. People come in and give or take money. Nothing too exciting. How was your day?"

Dodge paused. He wondered if Nikki noticed his hesitation.

"Pretty boring day. I interviewed a few people today. Nothing to write home about."

"What are you working on for the government?"

Dodge took another long pull from his bourbon. This time, to buy time to plan a response that didn't sound like he wasn't trying to avoid an answer. He could end her curiosity with the correct answer or expand it with the wrong one.

"Just some financial issues involving someone not paying their taxes."

He guessed Nikki wouldn't want to talk about financial crimes after working in a bank all day.

Nikki nodded and smiled and opened her menu.

The waitress came to the table with a pitcher of water and another drink for Dodge. She took their food orders and said they would be out shortly.

The couple's food arrived before Dodge finished his second bourbon, which was a good thing, as he already felt a buzz from drinking on an empty stomach.

Although he recalled having a filet just as tender at a restaurant in North Carolina a few years back, the Kobe beef steak was excellent. The chef prepared his sides of mashed potatoes and asparagus perfectly. Nikki had red snapper, whole and stuffed with lobster, with a small side salad. Dodge ate his meal and part of Nikki's after she said she couldn't take another bite. The extra food in his stomach allowed him to consume one more bourbon before paying for the meal.

The weather was warm and humid. The breeze intensified as they got closer to the harbor. Dodge saw lighting far out on the horizon. *Heat lighting, or a storm brewing far off in the distance.*

"Looks like it might storm," he said.

Nikki peered out into the blackness over the harbor.

"Just heat lighting," she said.

Dodge felt the first raindrop hit his face. Then another, and another.

"Heat lightning, huh?" he said.

"I guess I was wrong. I suppose we should find some shelter for the next couple hours. These storms rarely last more than a few hours."

Dodge looked toward *Kelly's Dream* anchored in the harbor.

"We might get caught in the rain and choppy waters if we take the dinghy to my boat."

Nikki smiled. "I might get seasick, too!"

"How far is your place from here?"

"Not too far." She pointed east. "Maybe a ten-minute walk."

The rain was falling steadier, with fewer voids between drops hitting their skin. The pair began walking toward Nikki's house, but ended up jogging the last few blocks because the skies let loose with a downpour. By the time they reached the front door of Nikki's home, they were both soaked. Neither had on a dry stitch of clothing, including shoes and undergarments. Once inside, Nikki stripped off all of her clothes and moved into the bedroom. Dodge wasn't sure what to do. Was it a sign to join her, or was she simply changing into dry clothes? He just stood in the entryway, dripping water onto the tile floor.

Nikki reappeared from the bedroom, wearing a robe and holding a towel. Her hair was still wet but hanging down, covering her shoulders. She looked amazing.

"Let's get you out of those wet clothes."

She stepped close to Dodge and began pulling his shirt over his head. He kicked his shoes off as she unbuttoned his pants, and the soaked fabric fell to the floor. He stepped out of his pants. A quick tug on his boxers, and they landed next to his pants. She dried off his naked body, starting with his head and moving down his chest to his stomach.

She stopped, stood up and kissed him hard on the lips. Dodge slipped his hand under one shoulder of Nikki's robe and slid it over her arm. Now they were both naked. They made love right there on the living room floor. Not once, but twice.

The storm never came, and the rain ended by midnight.

—⁓—

The sun shone through the patio windows, hitting Dodge in the face and waking him from a deep sleep. Nikki was beside him, sleeping with her head resting on his shoulder. He eased his arm out from under her head and rolled it onto a couch pillow they had knocked to the floor during the night's activities. He then went to the bathroom and brushed his teeth with his finger. Using his hand like a cup, he rinsed his mouth out and remembered that Nikki had put his wet clothes in the dryer. He got dressed and went back out into the living room.

Nikki was relaxing on the couch, in the bathrobe she had briefly worn the previous night, legs crossed, with a coffee cup in her hand.

"Got another cup?" Dodge said.

"Mug is on the counter." She pointed to a blue coffee mug sitting next to the coffeepot.

After pouring a cup, he sat next to her on the couch.

"What time do you have to be at work?" he said.

"Not until ten."

"Want to get some breakfast?"

"I can't. I have some errands to run before I go to work. Raincheck?"

Dodge nodded.

The two shared an intimate goodbye before Dodge left and began the long walk back to the pier. He needed to shower and change his clothes before meeting with Agent Williams. There was also the matter of another run at the duty officer staffing the US Customs office. He knew for sure the officer was lying to him, but he needed to get more information on who the Trey-Deuces might have placed at the docks. A name would be a good piece of leverage to use against the duty officer and show cracks in the system.

The dinghy had a full tank of gas and an extra can in the front for the generator.

"Sebastian always thinks ahead," he said to himself.

CHAPTER 14

DODGE ARRIVED AT THE FBI OFFICE early because he wanted to stop and get breakfast and coffee before the meeting. He didn't know if they would have time for lunch, and he didn't want to miss two meals, forcing an energy crash right when he might need it the most.

The plan had been to meet and discuss any news from Agent McCaffrey in Colombia. The two men would then devise a plan on how to meet with the Trey-Deuces.

During his time as a parole agent, Dodge had been a part of many raids, even the planning stages. But they always took place in his city, on his turf. He knew the layout and had days, if not weeks, to prepare a cohesive plan and coordinate with other agencies.

He and Agent Williams had none of that.

The mission would take place on the bad guy's turf, in the bad guy's city, and with little preparation time. There would be no coordination with the local police because Agent Williams didn't trust that the locals wouldn't tip off the Trey-Deuces. The two men would work alone. At least until Agent McCaffrey returned from Bogotá.

Oddly, this part of the plan Dodge didn't mind. He never enjoyed working in large groups. Too much left out of his control, and too much that could go wrong. Communications could break down, and friendly fire incidents were more common in large raid teams.

Agent Williams arrived at the office at 9:00 a.m. He had a cup of coffee and a bag of beignets. The oil from the beignets had soaked into the brown paper bag—a clear sign the powdered sugar pastries were fresh.

He sat across the conference room table from Dodge and slid the paper bag over to him. Dodge wasn't hungry, but never passed up anything resembling a donut. Especially one covered in white powdery goodness. He nearly choked on the first bite as sugar dust went into his windpipe, causing him to cough and drop the beignet on the table.

Williams smiled. "Always happens to newbies."

A sip of coffee cleared the obstruction.

"So, what did Agent McCaffrey have to say when you talked to him last night?" Dodge said.

Then he ate the rest of the beignet and wiped his hands on his pants, leaving white powdered sugar streaks—the telltale sign of a beignet breakfast.

Williams picked up his cell phone and looked at the screen.

"He never called. I figured he had a long day and crashed at the hotel after the meeting with the DEA."

"Maybe you should call the office and see if he's checked in today?"

Williams paused. "I'll try to call his cell again and see if he picks up."

He dialed the number and pushed the speaker button so both men could hear the conversation. The phone rang for several minutes, but there was no answer. Dodge could see the worry in his new partner's eyes. He had seen that same look in his chief's eyes, on more than one occasion, about his own wellbeing.

"I think you should call the FBI office and have them check his hotel to see if he checked in last night."

Agent Williams nodded and stepped out into the hallway, out of earshot, to call the FBI in Colombia. He returned to the conference room a few moments later.

"I spoke to the special agent in charge. He confirmed

McCaffrey met with him yesterday, and they talked about Jesús Martinez Delgado's drug-running operation. He also said McCaffrey was supposed to meet with the DEA after they finished."

"Is the DEA office in the embassy?"

"It is not. The DEA has its own office on the other side of Bogotá."

"Did he meet with the DEA?"

"I don't have that information yet. But the SSA in Bogotá will check on that for me."

Dodge felt a chill run down his spine. Agent McCaffrey not being locatable was a lousy situation for the FBI and McCaffrey. He worried the cartel had been tipped to Agent McCaffrey in Colombia and may have taken him for a trade. An agent for Maria Delgado's body.

He didn't want to place added stress on Agent Williams, so kept his fears to himself.

"He's probably just sleeping off the flight," Dodge said.

The two men sat in silence for a minute, each thinking the worst but not wanting to let the other know their doubts.

"Yeah," Williams replied. "Why don't we talk about how we'll handle the Trey-Deuces."

Agent Williams spread a map of Charlotte Amalie across the conference table. He pointed to the position on the map representing their current location at the FBI building. He then pointed to a spot that looked to Dodge to be about two miles from their current location, and said it was the Trey-Deuce's clubhouse. It was in an area Dodge had never stepped foot during his time on the island. Agent Williams said his only experience in the neighborhood came on a raid by the local police.

Dodge began counting the number of ways the mission could go wrong. After a half-dozen faulty scenarios, he stopped thinking about it. The two men were going to talk to the Trey-Deuce's leader, so they needed to play the cards they had, which wasn't much.

The two men sat on the ground, sweat dripping from their faces, staring at the hole they spent over an hour digging into the rocky ground. The older man pointed at the body wrapped in a white sheet—a sign he wanted the younger of the two men to do the heavy lifting of dragging the body over to the hole. The younger man protested, but the older man pulled rank, and that settled the argument.

Once the body was at the side of the grave, the two men pushed it into the hole and began back-filling. The younger man put two shovels full of dirt into the hole for every one shovel from the older man. After about twenty minutes, the grave was filled in completely. They then covered the spot with brush and grasses gathered from the area so it wouldn't be noticed by hikers or government forces patrolling the area.

The older man took out a cell phone and placed a call. The young man lit a cigarette and watched the older man talk to the boss on the phone. When he hung up, the older man yelled at the young one to grab the shovels and follow him back to the vehicle. They tossed the shovels into the truck's bed, and the older man handed the younger one the keys. The two men got in the truck and headed down the mountain road back toward town.

"What do we do now?" the younger man said.

"We go home. And you don't talk about this to anyone. Do you understand?"

The younger one shrugged.

"You put the gun and badge into the hole as I told you, right?"

The younger one nodded.

"Good. The boss doesn't care if they can identify him if they find his body."

The younger one said nothing and continued driving.

He dropped the older man off at a local bar and said he didn't want to drink. He said he needed to get home to his girlfriend. She was waiting for him to drive her to the market, and he didn't want to be late. The older man shrugged and walked toward the establishment.

The younger man waited until the older man was inside the bar, then reached under the seat and pulled a bag out from under the seat. He opened the bag and pulled out a 9mm Glock. The dead agent's gun was heavier than he thought it would be. The young thug had never owned a gun, but all the men close to the boss carried guns, including the older man.

The young man couldn't afford to buy one, and he didn't want to go into debt to the boss for a used piece of junk. Cops took the best care of their weapons, and in a business where guns meant power, he had a little now, too.

A quick look around told him the older man wasn't watching, and he put the gun back into the bag and shoved it under the seat. After pulling onto the road, he headed toward his house.

CHAPTER 15

DELGADO AND MELENDEZ STEPPED through the front doors of a one-room bar called Pepe's Place. A pool table sat in the middle of the floor, and Jamaican music wailed from a jukebox in the room's left front corner. The bar stretched from one side to the other, opposite the front door.

The layout is insufficient for a hideout, Delgado thought.

Seating was only available at the bar, placing every customer's back to the front door, which opened into a small room that was a sitting spot for a bouncer. Then another windowless door opened into the actual establishment. Once past the bouncer, a rival gang member could wait for their eyes to adjust to the light change before entering through the second door and laying waste to the people inside the larger room. But he and Melendez weren't here for a confrontation, only information.

Delgado shut the door behind him. Everyone at the bar turned in their chairs and collectively focused on the two strangers standing in their house. The bartender ducked out of sight through a door to the kitchen. A large man, wearing a dirty jean jacket with the sleeves cut off, stood and walked over, keeping the pool table between himself and the strangers. He remained there, silent, arms crossed and muscles twitching.

Delgado, sensing the tension and wanting to avoid a fight, threw his hands up in front of his chest and patted the air. The man in the jean jacket didn't move.

"We aren't here for trouble," Delgado said. "We just want some information."

A small man sitting at the center of the bar said, "You may not have been looking for trouble, but you might have found it, anyway."

Melendez crept his right hand toward the back of his jeans. Delgado touched his arm and shook his head.

"Are you the leader of this bunch?" Delgado said to the small man at the bar standing beside the man in the jean jacket with cut-off sleeves.

"I am," he replied.

"What is your name?"

"Fuck you."

A collective laugh rang out across the bar.

"I don't do that with men," Delgado said. "But feel free to use any of your friends in here. We are looking for some information about a little girl brought to this island a few days ago. I want to know who brought her here, and why she was taken." He paused. "I'll pay anyone who tells me what I want to know."

No one spoke. The guy in the jean jacket glanced at the little man who claimed to be the leader. Delgado recognized the look—*Should we tell him, or kill him?*

He stepped in front of Melendez and closer to the pool table. Partly because he wanted to block Melendez from view, and partly because he might need the pool table's slate top between him and the bullets that might come his way. He hoped Melendez had taken his cue and used the distraction to retrieve his gun from the small of his back.

The little leader said, "Why don't you take your money and get the hell out of here before something bad happens to you."

Delgado looked at the floor and shook his head.

"Do you know who I am?"

"Punta," the little man said.

"My name is Jesús Martinez Delgado."

The name fell dead on some gang members. But according

to the look in their eyes, the little man and the man in the jean jacket with cut-off sleeves knew who they were talking to.

Then all hell broke loose.

The little man yelled at the man in the jean jacket.

"Kill them!"

Melendez fired over the shoulder of Delgado, killing the man in the jean jacket. The sight of their comrade dead on the floor caused the other members to pause for a split second, giving Delgado time to draw his weapon and unload round after round toward the bar. He wasn't aiming. He was trying to put as much hot lead into the kill zone as possible.

Melendez shot the little man in the leg as he tried to scurry away, and then began shooting at the men still standing at the bar. It was over in about ten seconds. Most of the gang members were dead. The ones that weren't dead, Melendez executed by shooting them in the head. All except for the little man. Delgado wanted him alive. At least until he got some answers.

The fire department had extinguished the flames by the time Dodge and Agent Williams arrived at the Trey-Deuce's clubhouse. The metal frame of the sign that once hung above the door and lit up with the name *Pepe's*, now sat on the ground, charred and discolored. The rest of the building was reduced to a pile of smoldering embers, and the smell of burned flesh seemed to hang right at nose-level in the air around the scene.

Agent Williams flashed his badge to the officer handling the rope line and proceeded toward the fire chief's vehicle on the other side of the parking lot. The chief was a white man with red hair. He appeared Irish, which surprised Dodge. He imagined locals would have been placed into high-profile jobs in city government. Agent Williams said that was usually the case. But after searching for months and interviewing every applicant from the island, city leaders couldn't find a suitable candidate from the island, so they advertised on the mainland. Chief O'Sullivan had retired from his position in New York

City, moved to St. Thomas, and took over the fire chief job for Charlotte Amalie. His pale skin and freckles assured everyone he didn't come to the island for the beaches.

"What can I do for the FBI?" Chief O'Sullivan said.

Agent Williams identified himself and his new partner.

"What happened here?" he said.

"Fire. A hot one, at that," O'Sullivan replied. "It took two tankers to knock it down. Why does the FBI care about a local bar fire?"

"We're working on a lead for a missing girl," Agent Williams said. "Can you tell if it was arson?"

"There isn't much left of the structure. The heat at the center of the fire was intense. The only things left are the steel appliances. We likely won't find much evidence in that mess."

"So, it was an accident?" Dodge said.

"No. It was arson, for sure."

The two men remained silent, waiting for more of an explanation. O'Sullivan must have picked up on the signal, because after an awkward moment of silence, he continued.

"The bodies." He pointed to the burned-out shell of the bar. "There are like fifteen bodies in there. I had to send two recruits back for more bags."

"You found fifteen bodies inside?" Williams said. "They couldn't get out?"

"Hard to move when you are already dead."

"All fifteen were dead when the fire started?" Dodge said.

"Looks that way. We'll know more when the coroner can complete an autopsy of what's left."

"If the bodies are that cooked," Williams said, "how do you know they were dead before the building burned down?"

The fire chief led the two men over to a group of body bags lined up single file in the parking lot. He unzipped one bag.

"This one has a bullet hole in his head. He died farther away from where the fire originated and toasted less than the others."

Parts of a blue denim jacket were stuck to the victim's burnt flesh. It reminded Dodge of the jackets outlaw motorcycle gangs decorated with patches and wore everywhere.

Agent Williams examined the corpse. "They shot him at close range, in the head. Looks like he might have another hole in his chest."

"They executed him," Dodge said.

"Yeah."

O'Sullivan zipped up the bag and asked if there was anything else the FBI needed. Agent Williams shook his head and thanked the chief for his time. Dodge asked if they could get a copy of the completed arson report. The chief said he would call once he finished the preliminary investigation and had typed the report. They thanked the chief again, and the two men walked back to their car. Neither spoke the entire ride back to the office. They didn't have to, because they were thinking the same thing. Their collective worry for Agent McCaffrey had just increased tenfold.

CHAPTER 16

DELGADO AND MELENDEZ TRAVELED across town as fast as possible without drawing unwanted attention. The shootout at the bar was a mistake. The dead bodies inside the smoldering remains would inevitably draw attention from the FBI or Homeland Security, making time a precious resource.

During the ride to the northern outskirts of town, Delgado interrogated the hostage, who was brave at first and withstood the pain of the beating. But a man can only take so much. Delgado buried his finger into the gunshot wound on the little man's leg and twisted and pulled and pushed. He threw up twice from the pain before he spilled his guts. Then his torturer did what he promised. He stopped the pain with one round through the ear hole—guaranteed to hit all the important stuff in the brain and turn it into mush.

They drove to the northern edges of the city so they could dump the body. Delgado had no more room on the boat and didn't want to take the chance of fishermen seeing them lug 120 pounds of dead weight from the car to the dinghy tied up on the beach.

After pushing the little man's body out of the car and into a drainage ditch, the men headed southwest toward the beach and the dinghy. Delgado had gotten the information he wanted. He knew the FBI had identified his daughter. The Trey-Deuces had a man inside the local police department. The source had tipped gang leadership to the FBI's most recent visit, seeking information about the gang's clubhouse.

Retrieving his daughter's body would be near impossible now. The feds would guard it like Fort Knox. She was probably already on her way to Miami for safekeeping. It infuriated him, but he couldn't do anything about that now. But he could do something about the ones that had betrayed him—the ones behind his daughter's murder.

The little man had told him what happened. A Trey-Deuces member came to the man with a problem. The gang member said he had a cousin in Colombia who worked for a terrible man. A killer. The gang member's cousin had called him and said he accidentally hurt a young girl. A few members—laborers and drug mules—had gotten together for a party. There were drugs, alcohol, women, and everyone was drunk or high. One of the laborer's kids stopped by, and with him was a fifteen-year-old girl named Maria. Had Delgado been a fly on the wall, he would have seen exactly what happened next.

The boy and Maria stayed and had a few drinks, and he did a few lines of coca and became stoned out of his mind. The girl, Maria, wanted to leave, but a few of the partygoers thought it would be fun to mess with her. Three men took her into a room and locked the door. One man passed out in a chair. The other two began kissing her and grabbing her under her skirt. Maria screamed and kicked and fought, but she couldn't stop it from happening. She closed her eyes until her assaulters passed out from the effects of liquor, drugs, and exhaustion.

Maria laid on the bed, silent until she was sure the men were asleep. She could still hear the noises from the party downstairs. The front door wasn't an option. So, she took the only exit available to her and jumped from the window, onto the street, snapping her leg on impact. Her screams alerted the men inside, and they ran outside to see what was happening. Two men noticed the gravity of the situation, brought the young girl back inside, and woke the young boy she came with. The men kicked and punched the boy until he told them her name—Maria Delgado. Everyone knew the name Delgado, and one of the men pieced together who she was.

The three men were also beaten after learning who the girl's father was. The leader of the group decided they needed to make her disappear. None of them were mercenaries, and no one wanted to kill a child, so one man came up with a plan. They would need help from someone inside Delgado's organization. Someone with access to money and influence with security and customs officers.

Delgado knew human trafficking required dozens of payoffs across multiple levels. The drug lord had been paying off longshoremen for years. He knew the going rate for a kilo of cocaine. A live girl, a child, had to be ten times that. Too many people and too much money for dumb cargo loaders, deckhands, and dock workers. Someone would have a new television or gold teeth—an easy mark in a poor neighborhood.

Delgado would put feelers out to his lieutenants when he returned to the boat. The grieving father was getting closer to finding the men who betrayed him.

When the two men returned to the office, it was clear something had happened. The office was abuzz with agents on phones, and television monitors were showing news stories out of Colombia. Most of the broadcasts were in Spanish, but one set displayed a local channel covering breaking news, according to the banner moving across the scene.

"What the hell is going on?" Agent Williams said to the first agent that crossed his path.

"They found McCaffrey. He's dead, sir."

"What the hell are you talking about? Who found him?"

"The DEA got a tip from a local villager in Colombia about a mule showing off a brand-new Glock 9mm to his girlfriend. Apparently, she was so mad, she told her neighbor that her boyfriend had a new gun. She thought he had taken a higher-ranking job with the Delgado Cartel. The DEA and Colombian anti-drug forces talked to the kid to see if new guns were coming into the area. Most of the weapons that turn up in the hands of mules and runners are trashed-out Cuban or Chinese models with the serial numbers filed off. When they started questioning the kid, he got so scared his boss would find out the DEA was at his house. So, he handed the Glock over to the agent. The agent immediately recognized that the Glock was well-maintained and had law enforcement loads. A quick call to the FBI confirmed the gun was an agency weapon and assigned to Agent McCaffrey."

Dodge was silent.

"How long before we get his body back?" said Agent Williams. "I want to be the one to notify the family?"

"The State Department is filing the proper paperwork with the locals."

A booming voice echoed Agent Williams's name from across the room. Dodge looked over and saw a gray-haired man in a mainland suit made of cotton, staring at them. The suit screamed DC. Or maybe the Miami field office. A dead agent will always unite the brass looking for someone to blame. Everyone trying to save their ass and deflect the incident as far from them as possible.

Agent Williams began walking toward the suit, who then called out to Dodge.

"Agent Dodge, you come, too."

"Crap," he whispered.

Once in Agent Williams's office, the suit closed the door.

"Have a seat, boys. The name is Boyers."

He was from the Miami field office, for sure. He was wearing cowboy boots and a bolo tie. Miami is an urban area, but many agents transferred to the office from rural parts of the country to experience working large drug busts and RICO prosecutions.

Dodge once instructed a Miami sex trafficking training, and he noticed right away the local sheriff and many feds dressed like southerners. They love to wear hillbilly attire. They think it scares the locals. Makes the agents seem like outsiders capable of breaking Miami rules. But all the attire really did was make them stand out and put a target on their backs.

To each his own.

"What is this I heard about McCaffrey?" said Agent Williams.

"They found his body at about noon, local time. The kid with his gun led the locals and DEA to the body. He was beaten to death. Probably with hammers or crowbars."

The guilt registered on Agent William's face. He was the one who'd sent McCaffrey to Colombia, and maybe it was his fault McCaffrey was dead.

Dodge looked back at the suit, who was now staring a hole through him.

"Agent Dodge, is it?"

"It is."

"How the hell do you play into this whole thing?"

There was no way to gauge how much the suit knew, or if he was aware of the arrangement between him and Agent Williams. Dodge answered with as little information as possible to avoid throwing Agent Williams under the bus.

"I'm just here to help in any way I can."

"Cut the crap, boys. I know about the arrangement Williams made with you. Hell, I approved it. So, stop with the Abbott and Costello routine, and tell me what the hell is going on here."

Agent Williams told the suit everything. From the dead girl and her drug lord father, which he knew about. To the burned corpses of the Trey-Deuces, which he didn't know about. Boyers said it was his call to send McCaffrey to Colombia, even though it was McCaffrey's idea. No need to sully the dead's reputation. Besides, the boss's job is to take responsibility for the good and the bad.

That's another reason Dodge didn't aspire to be a boss.

After about twenty minutes, the suit had the whole story. He was quiet for what seemed like an eternity.

"So, what do we know?" he finally said.

Agent Williams replied, "I believe Jesús Martinez Delgado is on the island, sir."

"Why would he come here? And cut that *sir* shit out."

"To get his daughter's body," Dodge said. "Drug dealer or

not, he's still a father. I would have done the same."

Boyers stared at Dodge like he was deciding whether to believe him or tell him to pound sand. He pulled his hand through his thin gray hair and leaned back in his seat.

"Okay. Let's go with, Delgado was on the island. Let's say he is the one who slaughtered the...what do they call themselves?"

"The Trey-Deuces," Williams said.

"Let's say he is the one who charbroiled those *Trey-Douches* in that bar today. Why?"

Dodge said, "Well, I can only speculate that he's trying to figure out who kidnapped and killed his daughter. That's how I would react."

Agent Williams nodded.

"Do we think this Delgado fellow killed Agent McCaffrey?"

"It's too early to tell that, sir," Williams said. "We need to find out what happened in Colombia first. I assume the local office is interrogating the kid who had McCaffrey's gun?"

"They are," Boyers said. "They'll keep me in the loop. I'll tell you what I know as soon as I know it." He rose from his chair to leave.

Williams said, "I would like to keep Agent Dodge on board, if possible. He has been an enormous help so far. And frankly, without McCaffrey, I'm short a good investigator."

"Those were my thoughts, exactly," Boyers said. "I have already talked to his supervisor—a Chief Johnson—about him. He assured me Agent Dodge was precisely the man we needed on this case."

He gave the new guy a side glance. The kind a commanding officer gives a subordinate when he wants him to handle a problem off the books.

Dodge smiled as Boyers and his entourage left the office, leaving the two men in silence. They needed a new plan.

CHAPTER 17

FOR DODGE, WALKING AND THINKING went together like mustard on a hot dog. Losing a fellow officer was never easy. It struck at the heart of the entire law enforcement community. It was a message, and he was mad as hell.

He had understood the mess at the medical examiner's office. And he understood the killing of the Trey-Deuces. He didn't condone the actions, but he realized the tactical practicability. The guy at the ME's office was a liability. The Trey-Deuces...well, let's just say they needed a reminder of to whom they owed their wealth. Other gangs on the island wouldn't try to cross Delgado after that massacre.

The part that didn't make sense was, why murder a federal agent in Colombia. On his turf. That was the move of a desperate man, not the thought-out process of a ruthless cartel leader. Where was the upside? The US federal government doesn't run away when one of theirs is murdered. They come in full force. Agents in helicopters with .50-caliber machine guns mounted on the sides. Drones with hellfire missiles mounted under their wings, capable of hitting a target from two miles high and five miles away. Increased funding for the local military and police forces.

None of this was good news for Delgado. He was now the most famous man in the world. The wrong kind of famous. His face-on-a-deck-of-cards famous, like the US military used in Iraq when hunting down the top members of the Iraqi government after the 2003 invasion.

Cigarettes always calmed Dodge's nerves, and the store down the street had a nice selection of bourbon to go with the smokes. He needed a drink, and guessed Agent Williams could use one, too.

Agent Williams was sitting at his desk when he returned to the office, just staring out the window. Dodge knocked before entering and set the bottle of bourbon on his desk.

"Got any glasses?"

Agent Williams stared at the bottle, then reached into his desk drawer to retrieve two coffee mugs. He blew into each cup to remove the dust. Dodge pulled the cork from the top of the bottle, splashing an ounce into each cup.

"To Agent McCaffrey," Williams said.

Dodge didn't feel like eulogizing. He was furious, and the primal urge for revenge boiled deep inside.

He swallowed his bourbon, and the two men stared at the empty glasses. Agent Williams poured another shot for himself. Dodge shook off the second.

"What is the Bureau going to do next?" he said.

"The Bureau will do what it always does. They will bury the whole thing. Then issue a statement saying Agent McCaffrey was killed in a helicopter accident, or a car accident while visiting Colombia on personal time."

"Why would the FBI just not come out and say a drug cartel killed him? It isn't like the people in the United States would have some great uprising over a dedicated agent doing his job in a foreign land. Hell, I saw plenty of those boys die in the desert. Not one caused an uproar enough to roil a politician. It wasn't until the gains stopped being made, and IEDs started maiming troops in record numbers, that the civilians yelled enough to make the folks in congress nervous."

Agent Williams finished his shot of bourbon. "I would like to say the Bureau doesn't want to tip its hand to the Delgado Cartel. But I think we both know that isn't true. The director would score political points by going on CNN and telling the world the cartels have crossed the line and placing a bounty on the head of Jesús Martinez Delgado. Hell, the Midwest would practically dance in the streets."

Dodge said nothing.

"It's a new world out there. The drug war is at its most unpopular point in history. Mass incarcerations, black teenagers being killed in the streets—it all just plays badly on the news."

"What are you going to do?" Dodge said.

"I am going to work the Maria Delgado case. If that leads me to who is responsible for McCaffrey's death, then so be it."

"What do you want me to do?"

"That's a question I'm not ready to answer." Williams set his glass on the desk. "You were in the Air Force, right?"

Dodge nodded.

"What was your job?"

"Special security police."

"Did you ever do any tactical stuff while in the Air Force?"

"Some."

"Jungle training?"

"We had a few exercises in the Pacific Northwest—the best place stateside that we could imitate the jungles of wherever our next fight would be. I mean, we had been fighting in a desert for over ten years, but the service branches never forget where they came from."

Agent Williams said nothing. He stared out to a point somewhere in the distance, focusing on a thought or idea just out of reach.

Dodge had been known to have the same look in his own eyes. He understood what was happening. Chief Johnson had said he was precisely the man they needed for this job.

Agent Williams told his new partner to take the rest of the day. He needed to stay on top of the effort to bring McCaffrey's body back to St. Thomas, and then oversee the transfer to the mainland. McCaffrey's family lived in Indianapolis. It would be several days before his parents could receive the body and have a funeral—a closed casket, in this case.

Dodge thought about going to the bank to see Nikki but

decided against it. He just needed to think and rest on *Kelly's Dream*.

After walking the short distance to the pier, he slipped Sebastian another twenty. He knew he could use the money. Once onboard, Dodge poured a glass of bourbon. A long pour. He lit a cigarette and sat in the air conditioning in the cabin, protected from the tropical sun on deck.

He wasn't sure what would happen in the next few days, but how could he get justice for McCaffrey? The Bureau could never tie the murder to Delgado. He was way too cunning for that. These thoughts festered in his head as he watched the sun linger on the horizon and finally sink into the sea.

Why would Delgado murder an FBI agent in his home country, and then not dispose of the body in a more permanent manner? They could have burned the body or dumped it off a cliff or into a river and let the local wildlife devour the remains. An expert killer like Delgado should have known the entire US government would come crashing down on his head at the discovery of a dead FBI agent. Even the Colombian government, which looked the other way most of the time, would have no choice but to arrest him. He would lose.

It made zero sense. Something was wrong, but Dodge couldn't put his finger on it.

He lay back on the sofa and closed his eyes.

CHAPTER 18

THE WIND BLEW STEADY from the east. The sails billowed and pushed Kelly's Dream to the west and south. The captain tugged hard on the wheel, trying to correct the boat's direction, but it continued toward the rocky outcrop that riddled the shores of the Caribbean island.

Nikki stood in the cabin door, a look of worry on her face. The concern wasn't for her. Something else that troubled her. It was as if she knew something he didn't.

Lightning lit up the sky all around Kelly's Dream. The streams jumped from cloud to cloud like the water jets that shot from the Bellagio pool in Las Vegas. The wind's intensity picked up, and Kelly's Dream gathered speed. Dodge was struggling to control her direction as the boding rock formations ahead got closer. He could feel the boat shake around the center mast, and a violent buzzing came through the helm. He was losing her.

Dodge's eyes shot open, his cell phone ringing in his hand. He had put it in vibration mode while at the FBI office, and never turned the ringer back on. It took a minute to gain his senses before reading the number on his caller ID screen. Nikki.

He looked at his watch and noticed it was 8:30 p.m. Going out hadn't been in his plans, but he was now wide awake, drinking alone—the only other option for the night's activities. Nikki suggested meeting on *Kelly's Dream*, and that she would bring the food. He agreed and took the dinghy to the pier to pick her up.

Nikki brought Thai food from a little restaurant a block

from the bank where she worked. The vegetable entrée smelled strongly of curry and coconut, and a small brown bag held spring rolls with cabbage and shrimp. Dodge enjoyed the spring rolls but was not a fan of curry or meals made entirely of vegetables. He ate the food, not wanting to appear rude. Luckily, there were six spring rolls and four pieces of naan bread, which helped fill him up. She drank a half-bottle of wine, and Dodge had several beers to wash away the curry flavor lingering in his mouth.

After eating, they made love on the deck. It was a new-moon night with full cloud coverage shielding their activities from other boaters who might have been able to sneak a peek.

"So how was your day." Nikki ran her nails across Dodge's chest.

"Much better now."

"I'll take that as a compliment."

"It was."

The couple lay in the moonlight, quiet, for at least an hour. Finally, Nikki asked what was bothering him.

"We lost a good man today. Well, good as far as I could tell. I hadn't known him for very long."

"What happened to him?"

Stars began to peek through the dissipating cloud cover.

"He was shot and killed."

"Was he cop, like you?"

"He was. And he seemed to be a straight shooter, which is more than I can say for a lot of badges."

"Did he have a family?"

"His parents lived on the mainland. No wife or kids."

"That's good."

Dodge knew what she meant, but it still sounded callous. Nothing was good about any of this.

"I'm sorry. That is not what I meant."

Dodge shrugged.

Nikki gazed up at the sky. "What are you going to do?"

Bare-chested and only a pair of boxers as cover, he stood, pulled his pants on, and slid a shirt over his head. Slipped on his shoes, then looked down at Nikki. He now understood what he needed to do.

"I'm going to find who did it. I'll find who shot him, and I'll find the person who ordered it."

"What are you going to do, then?"

His voice cold, "I'll get justice for McCaffery and Maria. And anyone that tries to stop me will be sorry."

The usually beautiful face Dodge had become accustomed to changed. The corners of her lips sagged a little, erasing her perfect smile. The bronze tone on her cheeks seemed greyer. Her eyes, normally bright and wide open, appeared dim and closed off. She tried to reason with the man she had just made love to, but there was no changing his mind. The look in his eyes was that of revenge, not justice. She said she could not be a part of such an act, and that if he did this, it would likely be the last he would see of her.

"I'll take you back to the pier," he said.

The five-minute dinghy ride was silent except for the waves splashing off the watercraft's rubber sides. Nikki stepped up onto the pier and looked back at the man she had grown to care for. Then she spun away from him but stopped abruptly and removed a necklace from around her neck.

She tossed it to Dodge. "It is Saint Jude, the patron saint of lost causes. It will help keep you safe."

Dodge held the charm. The lights from the pier caused the gold coating to sparkle.

He squeezed it. "I'll get it back to you when I come back."

Nikki shook her head. "You can keep it. You need it more than me."

She turned and walked into the darkness. Dodge felt sad. Guilty, even. Then he remembered McCaffrey. The mission was more important than anything else.

He pushed the dinghy away from the pier and headed back to *Kelly's Dream*. He needed to get his weapon and ammo. The adrenaline in his blood made him too amped to sleep, so he might as well get a head start.

He dialed Williams's number. The agent was up, too angry to sleep. Dodge asked for his address, and said he would be there in a half-hour

—⁓—

Delgado and Melendez were crouched among the trees lining the beach. As a precaution, they had waited until dark before going back to the boat because of the events at the Trey-Deuces' hangout earlier that day. The drug lord knew it wouldn't take authorities long to figure out the fire was not an accident, and they would find the short man's body before nightfall. He knew the local police didn't have enough competent officers to put together the murders, the arson, and the medical examiner's office. But the American FBI would not only have that capability, but they also likely had already pinned him down as the primary suspect. It wouldn't be long before there would be men stationed at the airport, and orders sent to the Coast Guard to board every vessel sailing into and out of the marinas and seaports.

The two men waited in a thick wall of mangrove trees, looking out over the bay, toward their boat. They hadn't seen a single Coast Guard vessel or harbor police boat come within a half-mile of it but decided it would be best to wait for the cover of nightfall before dragging the dinghy out from its hiding spot in the mangroves. The moonless night allowed the men to traverse the waters to the boat, unseen.

Once onboard, Delgado and Melendez both fell to the deck, exhausted from the day's activities. The captain came up from the cabin area with a phone in his outreached hand.

"You had a phone call while you were gone, sir. They left a voicemail."

Delgado took the phone from the captain's outstretched hand.

"You didn't listen to the message?"

"I have no interest in your business. You hired me to get to the island and back. That is what I'll do."

Delgado nodded. The captain was a smart man, though he

still might have to disappear. Delgado would take no pleasure in executing an honest man.

He pushed the voicemail button and raised the phone to his ear. The captain headed back down to the cabin, still careful not to overhear anything that could make him a liability.

After a minute, Delgado flipped the phone shut and tossed it into the bay.

"What is it?" Melendez said.

"I have to go back to Colombia."

"Why? What has happened?"

"An FBI agent was killed in Bogotá."

"Good riddance, I say."

Delgado gave his second-in-command an icy stare.

"They found him on our land."

"Who would have given the order to kill a US agent on your land? A rival cartel trying to set you up?"

"Possibly. But I need to go home and deal with this. The US will have five hundred agents in Bogotá by the end of the week. All of them will be gunning for me. I can't control what happens there if I am here."

"I'll tell the captain we head out tonight," Melendez said.

Delgado placed his hand on his friend's shoulder.

"No. I need you to finish up here. I'll go back alone."

"We have nothing to finish here, sir. The FBI has likely moved your daughter by now, and the local police will soon know it was us who hit the Trey-Deuces."

"I want her body returned to me. Do you understand? I don't care how you get it done. Just do it." He paused. "And don't fail me, José."

Melendez nodded.

Delgado took another phone out of his pocket and ordered an air pickup at one of the abandoned army airstrips on St. John. Melendez went ashore to wait until dawn before going inland. He had enough cash to buy his way out of any trouble he could get into and find a flight back to Colombia.

Delgado paid the captain his share, plus the other two

men's shares, and said not to speak of what he saw. Delgado assured him they would know if he talked. The captain swore on his mother's grave that he would tell no one. Then Delgado boarded a two-seat Cessna and began the five-hour flight back to Colombia. He wasn't sure what to expect when he arrived, but he knew where to look for answers.

CHAPTER 19

DODGE APPROACHED THE FRONT DOOR from a path that snaked along the side of the modest ranch-style home. He could hear the gravel crunch under the weight of every step.

Agent Williams waited at the door. He wore a white T-shirt and a pair of baggy cargo shorts. Cops always looked strange out of uniform. It was as if the person was a part of the uniform, not the other way around.

Agent Williams held the door open, and his guest entered the home.

"What was it that needed my attention so much it couldn't wait until tomorrow?"

"You got a beer?" Dodge said.

Williams stood silent for a moment, then closed the door.

"Let's go into the kitchen," he said. "I don't want to wake the kids."

The two men walked through a long hallway, past a study which looked like an office. An agent in charge of a field office would undoubtedly have to work at nights and weekends from home. It was the price of being the boss—more pay, less free time.

Next, they passed what appeared to be the living room. There were toy trucks and construction vehicles scattered across the floor. Not so different from what Dodge played with as a child.

A bathroom, and what he guessed were two bedrooms, comprised the rest of the house.

Once in the kitchen, Agent Williams opened the refrigerator to grab a beer, and tossed it to his partner.

"Got an opener?"

"It's a twist top," Williams said.

Dodge twisted the cap off and put it in his pocket. He took a swig of the beer—an apple-cider flavor—taking time to form the words in his head before telling his new colleague about his plan.

Agent Williams stood silently, almost like he knew what Dodge was going to propose. But he waited for him to begin.

"We need to put this thing to bed, and we need to do it quickly," Dodge said. "Because once DC gets involved, things will be out of our control. The suits will send down a public relations officer and a cleaner. They will sweep this whole thing under the rug. McCaffrey will get a hero's funeral, TV cameras, and all, but he won't get justice, and neither will Maria Delgado. Someone will file the whole thing away and bury her case in a warehouse in one of the government's records repositories in an abandoned mine in Missouri."

Agent Williams nodded.

A sense of relief washed over Dodge. The only man he needed the okay from was on board with the beginning of the plan.

"What do you have in mind?" Williams said.

Dodge pulled out a chair and sat at the island next to him. He peeled the label from his beer while mulling over the next part of his plan.

"We find 'em and kill 'em," he said.

"McCaffrey was a good man, and a better agent," Williams said. "He didn't deserve to die like that and rot in the jungle." His head cantered to one side; eyes fixed on Dodge. " How do you plan to go about this?"

"There can't be a lot of moving parts. In and out."

"In and out? Sounds like you're saying we go to Colombia and try to kill Jesús Martinez Delgado. We don't even know for sure if he's involved."

"It was him."

"How do you know?"

"McCaffery was in Columbia to gather information on Delgado. He was picked up at the airport by DEA. It is more than likely—hell, it's probable—Delgado has men planted at the airport to report who comes and goes when the DEA is involved. We learned in the '80s, with Pablo Escobar, how cartels gathered information and kept track of every gringo that set foot in their territory. They have had years to perfect the technique. Not only would he have known McCaffrey was meeting with the DEA, but there are also likely locals that work for the DEA—secretaries and janitors—that are on his payroll."

"I can't go to Columbia on a search and destroy mission," Williams said. "My absence from the office would be missed. I can barely go to the bathroom without my phone ringing with a call from Washington or Miami. You would have to go this alone."

Dodge nodded. The wheels in his head were turning. He was putting together the who, what, and where.

The *how* might be an on-the-fly thing? Not having a finished plan before entering a fight broke about six of his rules. There was little room for error, and he would need to run every scenario on what could go wrong. It was impossible to control everything, but what he could control had to work perfectly.

"I know," he replied. "It's okay. I work better by myself, anyway."

Agent Williams let out a nervous laugh.

"You are going to go alone to kill a drug kingpin? One man versus an army in his country, on his land? Are you out of your mind?"

Agent Williams glanced across the kitchen, toward the dining room. Standing half-in and half-out of the light was a beautiful young woman. She looked to be in her mid-thirties, with blonde hair pulled back into a ponytail. She was wearing a pair of athletic shorts, which showed her long toned legs. A short tank top was all she had covering her upper body. She appeared to be groggy, as if she had just woken from a nap.

Agent Williams walked over and kissed her on the forehead.

"Sorry, babe. Did we wake you?"

"No, I was thirsty, and I heard you talking to someone. So, I checked on the girls to make sure they were not up watching TV with their dad."

She looked over at the strange man in her kitchen.

"Sara, I would like you to meet Paul Dodge. He is assisting us on a case."

Dodge nodded. "Hello."

"Are you here to help with that poor girl they found at the airport?"

"Yes, ma'am, I am."

"Well, I hope you find the person responsible. I can't imagine how anyone could do something like that to a child."

"With your husband working the leads, I'm sure we'll have the suspect in custody before long."

She wrapped her arms around her husband and kissed him softly on the lips.

"He is amazing," she said. "I'll let you two get back to business. Don't stay up too late, sweetie." She kissed him on the cheek and walked back into the darkness of the hallway.

Once she was out of range to hear their conversation, he asked Dodge, "Where were we?"

"We were at the part where I go to Colombia, and you stay here with your two girls and beautiful wife."

"You can't go alone. Besides, you didn't even know McCaffrey. Why the hell would you want to risk your life for a man you didn't know?"

Still thirsty from his earlier work out on the boat, Dodge downed the last swig of beer in his bottle.

"It doesn't matter how well I knew him. Every one of us wears a badge and deals with the bullshit every day. That makes us family, and I would gladly lay my life down for him and all the others out there doing this job."

Williams smiled.

"Besides, 1 plan on coming back," Dodge said.

"So did McCaffrey."

"I'm not McCaffrey."

The two men drank another beer and sat at the counter, discussing an evolving plan's details. Dodge would go to Colombia the next day to deal with Delgado. Agent Williams would stay on the island to continue working on the Trey-Deuces' murders and Maria Delgado's case.

Williams worried that Delgado was still on the island, trying to get to his daughter's remains. Dodge believed his plan would be to return to Colombia as soon as the news of a dead FBI agent in his home country hit CNN. He would have to be back to control his people. Without him, many would defect to rival gangs. Others would try to make a play for the leadership position. He couldn't risk being away while getting attacked from all sides.

"How do you plan to find him?" Williams said.

"With the one thing he wants the most."

"His daughter," Williams said.

Dodge tipped the top of his bottle toward his partner.

"He'll leave someone on the island to watch the ME's office," Williams said. "They'll make a play if you try to mover her."

"That's my thinking as well. Which is why you will move her in broad daylight. They'll wait until you're on the road. It'll be easier to isolate the car her remains are being carried in, and keep the other agents pinned in their vehicles. They know your resources are limited and will have planned for it. That is where you will have the advantage."

"How...oh, 1 see," Williams said. "We won't actually have Maria's body in the car?"

"Exactly. She'll be safely locked up at the coroners' office. The attackers will be so fixated on the car with the metal coffin, they won't even think about having someone check to see if the body was actually in it."

"How do you know that?"

Dodge took another pull from the brown bottle.

"I understand that kind of fixation," he said.

The two men spoke for another half-hour. They nailed down the who, where, and the how. Dodge would be on a plane to Colombia before 8:00 the next morning. Agent Williams would make the travel arrangements. He had been an FBI agent long enough to garner some personal favors. A plane trip should easy enough to arrange off the books. The rest of Delgado's men on the island would be in custody, or dead, before Dodge landed in Columbia, if everything went to plan.

Upon return to *Kelly's Dream*, Dodge packed a go-bag for his Colombia trip, starting with ammo and a weapon. Earlier, at Agent Williams's house, the two men decided it was not viable for Dodge to take a US government weapon on a revenge mission in another country. The act would break about a hundred international and US laws. Possibly land both of them in a Colombian prison, shortening their life expectancy considerably. So, Agent Williams had supplied him with a throw-down gun. It was a nice little Kimber .45 semi-automatic. Small enough to hide in an ankle holster or pocket, but powerful enough to take down anything he might encounter—man or beast.

Agent Williams also gave him three hundred rounds of ammo, and a double-edged boot knife for if things got up close and personal. Dodge would wear a GPS tracking beacon in his hat, allowing Williams to follow his progress from St. Thomas. Traveling by personal charter plane allowed the lone parole agent to stow his weapons in the private hangar if needed.

One of Agent Williams's friends who worked at State would pick Dodge up from the airport. They expected no incident at security, and he should be able to pass through without incident.

Next, he packed a set of extra clothes and boots. The plan was to be gone for only two or three days. But if he needed commercial transportation to get out in a hurry, clean clothes would draw less attention from the border guards, than jeans and a shirt covered with two days of grime and blood spatter.

He decided not to shave, in an attempt to blend in with

the locals. He was as white as they came, but it often surprised people how different a person could appear with full facial hair. Three days was not enough time to pull off a complete beard and mustache, but enough time to alter his appearance and not look so American.

His last task was to make sure *Kelly's Dream* didn't end up as some drug runner's offshore play toy. He wrote a short testament in which he decreed all his property to Anna. He had changed his life insurance policy to pay out half to Anna, and half to Kelly's family. It wasn't a lot of money, but it would provide enough to pay off most of their debts and have a little left over for a new car or whatever they might want to buy.

The backpack bounced as it hit the bottom of the rubber dinghy. He untied the line securing it to the sailboat and pulled the cord to start the motor.

The ride to the pier seemed longer this time. He noticed the other boats moored in the harbor. Most were bigger than *Kelly's Dream,* and a few had people sitting on the bows, watching the sun rise over the mountains. Some people got up every morning to watch the sun rise. It really was a spectacular sight.

The air around him seemed quieter than usual. Maybe it was just him.

His pal Sebastian was there to meet him.

"Sebastian." Dodge pulled even with the pier. "I won't need any gas for a few days. You think you can watch over the dinghy and *Kelly's Dream* for me? I should be back in a few days."

"No problem, boss. Anything you need me to do?"

"Just make sure the bilge pumps are working and start the generator once for me." He looked back at *Kelly's Dream.* "Don't want anything to freeze up."

Sebastian nodded.

Dodge tucked a hundred-dollar bill between his fingers and shook Sebastian's hand.

"Good luck," Sebastian said.

Dodge nodded and walked toward town. He planned to make one more stop before the sun rose higher in the sky.

Agent Williams sat at the dining room table; a file open in front of him. He scanned every document for information he could use as leverage against Delgado. He had called in a favor to a friend working at DEA headquarters in Arlington, Virginia, after the late-night visit by Dodge. He needed someone trustworthy on the inside to supply them with actionable intelligence. The information would help him bypass formal channels he could not use while running a mission off-the-books.

A by-the-books mission required filling out stacks of paperwork—requisition forms and travel vouchers with signatures of supervisors and their supervisor's. None of which he and Dodge had time for. It was imperative that what they were about to do was untraceable. Or they would end up jobless and blacklisted. And that was the best-case scenario. Worst-case would involve a story on CNN, and backroom deals between a foreign government and the State Department, turning the two of them over to avoid an international incident.

Just as he was about to close the file, his wife walked into the room. She looked at him, and he slid his chair back.

She sat on his lap and kissed him. "What are you doing in here? It's almost two in the morning."

He pushed the folder away. "Just finishing up some last-minute paperwork. Why are you still awake?"

"I couldn't sleep. Then I heard you out here shuffling around and thought I would remind you I was still a woman."

Agent Williams grinned. "I am well-aware of your woman-ness."

"That's not a word," Sara said.

"It is, too. I've used it in Scrabble before."

"You cheat at Scrabble."

He smiled and nodded. "I guess I sometimes do. But that's only because you're so smart."

She kissed him on the cheek and got up from his lap.

"If you aren't too long, I may still have some of that *woman-ness* to show you."

"I wouldn't miss it for the world."

Sara smiled, and as Agent Williams watched her walk back toward the bedroom, a sense of dread came over him. Not for himself, but for his new partner. What if he didn't return from Colombia? What if they never found his body? Or worse, his bloated corpse turned up on a local beach, half-eaten by sharks, and his mouth and eye sockets inhabited by crabs. The rumors would start before the ME had his body on the cold steel slab. Within days, tips would come in, and the body would be identified as Paul Dodge, an American law enforcement agent.

It would take less time to link him to the FBI. He had been in the office. Security footage would confirm dates and times, and he had been paid with taxpayer funds.

Sure, they could hide the payment for a few months. But it would get leaked to the press. These things always do. There would be hearings, and then hearings about hearings. Eventually, the truth would come out, revealing the revenge plot the two men had hatched at his dining room table.

The guilt of being responsible for the death of two agent's deaths would be the worst part. Williams wasn't sure he could live with the blood of two men on his hands.

He was about to phone Dodge to call the whole thing off, when his cell phone vibrated on the granite countertop. It was a message from his DEA connection. Homeland Security intelligence reported that an international cartel leader had taken a charter boat to the US Virgin Islands. It was believed that the cartel leader was searching for a young girl, possibly his daughter, who disappeared weeks earlier and was thought dead.

The FBI and DEA were asked to work their informants for any information that could confirm the information in the intelligence reports. The Drug Interdiction Unit of the US Coast Guard was tasked with stopping any suspicious watercraft in the ports and waters surrounding St. Thomas.

Agent Williams realized his fears of being caught were just that—fear. The FBI and DEA being asked to assist in the intelligence gathering concerning Delgado's current whereabouts could provide him with cover if anything went wrong. As a section chief, he could allocate resources and place agents in the field as he deemed necessary to accomplish the mission. He would be held responsible for any mistakes or line-of-duty deaths. Still, because Washington had asked for help, he would have more leeway than if he acted unilaterally.

He decided to keep the information his DEA colleague had sent him to himself. Partly because he wasn't sure how far Dodge was willing to go to avenge the death of an FBI agent he barely knew. But also, because he was a loose cannon. And a loose cannon was precisely what Williams needed against a drug kingpin.

He wouldn't know if he made the right choice, until it was all over.

Agent Williams placed the file in his briefcase and headed for bed. Sara was still awake and waiting for him, wearing a T-shirt. Just a T-shirt.

He closed the door and pushed the lock to keep out curious children.

CHAPTER 20

DODGE HAD SPENT A SHORT TIME standing across the street from Nikki's house, trying to decide if he should knock or just leave the envelope, which was addressed to Detective Renquest.

He decided to leave it on her doorstep, with instructions on how and when to mail the package. He slid a twenty into the fold of the envelope to cover any postal charges, worried that if Nikki saw him, she might talk him out of what he was about to do. That could never happen. Promises were made, and handshakes were given. A man's word was his bond. It was how deals were made when money didn't change hands.

It was 8:30, and sun had broken free of the tops of the mountains, highlighting the small runway. His only baggage was a small duffel bag, and a backpack slung over his shoulder. The airplane sat at the east end of the runway, its engines running. The pilot stood at the base of the ladder. No other passengers were in sight.

It was a two-man job. One for air, and one for land, just like the military would have executed it. The pilot wore paramilitary-style black fatigues, with a baseball cap and dark sunglasses.

His first glimpse of the pilot caused Dodge to laugh to himself. The guy looked right out of a movie about the CIA or DIA. Nothing conspicuous about a guy dressed in all black, standing at attention at the end of an abandoned airstrip next to a plane with no tail identification.

Once inside the cabin, the pilot had the door shut and

secured, and the plane taxiing within three minutes. A real professional. He didn't speak, and his sole passenger didn't ask questions.

During covert black flights, it was best if both parties were unaware of the other person's name, like in a double-blind study, so no one could rat out the other if caught. They can threaten or torture all they want, but you can't give up information you don't have.

The twin turbo engines roared to full power, and the wheels lifted off the runway. After ten minutes, the aircraft was at ten thousand feet, and they were on the way to Bogotá, Colombia. The pilot looked back and flipped up two fingers, signaling that they should be on the ground in two hours. A nod indicated that Dodge understood.

He laid his head back and closed his eyes, using the time to run through the timeline of what he needed to do. Once on the ground, he needed to get past security with his weapons. Facing an armed cartel with no weapons of his own was a suicide mission. And while there was always a chance, he might not make it home, a lack of preparation would not be the reason. He needed to figure out how to secure untraceable weapons if he had to leave his behind at the hangar.

A quick meeting with the DEA agent who found Agent McCaffrey's weapon was first on the agenda, as well as a talk with the drug mule who stole it. Any intelligence from the kid might help him when he caught up with Delgado.

The next thing was how to get a ride into the mountains and near the Delgado compound. Once there, it was all a crapshoot.

His eyes heavy, and with a long day in front of him, Dodge drifted off to sleep about an hour after takeoff. The rough descent into Bogotá woke him from his slumber and nearly knocked him out of his seat. Out the window, he could see nothing but clouds and rain. Lightning flashed all around the small aircraft. They had flown right into a storm, resulting in the pilot speaking for the first time.

"Change of plans. We're not landing in Bogotá. Storms too bad. We need to divert to a small strip outside of town."

"Does the guy from State know we're changing locations?"

"I don't know. I just know that we don't have enough fuel to circle for an hour."

"Can you get him a message?"

"Not until I'm back in the air. I don't want to give up your position if the bad guys are monitoring local air traffic signals."

The plan was falling apart already. *At least I have my weapons.*

Then the sound of metal hitting metal blasted his ears. The plane shook and tossed right, then left. He gathered himself and peered out the window across the right wing. Smoke and fire tailed out from where the engine used to be. It was gone, and the plane was reacting the way an aircraft with one engine acts—tilting to one side and losing altitude quickly.

Dodge jumped from his seat and bolted to the cockpit. The pilot was fighting the controls, trying to keep the plane from nosediving into a death spiral. He killed the power to the remaining engine, and the plane momentarily righted itself. They were gliding now, and Dodge knew the plane wouldn't remain airborne for much longer. It's simple physics. Speed plus momentum equals lift.

"What happened?" Dodge said. "Feels like we lost an engine!"

"We took a round from something. I think it was a shoulder-mounted rocket."

"Who the hell would shoot rockets at us?"

"Someone told them you were coming." The pilot pulled a parachute from under his seat and tossed it to Dodge. "You know how to put one of those on?"

"Yes!" Dodge yelled over the chaos of warning alarms blaring in the cockpit.

Dodge slipped the leg straps of the chute over his legs, and they rested snugly in his groin area. Then he pulled the pack up over his shoulders and buckled the harness in the front.

He looked up at the pilot. "You going to put one on?"

"Only as a last resort. If I can get it on the ground, I need to make sure the plane is scuttled. No need to leave anything for the greasers."

Dodge reached out his hand. The pilot shook it and wished him good luck.

The ex-Air-Force officer then did what he had done a hundred times before. He jumped out of a plane with no idea what was below him.

His chute opened perfectly, pulling him up against gravity for a few seconds, before slowing his descent. There was nothing below him but clouds. Dodge had no way of knowing if trees or water or houses were going to break his fall. He pulled his legs up to his chest to help break the coming impact. A broken leg would end the mission, and likely lead to his capture.

He peered into the surrounding clouds, searching for any sign of the plane and its pilot. His ears strained for the sound of engines restarting or metal shearing into pieces as it hit the forest canopy.

Nothing but the sound of wind rushing past his ears. Then the ground came into view.

The muddy soil was upon him before he could react. Had he not prepared for the landing by pulling his knees up close to his body, the result would likely have been broken a leg.

His right foot got stuck in the mud, preventing him from performing a roll as all military parachutists are trained to do upon impact. The roll helps prevent injury by absorbing some of the landing energy and spreading it across the whole body, dissipating in the extremities. But the wet ground served the same purpose, and the landing was reasonably soft. A quick pat down of his extremities reassured Dodge that he had no serious injuries.

The jump from the plane had been so hasty, he almost forgot to grab his backpack, which contained his weapon and extra ammunition. He had three hundred rounds of 9mm ammunition, plus two full magazines. Unfortunately, during the rush to exit the failing aircraft, he didn't manage to grab his duffel, which contained his extra clothes and other weapons and ammo.

Dodge pulled the chute in, rolling it up as he sprinted for the tree line. He kept low and moved across the open ground, scanning for any signs of hostiles or his pilot. He saw neither. Once in the safety of the tree line, wet and tired, he knelt behind a tree and waited for ten minutes, watching for anyone searching for him.

First, he would check the open ground for signs of the plane and its contents. He would then head toward where the searchers came from. They had to come from a town or compound close by. It was as good of a plan as any.

Straight to the source.

———∿∿∿———

On St. Thomas, Agent Williams had just gotten word that the plane carrying his partner never landed in Bogotá and dropped off radar a half-hour ago. Its current position was unknown, and a choice had to be made to trust that Dodge survived, or make the call to Washington, changing a search and destroy mission into a recovery mission.

He decided it was best to wait for contact from his man in the field. If there was no contact by nightfall, he would be forced to call his superiors in DC and beg for help.

Agent Williams grabbed his briefcase off the kitchen table and slid his weapon into its holster. He latched his FBI badge onto his belt and walked to the front door, where he paused before opening it. Looking back over his shoulder at the home he hoped to come back to when this day was over, he let out a sigh and opened the door.

A dark-skinned man with muscular arms stood on the stoop to greet him.

Agent Williams fought the instinctive reaction to reach for his weapon. He had no desire to start a shootout where the backdrop was his children's bedrooms. Besides, the man's weapon was secured in a holster on his right hip, and he had made no move to retrieve it.

"Agent Williams. I was hoping you hadn't left for work yet. I apologize for the intrusion."

Williams peered over his shoulder, down the hallway leading to his children's bedrooms, and then back at the man, wearing a look of concern.

The man appeared to understand and asked him to shut the door. Then he suggested they talk out in the open, in full view of neighbors and passing cars. Agent Williams gladly took the offer to move any danger further from his family.

"Thank you," Williams said, after the two men were standing in the middle of the driveway.

"I have three children of my own. A little older than your two." The man glanced over Agent Williams's shoulder, back toward the house. "Their mother isn't as pretty as yours, but she is a fine cook." The man laughed as he rubbed his round belly.

"Who are you? Williams said.

The man wore a smile that looked more like a grimace.

"Who I am is unimportant. Who I work for is important."

"Who is it you work for?"

"That is a question to which you already know the answer. Would you like to know some answers to questions you don't know?"

Agent Williams glared at the man, trying to figure out what kind of game he was running.

"You work for Delgado. So that would make you José Melendez. I can't imagine him trusting anyone else to send to an FBI agent's home."

"That's good, Agent Williams. We know each other's names, so let's get to business. You have something my employer wants."

"I don't know what you are talking about."

Melendez showed signs of impatience, but the smile quickly returned to his face.

"We are both professionals," he said. "Let us continue to keep this meeting as such, and not sour the day by saying things we both know aren't true. Again, you have something that belongs to my employer, and he would like it returned."

Agent Williams decided not to try the man's patience by continuing to lie to him.

"He would like the body of his daughter returned."

"He would consider it a personal favor if the body of his beloved daughter, Maria, is returned so that he may bury her and grieve as a father."

"I am not in any position to do favors for an international drug dealer. Besides, we have another problem. One of my agents was killed in Colombia by some of Delgado's men. There is currently a manhunt underway for your boss, and my bosses in Washington, DC, are on the warpath. They want to send in an aircraft carrier and level the whole damn jungle. And they just might. Unless your boss surrenders to the Colombian National Police by week's end. If he surrenders, I'll see about getting his daughter's body released."

Melendez looked at the ground, and then back at Agent Williams.

"How is your man in Colombia doing? I heard there was a small plane crash outside of Bogotá this morning. They found no survivors. No bodies. The plane was not identifiable and burned beyond recognition."

Agent Williams felt a knot in the pit of his stomach rise to his throat. He could hardly take in a breath as anger surged throughout his body.

"If anything happens to Agent Dodge, I swear to you, I'll hunt down you and your boss and make him wish he'd never been born."

Melendez held his hands up in front of his body, patting the air to let Agent Williams know he was admitting a mistake.

"I assure you, my employer had nothing to do with the death of your agent, or the plane crash involving Agent Dodge. I was merely showing you that nothing happens in Colombia that we aren't aware of. In fact, my employer is already back in Colombia, leading the search for your missing pilot. He believes he'll have them both by the end of the day. I needn't tell you that Colombia is a perilous place. Many groups would enjoy catching a couple Americans and selling them to the highest bidder."

"Why would Delgado want to find them? If he hadn't issued orders to shoot them down, they could have been picked up as soon as they left the airport."

"You misunderstand me, Agent Williams. We didn't shoot down your friend's plane. But we may know who is responsible for that, and the death of your other agent."

"And let me guess, you will turn over those responsible, in exchange for the return of Maria Delgado's body."

Melendez stood quietly for a moment. "No, Agent Williams. Those responsible for the death of your friend and the downing of Agent Dodge's plane are the same people involved in the demise of young Maria. They will be dealt with internally. I can assure you; they will receive the harshest punishment imaginable."

"So, what is it you can give me in return for her body?"

"We will return your man to you safely. We have already rid you of a problem here on the island."

"The Trey-Deuces. That was you?"

Melendez said nothing.

"How do I know this is not some trick, and as soon as I give you Maria's body, you kill Dodge?"

"You don't. My employer thought you may react in this way. So as an act of good faith, you get to keep me. As soon as Agent Dodge is safely back in your custody, you will set me free. If he dies or doesn't return, you may use me to your advantage."

José Melendez put his weapon on the ground and dropped to his knees, placing his hands on the top of his head. Agent Williams inched toward Melendez, scanning the area for an ambush. There was none. He put Melendez in cuffs and sat him in the back of his car. Then he headed toward town and the FBI office.

Agent Williams wondered if this was the right thing to do. He trusted Dodge was still alive and had no concerns if he succeeded in his mission to kill Delgado. There would be no sleep lost over a dead drug dealer and murderer. Whether Delgado pulled the trigger that killed Agent McCaffrey, or one of his men did, it didn't matter to Williams. The agent's death landed squarely on the shoulders of Jesús Martinez Delgado. It was his actions and greed that caused McCaffrey's death, along with thousands of others that fell prey to cartel violence and the ill effects of drug addiction. That was the price of being in charge.

CHAPTER 21

THE PLANE CARRYING DELGADO landed at a private airstrip ten miles from his compound in the mountains, three hours after takeoff. During the flight, he had received a text message from José Melendez, informing him the plan was on schedule.

Delgado was hesitant at first, using Melendez as a proof-of-life pawn. But Melendez insisted it was the only way the FBI would trust him and play along.

The thought of Melendez betraying him crossed his mind but disappeared just as quickly. José Melendez was as loyal as they came. He was someone Delgado would never let rot in an American prison. Deal or no deal, he would make sure Melendez would be returned to his side, unharmed.

A helicopter was waiting at the airstrip, its rotors spinning, forcing Delgado to hold his hat as he walked beneath. The pilot readied for takeoff by supplying the turbo engine with more power. The rotors' increased speed created a wash strong enough that forced Delgado to clamp his hat to his head as he climbed into the safety of the cockpit. He put on the headset—designed so the passengers and pilot could communicate over the engines' roar—and ordered the pilot to head for the compound. The pilot nodded and pulled back on the stick. The engine sputtered for a second, and the machine lifted off the ground. The chopper spun one hundred eighty degrees, and the pilot increased the throttle. The aircraft reached fifteen hundred feet in thirty seconds.

After five more minutes, Delgado saw the clearing in the

jungle that outlined his property. He was always impressed while viewing the two-hundred-acre property from the sky. It took millions of dollars and five years to build. Now, someone was trying to take it all away from him. He would never let that happen.

Once on the ground and clear of the humming helicopter, Delgado began calling all his lieutenants. He ordered them to report to the compound within the hour.

Melendez was usually the one who contacted his underlings. He was the go-between for the workers and management. Receiving a call directly from the El Jefe meant there was a serious problem, and blood would likely be spilled.

The moment was not lost on the drug lord. He guessed that the responsible party for his daughter, and the FBI agent's death, would not show. He would then use his many resources to hunt the guilty party down and make an example of them—a warning to the rest of his people. If you mess with the bull, he'll torture you and then dismember your corpse before sending the pieces, one by one, to your family for many years, as a constant reminder of their loved one's treachery.

—◇◇◇—

The terrain had been muddy and almost impassable, even on foot. But Dodge made it to Bogotá in a couple hours. He guessed that the group searching for him must have found the downed plane and assumed both he and the pilot were dead. They would eventually find out he was still alive. But once in the city, he just needed to get to the US Embassy to meet his State Department contact.

Safely in the town's suburbs, he hailed a cab and asked to use the driver's cell phone. The driver said he didn't have a cell phone. But a hundred-dollar bill slipped through the slit between the plastic dividing glass and the seat caught his attention. The driver looked at Dodge in the review mirror, then took the bill. He pulled a cell phone out of his shirt pocket and passed it back to his new passenger.

The first call was to his contact, Mr. Brown, at the US Embassy. There was a long pause before a man's voice came over the phone.

"This is Brown."

"Brown, this is Paul D."

"Where the hell have you been? We got notice that a small aircraft went down just outside the city. The locals confirmed the crash site and said no survivors were expected. How did you get out?"

"It wasn't by choice. A damn rocket hit our plane, and the pilot nearly threw me out before it crashed."

"Where is the pilot? Did he go down with the plane?"

"Why don't you pick a place to meet, and we can discuss it over a meal and a beer. Hiking through the jungle made me hungry."

"And thirsty, I would imagine," Brown said.

Dodge gave the cab driver the address Brown had provided him and handed the phone back through the slit at the top of the seat. Fifteen minutes later, he was sitting at a table with a cold beer in his hand, at a dive bar, ironically, near the airport. Brown sat across from him, sipping from a bottle of water. He let the exhausted parole agent nearly finish his meal before asking him about what happened on the airplane.

"I don't know what hit us. The pilot said it was a rocket. And with him being a spook and all, I guessed he would know what a rocket hitting a plane would feel like."

"Who said he was an agency asset?" Brown glanced around the bar to see if anyone was paying too close attention to what they were saying.

Dodge put the last bite of meat into his mouth and chased down with a mouthful of beer.

"I was in Afghanistan and Iraq while in the Air Force," he replied. "I was around enough agency people to know one when I see one. Besides, the tail of the plane had no identification number, and there are only a couple groups that operate black planes."

Brown nodded. "Did you see the pilot bailout?"

Ashamed to have left a man behind, Dodge looked down at his plate to avoid eye contact.

"No."

"You are saying, you didn't see him leave the plane?"

"All I can say is he didn't jump with me. He said he needed to make sure the plane was scuttled if he couldn't get it back into the air."

"Protocol," said Brown.

"As soon as I hit the ground, a group of men came out of the jungle. Maybe twenty or thirty. All armed, and definitely looking for something."

"Could you see what they were wearing?"

Dodge thought back to when he was hiding in the tree line.

"I don't think any were wearing military uniforms. But I can't be sure. I was still a little dazed from a hard landing."

"I thought you Air Force boys were trained to jump from airplanes?"

"We are trained to get the hell out as fast as possible. Landing alive was just a bonus."

The two men finished their drinks, and then Brown paid the check. A total of four dollars.

Dodge had forgotten how much cheaper it was in foreign countries. A half-pound of meat, plus rice and a beer, cost him under five bucks. Unfortunately, things would become more expensive once he was in the mountain villages. Information always comes with a high price. Doesn't matter what part of the world you're in.

They left the bar, turning south toward a late-model sedan parked nearby. Dodge got into the passenger's seat. Brown started the car and eased the nose of the car into the street. A rusty beat-up pickup truck, with an older gentleman at the wheel and a younger man in the passenger seat stopped to let them merge in. Dodge nodded at the driver before turning his attention back to Brown.

Brown, using his free hand, reached into the back seat

and handed his passenger a brown paper bag. Dodge opened it and emptied the contents into his lap. The bag contained a stack of bills totaling ten thousand dollars, and a cell phone with GPS tracking capabilities. All he needed to do was dial 999, and the phone would send an alert notifying Brown to his position. Brown could then send in a small contingent of special operators to rescue him.

"Saved by a bunch of jarheads? I'd rather be dead."

"That will be the likely outcome if you're in a position where you have to dial that number. It's more of a recovery tool. Like the black box on an airplane. Helps us find something to stick in your casket."

Dodge bellowed a laugh. He was nervous, but he didn't want Brown to know.

He knew what he had just heard was true. He would probably end up dead, and they might or might not find his body. Which reminded him...he needed to call Agent Williams and let him know he was on the ground, and the plan was still a go.

"Is this phone traceable?"

"Completely clean," Brown said.

"Can I call out of the country?"

"Why? Need to tell your girl you won't be home for dinner."

"Something like that."

"It is set up for international calling."

"Good." Dodge dialed Agent Williams's number, which he had memorized before leaving St. Thomas.

The call was answered on the first ring.

"Agent Williams here. Who am I speaking to?"

"It's Dodge. I just wanted to let you know I'm on the ground and in play."

"Dodge! Damn good to hear your voice, man. I was going to give you until the end of the day, and then call in the Marines."

"I'm good. A little worse for wear, but I have all my supplies, and my contact is dropping me off at the outskirts of town. From there, I should be at the location by morning."

Agent Williams paused. "There have been some developments here."

He described José Melendez showing up at his house, and his story that a coup was underway in Colombia to take power from Delgado. He decided to leave out the part about the deal he had made with Melendez and Maria Delgado's body. He figured Dodge might need the leverage if things went south.

"Well, that changes things a bit," Dodge said.

"What do you plan to do?"

"There's no need for me to sneak through the jungle now. He obviously knows I'm coming and will probably already have double the protection around the compound for fighting off any attack from his own men."

"So, you just going to ring his doorbell?"

"I won't need to get that close. I'll call you when I get a chance." He hung up.

Brown stared straight at the road ahead, but he had been listening. He was trained to listen.

Dodge looked around at the car he was in.

"This a Volkswagen?"

"Diesel," Brown said.

"All-wheel drive?"

"Yep. Pretty good on mountain roads. What do you have in mind?"

"Might need to borrow her for a day."

"Sorry. Can't do it. This car is official State Department property." Brown pulled off the side of the road and parked in front of a small restaurant. "I have to go to take a wiz. Make sure the car is not stolen."

Brown got out of the vehicle, leaving the keys and the engine running, and walked into the restaurant. Dodge smiled before sliding into the driver's seat. He put the car in drive and punched the gas, shooting rocks and debris across the hood of the car parked behind him. He glanced in his rearview mirror at an old man running out of the restaurant and yelling what could only assumed were insults directed at him.

Brown would likely wait a half-hour before calling his office to report the theft. By that time, his car would be well into the mountains, and police would check the surrounding area before giving up the search. A gringo's stolen car probably rated low on their list of priorities. Dodge had little to worry about from behind. He needed to start thinking about what lay ahead.

CHAPTER 22

THE MAN SITTING IN THE COPILOT SEAT knew the car would remain in view for about five miles before the road became obscured by the jungle canopy, as it wound its way around the mountain. The plan called for a rendezvous team to disable the vehicle as soon as it entered the section of road covered by the thick jungle trees.

They were under strict orders not to hurt the driver. Delgado was insistent on this point. The penalty for any harm that befell the driver was death. Not just for the person responsible, but for all of them. Therefore, the moment Dodge entered the road's forested section, the rendezvous team targeted the car's tires and not the windshield.

A few years ago, Delgado ordered one of his lieutenants in the US to leverage some police equipment from a Los Angeles Police detective who had fallen behind on his payments. The detective stole some riot gear, flash-bang grenades, and a case of tire stops. They make tire stops from collapsible lightweight metal that expands across a roadway, in front of fleeing vehicles. The metal frame was covered in rows of hollow metal tubes that broke off as the car tires passed over the device, puncturing the tires and remaining stuck in the rubber. Hence, the air freely escapes, and the tire goes flat in a matter of seconds. He had seen them used on American television shows and thought he might have a use for them one day.

The team lead ordered the tire stops deployed just before the car approached their location. He didn't want to give the driver time to react and miss the device. Nor did he want the driver to swerve, miss the trap, and career into the ditch and hit a tree—a move that might kill him, or cause severe injuries at the least, which would set Delgado's promised killing spree into motion.

The car approached, and the trap slinked across the road. There was a deafening pop as dozens of the hollow needles punctured the rubber, forcing the air out of the pressurized tire interior. The device caught the back tires as they slid across its surface, the needles sticking into the tire's tread, and the device frame lodged between the rear fender and the tire. Sheet metal tore from the car, producing an ear-piercing screech as the vehicle tried to push forward. It came to rest about a hundred feet from where the tires first ran over the stop strip.

Three men from the rendezvous team, weapons pointed, approached the vehicle. The airbags had deployed when the front tires dove into the ditch, and the car's front bumper contacted the hard earthen embankment. The lead man moved to the driver's side door and pushed the side air curtain out of the way, using his rifle's barrel, revealing the unconscious driver. He raised a hand and waved the rest of the team over to his position.

The three men extricated Dodge from the vehicle and laid him on the side of the road. One man removed a canteen from his backpack and poured its contents over the groggy driver's face. Dodge sputtered and opened his eyes, darting them side to side, trying to locate a point of reference or the immediate threat. The three men stood over him, rifles aimed at his head.

A fourth man approached as the three made space for him.

"Agent Dodge. We apologize for the damage to your car. We needed to talk to you, and I'm sure you wouldn't have stopped for a group of armed strangers on a dangerous mountain pass."

"You could've tried," Dodge said.

"We are under strict orders. You are to be brought in unharmed. If you do not cause us any trouble, my employer gives you his word—you will not be harmed."

"Do I have a choice?"

The man smiled and shook his head.

As one man stretched an arm out to help Dodge off the ground, a voice crackled on the radio attached to the team lead's belt.

"Be aware. A small truck is approaching from the south. It is about two hundred meters back. Two occupants. Appear to be local."

The rotating blades of the helicopter could be heard in the radio's background transmission. Dodge looked overhead, trying and spot the chopper, but his eyesight hadn't fully returned. His ears were still ringing from the impact between his head and the airbag.

One man in the group pulled a phone from his pocket and pushed the screen with his finger a few times, before passing the phone to the leader.

"I know that rusty piece of shit," the leader said. "It belongs to Pedro Ruiz. He's an old head, but mainly does enforcement and money collections for the boss. He has a partner, Antonio *something*. An addict Pedro uses for labor."

"What do you want us to do about them?"

"Funny thing. Rumor has it, Antonio's girlfriend turned him in to the DEA for having a new Glock 9mm. Where do you suppose an addict gets a new Glock? I was about to pay him a visit when the boss called and placed me on this job."

"You think he's a rat," one man said.

"What do you say we find out? Shoot the old man and bring me the boy."

"Yes, sir!"

Two of the men sprinted down the road, around the bend, and out of sight. A few moments later, a trio of gunshots rang out. Then silence.

After about five minutes, the two men appeared on the road with a young man in dirty clothes, propped up between them. His feet were dragging behind them, and he was wincing in pain.

The men reached the rest of the group and dropped the boy on the ground next to their captive's feet.

"One round ricocheted and struck him in the leg," the first man said.

"Just a superficial wound" said the second man. "He'll be fine."

"Good," the leader said. "Load Antonio and the American into the SUV, and signal the chopper to return to the compound."

It took the group a half-hour to make it to the outskirts of the compound. Once on the property, the roads became paved, and the ride was considerably smoother for the remainder of the trip. It was apparent that whoever lived here was filthy rich. Half the streets in the cities comprised cobblestone, and none of the country or mountain roads were finished in asphalt or concrete. Colombia was a poor country, except for the businessmen, politicians, and drug lords. Especially drug lords, who collectively had more money than most Central and South American governments combined. And it wasn't even close.

The lead vehicle, followed by two more black SUV's, pulled up to a mansion. The entire front of the home was framed in glass, from the top of the highest roof peak to the lowest spot on the ground. Dodge wondered if it was made out of bulletproof glass but decided the weight of that much ballistic glass would require a foundation buried fifteen-foot deep, with a framing system made of structural steel. Logistically, it seemed impossible to get semi-trucks up the narrow mountain roads with loads of steel I-beams.

No, it was regular old glass. The person who lived here was not afraid of anyone. That didn't bode well for anyone brought here against their will.

The front door opened, and two armed men took up a post on each side of the entrance. Then a large man, who looked to be made of steel, stepped out of the entryway. He carried himself like a leader, a commander of troops, much like Dodge had experienced in the Air Force. The main difference being, the men and women in uniform followed out of respect. Delgado's men followed him out of fear.

The man reached out and shook Dodge's hand with and iron-tight grip. A sign that he was in charge and would call the shots.

"Agent Dodge. It is good to meet you," Delgado said.

His English was better than many Americans.

"The pleasure is all mine," Dodge replied.

"I hope my men didn't scare you too much. They were under strict orders to bring you to me, unharmed." He looked around at his men.

None of them made eye contact, except the team leader, who nodded.

"What do you think of my little mountain retreat?"

"It's a bit gaudy for my taste. But hell, I live on a boat."

"Ah, *Kelly's Dream*. I could never live on a boat. Not enough room to stretch out. I like to take long walks across my mountain. It gives me time to think. How about you, Agent Dodge? Do you like to walk?"

"I do. But usually in the company of a beautiful woman."

Delgado burst into laughter. "Yes, the bank girl is quite a beautiful woman."

Th e cartel leader had a network on the island, and they had been tracking the good guys for days, depriving them of any advantage. He had been in control the entire time. But Dodge still had one card—the name scratched into the inside of the shipping container: J-U-A-N. He would hold that information to secure his safe release.

Boom! The concussion from an explosion pummeled his eardrums.

The battle-tested veteran dropped to one knee and covered his head for protection. The team leader fell alongside him, the front half of his head missing, except for one eye that remained open and stared at him.

Dodge waited for the following sniper shot to come, but it never arrived. He looked up at Delgado, who stood staring at the other men who had dropped their weapons to the ground. The boy from the truck was now standing beside his boss. There was a resemblance between the two men. Distant but distinct facial features gave away the family ties. Both men smiled, then reached out and helped Dodge to his feet.

"I am sorry you had to see that, Agent Dodge," said Delgado. "But Juan had betrayed me. He knew about the dead FBI agent, and lied to me about what his part in it was. I can't have trust issues within my inner circle. As a military man, you certainly understand?"

Dodge nodded. He now had zero cards to play.

He turned his attention to the kid from the truck.

"The boy is related to you?"

"He is a cousin." Delgado put his hand on the boy's shoulder. "It is by marriage, but family is family. It's not his fault he's dumb. His parents didn't prioritize education, and instead used him as a tool to feed their drug habit. They even sold him once to a pedophile for cash so they could buy more coca."

"And you saved him," Dodge said. "Was that for you, or for him?"

The smile disappeared from the drug lord's face.

"I admit, I benefit from his predicament and small brain. However, he is taken care of, and will never be used by anyone ever again."

"Except you," Dodge said, wishing he could take it back as soon as the words crossed his lips.

A sharp tongue with someone who just shot his own man in the head was not a good idea.

"In this case, Agent Dodge, you are correct. I used the boy to my advantage. Rumors had been circulating for months about a coup against me. I knew someone in my inner circle planned on betraying me, but I could not find out who. When Maria went missing, I knew a move had been made. But I was a father, and I showed weakness by acting like a father and chasing my child. I should've sought vengeance for the traitors. That was my first mistake."

Dodge realized Delgado may not have all the details about what happened to his daughter. He only thought she was kidnapped and died somehow. Once again, he had a card to play when the time was right.

"What was your second mistake?"

"I just took care of it." Delgado pointed at Juan's corpse on the ground.

"How did you figure it out?"

"It was something one of my lieutenants said to me while we were in Saint Thomas. He asked who possessed cojones large enough to think harming my daughter would go unpunished. There were only two people I could think of. Juan and José Melendez. Both men had my complete trust, but only one had the desire and ambition to make a move on my business.

"Well, the FBI knows that a man named Juan was involved in your daughter's kidnapping and eventual death," Dodge said. "His name was carved into the inside of the crate your daughter died in."

Delgado shook his head and spit on the body lying at his feet.

"He'll be left for the animals of the forest. Cowardly traitors do not deserve a righteous burial."

"But we still have a problem," Dodge said.

"The dead FBI agent," Delgado replied.

"Yes. And the shooting down of my plane. I would like to have my pilot back. Alive would be preferable. But if he died in the crash, returning with his body is my responsibility."

"I am afraid I can't help you with what you require. I am not responsible for the FBI agent. That was Juan and his crew." Delgado pulled his pistol from its holster and held it out for Dodge. "This is his crew right behind you. Take my weapon and have your revenge. They knew what would happen when they betrayed me. Go ahead. Kill them all and avenge your comrade."

Dodge's gaze never left Delgado's face. He had no intention of engaging in a battle for bravado.

"What about my plane being shot at, and the location of my pilot?"

"Once again, I know nothing about your plane being shot at—"

"*Shot down* by a damn rocket."

"*Shot down*, then. But it doesn't change the fact I had nothing to do with it, or your pilot's current condition."

"What is his current condition?"

"He is alive. However, he is not my concern, as it is not my men who have him."

"Who is holding him, then, if not you?"

Delgado looked at his two bodyguards and nodded. The men rounded up the rest of the dead man's team and led them around the corner of the house, forcing two of them to carry Juan's body as they disappeared out of sight. Dodge guessed the whole group would be dead right after they dug their own graves.

Play stupid games, win stupid prizes.

"Very violent men," the drug lord replied." Men not to be messed with. Why do you care about the pilot so much? You don't even appear to know his name."

"It's a military thing. You don't leave men behind."

"Honorable, but foolish. You survived, and I would advise you to keep it that way. But the choice is yours, and I can't help you in your quest to find your friend."

"Your daughter was not just kidnapped. She was assaulted and left to die on a shipping dock in the middle of a hurricane. The people that left her there could have saved her, but they let her die. Alone, and gravely injured. And the FBI secured her body after your attempt failed a few days ago."

Delgado's face turned red as blood rushed to his skin's surface. He clenched his hands but didn't reach for his weapon.

"Do you know who took my Maria?" he boomed, and the words echoed off the surrounding hillside.

"Based on the mess you left at the Trey-Deuces' clubhouse, we know you think they were involved. We also know it would have taken a dozen men to move that container through both ports. They needed to bribe canine handlers and security guards. It would've taken a lot of money."

"You are correct, Agent Dodge. I already know this. Do you have any information I haven't found on my own?"

"We believe—"

"The FBI?" Delgado said.

"I should say, I believe Juan used the situation with your daughter to his advantage. He knew you would leave Colombia to search for your daughter and her captors. He would have several days to gather some men loyal to him, and when you came back, force you to retire. Or just kill you and take over himself. He was not the one behind the plot to take your daughter, though he was likely involved or knew about it. That was someone else, but he had Agent McCaffrey murdered, knowing US authorities would put you at the top of their list."

"You know this for sure?" Delgado said.

"I believe this is the most likely scenario. Juan betrayed you, but he is not responsible for Maria's death."

Delgado nodded and looked around at the mountains surrounding his fortress.

"We should go inside. I may have many new enemies. Enemies that can gain access to my home." He turned and walked through the portico and into the entryway of the mansion.

Dodge followed, trying to think of a plan to assure his survival, at least for the next few hours.

CHAPTER 23

THE TWO MEN SAT IN A STUDY toward the back of the house. It rivaled any Dodge had seen on TV shows about the great American socialites of the late eighteenth and early nineteenth centuries. The room was covered in dark wood, with floor-to-ceiling bookshelves comprising three of the walls. Each bookcase was filled with fiction novels, general knowledge titles, a section of what appeared to be texts with titles in Spanish, and an entire section dedicated to everything Americana. A stone fireplace an average-sized man could walk into and turn around in, covered the entire fourth wall. And right in the middle of the stone chimney was a portrait of Simon Bolivar. Though he was Venezuelan by birth, Bolivar lead the fight for Colombian independence.

It had long been rumored that all cartel leaders had a picture of the national hero hanging in their homes. Many felt some sort of connection to the man and may have felt the portrait gave their illegal enterprises some kind of legitimacy. Dodge called bullshit. Cartel leaders were men of greed and ego. Ruthless, impassionate killers are only concerned about their own reputations and increasing offshore bank accounts—sycophants, every single one of them. Including the man he was talking to at that moment.

But none of that mattered now. *This* sycophant had something Dodge needed, and that was time. And maybe a few guns.

"So do we have an agreement?" he said.

Delgado grabbed a cigar from a humidor that probably cost a year's salary for most residents of Colombia. He held out an open hand as an invitation for Dodge to take a cigar. Dodge accepted and placed the cigar in his shirt pocket.

"I'm more of a cigarette guy, but I'll take one for later. I can torch it up once I am safely back on Saint Thomas."

Delgado sat in a brown leather high-back chair, cigar in one hand, and a brandy held loosely in the other.

After a minute, he said, "I agree with your proposal. I'll provide you with a vehicle to exit the mountain. I'll guarantee safe passage to town and anywhere within my lands. You may have your choice of two weapons from my armory and all the ammunition you can carry. You will find the men responsible for my daughter's death, and have her body returned to me. When you have the traitors' names and locations, you will notify me on the cell phone I gave you. Once you tell me the information I desire, I'll tell you who has your pilot and where he is being kept. From there, your journey is your own."

Delgado reached out and squeezed Dodge's hand so hard it made his knuckles pop. Then he pulled Dodge close and whispered in his ear.

"If you betray me, I'll kill the bank girl, Agent Williams, his family, and anyone else I can find that you care about. I'll dig up your dead relatives and shoot them in the head just to prove a point. Do we have an agreement?"

"Understood," Dodge said.

Delgado released his hand and smiled. "Good! Let's get you some guns for your trip."

With a push of a button on his smartphone, Delgado activated a hidden door on the study's east wall. The door pushed out and slid to the left, damn near silent. It was made of what appeared to be carbon fiber coated in a high-tech Kevlar material Dodge had only heard about a few years back, from one of his DoD buddies working at the Pentagon. Even then, the product hadn't seen the battlefield, and was never intended for civilian, or even law enforcement, use.

But what Dodge saw within the room concerned him most.

—⁓—

As Dodge entered the safe room, José Melendez was sitting in a holding cell at the FBI office in Charlotte Amalie. He was technically not under arrest but had told Agent Williams that he would gladly wait in the cell if it put the agent's mind at ease. Melendez just asked that he be able to keep his cell phone, in case Delgado tried to contact him. He told Agent Williams that if his phone rang and there was no answer, they would execute Williams's partner. Melendez assured him that his men knew exactly where Dodge was, and could move on him in a matter of minutes. His lifeless body would be hung from a tree in the jungle, where birds would pick at his corpse until his skin could not hold the joints together, and the body would fall to the jungle floor. Scavengers and jungle cats would finish the remaining evidence. No one would ever hear from him again.

A few hours passed before the phone buzzed in his pocket. Melendez placed it to the ear closest to the wall, hiding it from view, so it would appear as if he was just a man lying on a cot, talking to himself. He listened carefully to the man on the other end of the call, whose voice sounded panicked. His lungs sounded like they were working overtime as heavy breathing filled the man's phone mic.

"Slow down," Melendez said. "I can't hear you over all the breathing noise."

"I can't slow down!" the man yelled. "They are right behind me."

"Who? Who is behind you? Where are you at?"

"I don't know. Somewhere in the jungle near the compound."

"What the holy hell are you doing at the compound?"

Melendez realized his voice had risen to a level where one of the agents might have heard. He turned his head but saw that no one was paying him any attention.

"Where the hell is Juan?" he said.

"Juan is..." the sound of branches and leaves smashing

against the phone muffled the rest of the answer.

"Where is Juan?"

A few seconds passed before the man answered.

"Juan is dead. El Jefe murdered him."

Melendez flinched. In his heightened state of alertness, it felt as if he had levitated off the cot.

"What do you mean he's dead? What the hell happened. You were supposed to find the American and kill him, then feed his body to the Caymans."

"The boss knew he was coming and called Juan to get the American and bring him back to him. He said if the American was harmed, he would kill us all. Juan changed the plan and said he would kill the American and El Jefe at the compound. It would make it look like the American agent came for him, and they both died in a shootout."

Estúpido. The plan was to kill the American in an ambush. Then Juan was to kill two of his men and leave them at the scene so it would look like Dodge got off a few good rounds before being shot himself. The locals would blame Delgado, and he would be hunted down. One dead American was bad enough, but two would force the Americans to react. Possibly with a drone strike. It would be quick and precise. Delgado always said Juan had a grown-up ambition and a child's brain.

These thoughts sped through Jose's mind as he lay on the cot. Then he heard the dogs.

The man running through the trees would not escape the dogs. His boss had purchased the German Shepherds from a local police department when the animals became too aggressive, even for Colombian police standards. A little food deprivation, and shocking with a cattle prod, and the dogs were ready to hunt anything he scented them with. Their only job was to hunt and kill. No pulling back. No latching onto a leg or arm and tugging. It was about fear—the fear of being torn apart by crazed animals.

Melendez hung up the phone. It would be over soon.

Agent Williams had sat in his office for most of the day,

only coming out to check if there was any word from Dodge. Melendez could tell the seasoned agent was worried. And he had a right to be. Delgado was ruthless, as Juan and the man in the jungle had discovered.

His boss had Agent Williams's man. The status of his condition was the X-factor. If Dodge was dead, Melendez knew he would soon to be joining him. Even if Agent Williams didn't have him shot right there in the cell, spending the rest of his life in an American prison was not an option.

It wouldn't take long for his boss to fill in the gaps. Eventually, someone would talk. That was the thing about junkies and low-level foot soldiers. They always gave up their comrades if the right tactic was used—like beheading a wife or parent. That one had worked for cartels for decades. Melendez pictured his mother lying on the ground in a pool of blood, flies laying eggs, and bugs slowly devouring her corpse. As a deterrent to others who think about betraying his employer, her head hung from a tree in the rural village where she lived.

Melendez shook the thought from his mind. He could not allow himself to go there. Adapting to the situation is what would save him.

He pulled the phone out of his pocket. This time, he didn't try to hide his call. No one was paying him any attention, anyway. If the cell door was open, he was sure he could have just walked right out without anyone noticing.

He dialed the number he had memorized. The phone rang twice before it was answered.

"You must kill the American," Melendez said. "The one they call Dodge. We know who took your daughter. It was Juan, your head field ops man. The FBI is planning an assault on the compound, with the DEA and Colombian forces."

"I am aware of Juan's betrayal. He has been dealt with. As for the American, I have promised him safe passage. He is not to be touched."

"Why would you help the Americans?"

"We made a deal. He'll find those responsible for my

daughter's murder, and I am going to let him know where his pilot is. I have supplied him with weapons, ammo, and a vehicle."

"The American can't be trusted. He'll betray you."

"If he does, we will kill everyone he knows and loves. My men in Bogotá are already compiling background information on Agent Dodge. By the end of the day, I'll have his address, mother's name, ex-girlfriends' names, and anything else we need if he breaks his word to me."

Melendez began to worry his plan might not work.

"Where are you at?" Delgado said. "I may need you ready on the boat at a moment's notice. When I send word, I want you to kill the captain and burn the boat. Do it in open water so the sharks take care of the captain and the other two bodies. Understand?"

"I do. I can be at the beach in forty-five minutes."

"Good. And José, don't let me down. If you do, my dogs will feast on your entrails."

Melendez flipped the phone shut and tossed it on the bed, then yelled for Agent Williams.

"Stop yelling." Williams approached the holding cell. "What do you want?"

"I am afraid things have changed. I just got a call from one of my men at my employer's compound. Your friend is being held there as we speak. My man has informed me that Delgado plans to kill your friend. He has already purged at least two members of his best tactical team, and is threatening more. I'm afraid he is consumed with grief, and his next move will be to kill the American agent."

"You're sure this is true, and not just a ploy to get us to act?"

"I've been with him for twenty years, and I have never seen him this...how do you say it...unpredictable."

"And you're turning on your boss because you like me and care about Agent Dodge? Or are you next in line to take over as El Jefe?"

Melendez thought for a moment. He needed to give something to gain Agent Williams's trust.

"I understand your hesitation, so I'll give you two bodies."

"Why should I care about two dead guys in Colombia?"

"You shouldn't. But the two I am talking about are here on Saint Thomas."

"What the hell are you talking about?"

"Have your Coast Guard go to the inlet off the west side of the island, north of the airport. There they will see a fishing charter boat anchored in the bay. It flies a Puerto Rican flag."

"And the bodies are on that boat?"

"Yes. And so is the captain who witnessed both murders. He also has a sizeable amount of cash on him, intended to keep him from talking. Take the money and his boat, and he'll talk."

Melendez could see the gears turning in Agent Williams's head. The idea of two dead bodies on his turf would create a powerful argument for the American government's intervention, which could play into Melendez's hands. A strike would take down Delgado, his compound, and many men. But the drug trafficking infrastructure, supply chains, men loyal to Melendez outside the compound, and of course, the never-ending demand for the product in the United States would survive. As the new leader of the cartel, he, José Melendez, would build the empire back in a matter of a year. Then things could be run his way— the right way.

"If you're lying to me," said Agent Williams, "I'll shoot you right here. If Agent Dodge is dead, I'll shoot you. Do you understand?"

"Then you better hurry and make the call to the Coast Guard," Melendez said. "My life depends on it."

He watched as Agent Williams pulled out a cell phone and dialed while walking back to his office. Melendez studied him, trying to read his lips through the open blinds on the window facing the holding cell. He thought he made out the words, *two bodies* and *cash*, before Agent Williams saw him staring and closed the blinds.

He seemed to have taken the bait. It would only be a matter of time now. Even if Melendez's' man in Colombia contacted the FBI to let them know Dodge was safe, the foundation was laid. The empire would soon be his.

CHAPTER 24

THE SAFE ROOM IN DELGADO'S HOME was lined with racks and shelves holding every kind of weapon imaginable: military-grade assault rifles and pistols, both semi-auto and revolvers of all calibers and sizes. He even had two rocket-propelled grenade launchers. It was a gun nut's dream.

To the eyes of a trained law enforcement officer, everything in the room was utilitarian. Firearms served one purpose—to kill.

Delgado looked over all the merchandise in the room before pointing to a Glock 9mm, an MP4 close-quarters assault rifle, and extra mags and ammo for both. For good measure, he added a derringer that shot small shotgun shells, .410 gauge, for emergencies. It wouldn't kill anyone, but it would certainly buy him time.

Delgado ordered one of his men to place the weapons in a black gym bag, and the men left the room and headed toward the garage. Delgado's man tossed Dodge the keys to an average-looking American SUV, and placed the bag of weapons in the back seat. The newly freed hostage hopped in the driver's seat, backed out of the garage, and down the winding mountain road leading to town.

The drive took two hours. There were several vehicles stopped where the rendezvous team had intercepted him earlier in the day. His car was gone, but debris from his accident was scattered throughout the ditch. People were sorting through the parts for anything reusable, recyclable, or sellable. That's how it is in impoverished places around the world. Nothing ever went to waste. Dodge assumed that if he were in that ditch, someone could find a use for him as well. Probably pig feed for a pig or garden fertilizer.

About a quarter-mile later, he passed the spot where the team of armed men had grabbed the young man and killed his partner. The rusty old truck sat off the side of the road. There were skid marks on the pavement where someone had used another vehicle to push the truck from the side of the road. The old man's body was still slumped over the steering wheel. Apparently, he was of no use to anyone.

Once in town, Dodge headed toward the US Embassy to contact Brown. He wouldn't be happy about his car's fate, but Dodge guessed he would forget about the car once he found out the money and guns were also missing.

The thought made him smile. He felt the guns given to him by Delgado were worth more than the car and the cash.

The jar of hitting a massive pothole brought his mind back to the task at hand. He needed to call Agent Williams and tell him about his meeting with Delgado and the deal he had struck with him. Unfortunately, the phone given to him at the compound was programmed to dial only one number—Delgado's.

All of this gave Dodge a strange feeling in the pit of his stomach. Something about what his captor had said to him, about there only being two people that had the guts to take his daughter and his empire from him. One man was now dead, and the other was in a cell at the FBI office in St. Thomas, with Agent Williams. Something about José Melendez showing up at Williams's home just seemed off.

Dodge pulled over at the bar where he had left Brown over six hours ago. The sun had dipped behind the mountains, and dusk was settling in. He parked and went inside to see if Brown was there or had left anything for him.

After Dodge slipped the bartender his last twenty, the man said the American government man ate lunch and asked to use the phone to call a taxi. He left shortly after that and hadn't returned.

Dodge thanked the bartender for the information and asked if he could use the phone.

"It'll cost ya another twenty."

Before the guy could react, the more agile parole agent reached across the bar and snatched out of his shirt pocket the twenty he had given the man a few minutes earlier, slamming it onto the bar.

"You can have it back if you let me use the phone."

The bartender nodded, pointing toward the end of the bar, where an old rotary phone sat with a drunk slobbering all over the receiver, trying to talk to someone. Dodge strode over to the drunk and kicked the chair's legs out from under him. The chair flipped on its side, causing the intoxicated man to hit his chin on the bar before crumpling to the floor. The phone's receiver hung by its cord, swinging along the front of the bar. Dodge grabbed the line and pulled the receiver up, then clicked on the disconnect button and dialed the operator.

The parole agent didn't speak Spanish, but figured the operator would understand *United States Embassy*. She did, and within a few minutes, he was talking to the switchboard operator at the embassy. When the operator asked who he wanted to speak with, Dodge realized he didn't know Brown's first name. One of the five most common names in the States— Brown. He figured the only thing that could be worse was if the name was Smith or Jones. Still, he told the operator that the name was Brown, and apologized for not knowing his first name. When she asked for his name, he simply said, "Dodge."

Elevator music came through the earpiece, and he caught his foot tapping to a familiar tune. After a moment, the operator came back on the line.

"Mister Dodge, I'll patch you through to Mister Brown."

Must not be as many Browns in Colombia.

A familiar voice came on the line.

"Dodge, I had just about given you up for dead. Where have you been?"

"Just doing some sightseeing in the mountains."

"You brought my car back, I hope."

"Honestly, I thought you would be more concerned about the money."

Brown laughed. "We piss more money than that away in a day. Besides, we seized it from a drug smuggler at the airport. The car, however...I liked that car."

"Keep an eye out. You might see it driving around town."

"Anyway, glad you're alive. How'd you escape?"

"About that. He let me go."

"And why would Delgado just let you go?"

"I told him I would find everyone responsible for what happened to his daughter."

Brown laughed. "That's all!"

"I know. But if I can give him a name, he'll tell me who's keeping my pilot and where I can find him."

"Making deals with drug dealers. Nothing bad has ever come from that."

"This all started with a dead girl, and it should end with her as well."

"What can I do to help?" Brown said. "Just don't ask for another car."

"Already got the car covered. What I need is information. Do you or your DEA friends have any contacts down at the cargo area of the airport?"

"I can make a call. How can I reach you?"

"I'll call you."

"OK. Give me a couple hours, and I should have something for you."

The receiver clicked as it rested back in the phone's cradle. The drunk on the floor was coming out of his nap, and Dodge decided it was a good time to leave. He nodded to the bartender and stepped out into the dark night.

Now, money was the main issue. Information was never free, and he needed a lot of information.

Looking at the car Delgado had given him parked across the street gave the skilled operative an idea. He went back inside the bar and asked if anyone knew a local place that bought used cars. An old man sitting at a table in the far corner stood and said he had a cousin that would take the car off his hands for cash.

"American dollars," he said.

The man's English was broken, but good enough understand the address and directions.

Then Dodge left the bar for a second time that night.

The address was just a few blocks from the place he had just left. He made a right turn at the first street, then two lefts, and he parked in front of a warehouse-looking building with roll-up-type doors lining its face. Each garage door had a street number, and a name spray-painted on its face. The one for the old man's cousin was the third door, 1724. Pedro Sanchez was painted on the door in black spray paint.

Appropriate. Dodge stepped out of the car and approached the building. A camera was mounted above Pedro's door. The flimsy sheet metal rattled as his fist made contact with the door. Then he stepped back and waited for someone to come. Two minutes later, he heard footsteps coming from the other side of the door, followed by the sound of a metal security latch disengaging. He took one more step back and placed his hand in his pocket to grip the derringer .

The door rolled up. A young boy looked up at the man in in front of him and smiled. He yelled something in Spanish over his shoulder, then ran back into the shop on the other side of the door. Dodge hustled to keep up with the child, keeping a tight grip on the pistol in his pocket.

The shop was about a hundred feet deep and fifteen feet wide. There were four cars in different states of disassembly, parked two by two. At the far end of the shop sat a man at a rusty metal desk. He wore blue overalls and smelled of grease and gasoline. What few teeth he had were brown from years of neglect and what appeared to be chewing-tobacco use.

The man stood and held out a hand. "I am Pedro. When my cousin called and told me an American would come to see me, I said, *an American?* Why would a gringo want to do business with Pedro?"

Once again, Dodge was impressed with a local's grasp of the English language.

"Same as anyone else," he replied. "I need some quick cash."

Pedro spit on the floor beside him. "Let's see what you have to offer."

Dodge led Pedro into the dark street and pointed to the SUV parked two spots down from the storefront.

"There it is." Pedro walked around the vehicle, kicking the tires as he passed each one.

Dodge laughed. "In America, that's a saying. No one actually kicks the tires."

"The roads in Colombia aren't like those in America. Suspension is the first thing to go, so it is my biggest moneymaker. There is always a need for good suspension parts. Especially four-wheel drive." Pedro walked back and stood beside Dodge. "Where did a gringo like you get this car?"

"Does it matter?"

The man shook his head and smiled. "Not really."

"What'll you give me for it?"

Pedro went into full car salesman mode. He slid his foot around in the dirt, ran his hand through his greasy black hair, then made several grunts and moans before turning back to Dodge.

"Twenty-five hundred, US dollars."

"Make it three thousand, and I'll throw in this pretty little derringer. Dodge pulled the gun out of his pocket and watched as Pedro's eyes grew to twice their size.

"Got any bullets?"

"Yep."

Pedro slapped his new friend on the arm in a gesture to seal the deal. The two men walked back to the desk at the far end of the shop. Pedro opened a drawer on the bottom left side and removed a small metal box with a padlock securing the lid. He pulled out a stack of one-hundred-dollar bills and counted to thirty, laying each pile on the desk. When Pedro reached thirty, Dodge slid the piles together and placed the money in his pocket, then handed over the derringer after unloading the shells. *No need to tempt anyone.*

Pedro took the little gun and pointed it at the wall, making a *bang* sound with his mouth. He then stuck the gun in the box and placed the padlock through the latch, securing its contents once again, before putting the box back in the bottom drawer.

"Thank you, my friend," Pedro said.

"Since we're now friends and all, can I use your phone to call a taxi?"

"No taxi is coming down here in the dark. It is not a nice place. I'll have him give you a ride to where you need to go." Pedro snapped his fingers at the young boy and pointed at the street. "Get El Caballo."

A few minutes later, a jet-black sports car skidded to a stop just outside the shop's door.

"The boy will take you to where you need to go. I would not stay in this place too long. A white gringo with a pocket full of money is a...how do you say...easy target."

Dodge said thanks and grabbed the black duffel bag from the back seat of the SUV. He nodded at Pedro and got into the sports car. The young boy could barely reach the pedals. Still, he put the car in gear and pressed the accelerator, powering them down the street, and eventually, to the main highway that traversed town.

The boy dropped off the tired and dirty parole agent at a non-chain motel near the city center. Dodge guessed the people holding the pilot would stake out the larger Americanized hotel chains searching for him. People like to stay where they're comfortable. At places that remind them of home. For

Americans, that means looking for American names on the sides of buildings. He did the opposite. He picked a modest motel with a local name and signed in under a fake name and paid for the room in cash.

He made sure to slip an extra hundred to the clerk, who looked around before placing the bill in his pocket. He gave Dodge a key to a unit facing the street, but one that had a back door to the courtyard. An escape route, if needed.

Dodge could tell the clerk was well-versed in the routine, as he only said, *thank you,* throughout the transaction.

Once in the room, the first thing was a quick call to Brown to see if he had made any headway on names of cargo workers who might have had a part in Maria Delgado being in that container. Brown said his DEA friend had several sources at the airport and would send a list to Brown over a secure email channel in the morning.

Dodge also asked if Brown would call Agent Williams in St. Thomas and give him his cell number.

Once he hung up, Dodge showered and put on clean clothes he'd purchased earlier that day at a store around the corner from the hotel. It was after 2:00 a.m., and his eyes shut as soon as his head hit the pillow. He dreamed about *Kelly's Dream,* and Nikki, and Anna, and Kelly, the woman responsible for his lodgings in St. Thomas. All the things he cared about.

Dodge slept soundly until his room phone rang at nine the next morning.

CHAPTER 25

AGENT WILLIAMS SAT ABOARD the Coast Guard's interdiction boat as it rocked back and forth in the rough waters off the shore of St. Thomas. He had passed on to headquarters the information that José Melendez gave him about the fishing charter Delgado had used while he was on the island. They notified the local Coast Guard station, formulated a plan, and the drug interdiction unit hit the boat at 5:00 a.m. the following day. Once the boarding team secured the ship, the officer in charge called Agent Williams and sent a dinghy to the nearest beach to pick him up. The operational command was under the Coasties until the parties were on land. Then the FBI would take jurisdiction. Agent Williams was just an observer while on the water.

The constant rocking of the boat took its toll on Williams. He had never been one for boats and water. In fact, he didn't even like to swim. He could swim like a fish, but never felt comfortable in water.

He swallowed a motion sickness pill before leaving shore, and couldn't help but think how bad it would have been if he hadn't premedicated. He imagined being on board the larger fishing charter might help since it was a bigger boat and its keel rode deeper, causing less swaying.

Once on the fishing charter, he found he was right about the rocking. But the rotten smell of decaying flesh from the bodies of two men wrapped in plastic that the Coast Guard had found on board and laid out on the deck caused his stomach to force up the coffee he'd drank earlier. The captain's unwrapped corpse lay beside them, a small round hole in the center of his forehead. Likely a .22 caliber. *Professional hit.*

"Most likely Delgado covering his tracks," said the officer in charge.

"How long have they been dead?" Agent Williams said.

"Won't know for sure about the ones in plastic until the medical examiner gets them on the slab. But the captain here has been dead anywhere from twelve to twenty-four hours, based on the rigidity of the limbs. Rigor mortis has come and gone, and the body has started bloating."

"Did you find anything else worth noting about the boat?" Agent Williams said.

"It was clean. Too clean, if you ask me. We would've noticed something was off had the boat been encountered at sea. Not a single fishing pole above deck. We found no bait on board, either. There hasn't been a single fish brought on board this ship in at least a month. You just can't get rid of that smell."

Agent Williams noticed the burn from stomach acid rising into his throat.

"How the hell could you smell fish over this stench," he said.

"When you've boarded as many trollers and charters as I have," said the agent in charge, "you learn to notice different smells."

"If you say so." Agent Williams climbed back onto the small coast guard boat. "I'll get the medical examiner down here. Once he has the bodies, bring the chain of custody paperwork to the FBI office, and I'll sign for the bodies, along with any evidence you dig up."

The agent in charge nodded. "Will do, sir."

A young Coastie took Agent Williams to shore in the dinghy. It was all he could do to keep from throwing up right in the inflatable boat. Once on shore, he pushed the rubber inflatable off the beach, along with the Coastie, and found a bench to rest on until he lost his sea legs. The sun was blistering, making the sickness in his stomach that much more unbearable. He sat on the bench, taking deep breaths and exhaling slowly, until the urge to vomit had subsided. Just as he stood to walk the short distance to his agency cruiser, his phone rang. The number showed the call was coming from the FBI office on St. Thomas.

"This is Agent Williams. What is it?"

"Sir, you need to get back to get back here, *right now.*"

"What's going on?"

No reply.

"What's going on?" he said again.

After a few seconds, the agent replied, "We are under attack. I repeat, we are being attacked."

"Who? Who is attacking you?"

"I don't know. The damn..."

The phone went dead.

"Shit!" Agent Williams shoved his phone into his front jacket pocket, fumbled his keys before securing them, and then jumped into the driver's seat of his black sedan.

The engine roared to life, and he flipped the switch on the console, activating his red and blue flashers mounted in the front grill and back window. The tires broke free of the pavement, throwing rocks and sand high into a rooster tail behind his vehicle as he sped away.

It was still early morning, and traffic was light, even for a weekday, allowing him to catch most of the stoplights on the main roads, which increased his response time by a few minutes—minutes his men might need.

Fifteen years of training told him to stop a block or two before the office and walk the rest of the way, using buildings and vehicles parked on the street for cover. Don't blindly run into a firefight, guns blazing like some action-movie hero. Real-life didn't work that way. That television crap got you killed, but fifteen minutes of adrenaline proved the deciding factor.

He pressed the accelerator harder, sliding around the corner leading to the main entrance, looking for anyone with a gun, not wearing a police uniform or a suit. He found his target and slammed his car into the right side of the closest bad guy he saw.

The man bounced off the rear fender, spun around, and tried to regain his balance. His reaction was half-a-second too slow, as the rear of the three-thousand-pound car beat him to the spot. One of the rear tires slid over his legs, and with one last spin, pulled his body up between the tire and the wheel well, snapping his neck with one slam to the pavement.

The commotion caught the other attackers by surprise. Two of them turned and ran. Three stopped shooting at the building, refocusing their sights on Agent Williams. One round hit the windshield, but Agent Williams was splayed out across the front seat, below the line of fire. He had no plan on shooting back at the men on the street. His move was a diversion. As special agent in charge, he knew the standard operating procedure in the event of an attack on a government office. First, the front entrance would be sealed when steel curtains dropped from the ceiling in under two seconds. Next, all prisoners and civilian employees would be secured in the armory, which was just a bank vault converted to hold guns and ammunition. Last, four men would deploy to the roof of the building with sniper rifles.

Agent Williams's diversion allowed his snipers to get off six shots. All kill shots to the head. He tucked into himself to maintain a low profile on the seat. Then it went quiet. He fought the urge to pop his head up and take a glance. No need to give a juiced-up twenty-five-year-old sniper a reason to turn his head into a canoe.

When he heard a voice from the office's direction yell, "Clear!" Williams crawled out of the car and surveyed the damage.

—◦◦◦—

The old rotary phone camped out on the nightstand came to life. Its ring sounded like church bells, causing Dodge to slap his hand on the table until the receiver fell to the floor.

He picked it up and grunted, "Hello."

"This is the front desk. There is a man here to see you. I told him I would see if you were still staying with us."

The voice was from the same clerk staffing the desk when he had checked in the night before. The C-note turned out to be an excellent investment.

Dodge grabbed his Glock from the nightstand and racked the slide to chamber a round. He wondered if the clerk had heard the pistol's action cycle.

"Is this man a local?"

"No," the clerk said. "It is a gringo. Like you."

Dodge paused. "Give me two minutes, and then send him to my room."

"Are you sure? He's got a gun."

"Yes. Two minutes." Dodge hung up.

When the man knocked on the door, Dodge didn't answer the first time. The man knocked again. Dodge, positioned himself in a chair opposite the door swing, with his shotgun pointed waist-high to an average man, toward the door.

"Come in," he said.

The handle turned, and the door swung inward toward his position. A head pushed through the opening.

"Agent Dodge?"

He dipped the barrel of the shotgun. "Brown! What the hell are you doing here?"

Brown's gaze focused on the shotgun pointed at his midsection.

"Don't shoot me with that thing. My wife will get rich and retire on a boat on a Caribbean island."

"It's overrated," Dodge said. "Besides, someone always comes along and ruins the fun. This time, it's you."

"Well, I thought you might need a ride. You can put the gun and your *bag* in the trunk of my official US State Department car."

"Smart. Diplomatic immunity, and the car is official US property. No one can search it."

"Membership has its privileges," Brown said.

"I got time for a quick shower?"

"Sure. I'll get some coffee from the lobby."

Dodge laughed. "I don't think it's that kind of hotel."

"The guy at the counter was drinking some. I'll see if he'll make a few cups to go."

"That probably wasn't coffee."

Brown left the room, allowing Dodge to shower and shave. He put on the clothes he was wearing earlier, disassembled and cleaned his pistol, and topped off the magazine, replacing the shell he ejected earlier. His mood was good. Despite being in a foreign country, not speaking the language, and his only connections in the country being a drug lord and a spook, he gave himself a seventy-five percent chance of surviving. *Good odds.*

Brown returned to the room with two glass bottles of soda—one diet, the other original.

"Leaded or unleaded." He held out the soft drinks.

"They started putting coffee in bottles, I see." Dodge reached for the bottle containing the diet version.

"We should get moving," Brown said. "Longshoremen work long shifts and tend to be less punch-you-in-the-face-for-asking-them-a-question before a full day's work."

Dodge put the black duffel bag containing his Glock and extra magazine into the trunk of the car. Then the two men drove for about twenty-five minutes, maneuvering through cityside streets and back alleys. Brown said the route was to avoid traffic. Dodge guessed he had other reasons for staying off the busy roads. Whatever the reason, once at the airport, Brown drove the perimeter of the fence and stopped the car when he came to a spot just inside the fence that appeared to be used as a break area for employees.

Sitting at a picnic table, smoking a cigarette, was one of the largest men the veteran parole agent had ever seen. He had to stand six-foot-five and weigh three hundred pounds, with a squared-off jaw and a head the size of a watermelon. His arms were covered in tattoos. In the US, it was referred to as having sleeves. On this fellow, it was likely a record of his criminal conquests and subsequent incarcerations.

As Brown pulled up next to the fence, directly behind the picnic table area, the large man stood and walked toward them. Brown asked Dodge to wait in the vehicle while he got out to speak to him.

"These guys can get a little jumpy around new people."

It was evident the two men knew one another. A cordial introduction concluded with Brown passing the small white envelope through the slot in the fence, to the tattooed man. The man put the envelope into his pocket without opening it, signaling he trusted Brown.

After a few minutes and a couple side glances toward the car, Brown waved Dodge over. The man with the tattoos spoke only to Brown.

"What does he want?"

"Information," Brown said.

The man studied the new arrival and said, "Gonna cost him."

Dodge reached into his pocket to pull out some of his car sale proceeds, but he caught a side-eye glance from Brown and slid his hand up to adjust his belt.

"Doesn't work that way," Brown said. "I gave you all you're going to get. And try to shake me down again. I'll make sure your employers know who has been feeding the American government cartel information for the last year. Do they like snitches?"

The man shook his head.

"Good." Brown glanced at Dodge and nodded, then looked back at the tattooed man. "This man is going to ask a couple questions. Answer them, and we will be on our way. Lie to him, and well..." He paused for effect. "We already covered that."

Dodge told the man who he was. It didn't matter if the guy knew his name or not. The most ruthless man in the Southern Hemisphere knew where he lived. This fellow didn't make the top ten concerns list at the moment, tattoos or not.

Dodge then asked about the container. He described it and told the man when he believed it had been left at the airport. To help drive the point home, he added the part about a drug lord's daughter being stuffed inside and left for dead.

"I don't have anything to do with any dead girl," the man said.

"Maybe not," Dodge said. "But you know something about it, don't you? I can promise you that Delgado will not differentiate between those who had a hand in it, and those who knew and kept quiet. I saw him shoot his righthand man in the head today."

The tattooed man looked straight at Dodge. "José is d-dead?"

Dodge realized he now had confirmation of one person responsible for Maria Delgado's death. He thanked the man and tapped Brown on the arm.

"Let's go."

Brown nodded, and the two men got in the car, turned around, and headed back alongside the property fence toward the road. They managed to drive halfway before a forklift moved out of a gate, directly in their path. Brown slammed on the brakes, and the car came to rest twenty feet from the yellow machine.

"Damn," Brown said.

A glance to the rear of the car showed no one was coming from behind. Only more fence and airport runways. Dodge then spotted a familiar face approaching from inside the secure area. It was the tattooed man, and he had two others with him.

"Hey, look." Dodge pointed at the approaching men. "It's your friend, Tiny."

"He does have friends. I figured no one liked him."

"Even assholes have a friend or two."

"Where is your gun?" Brown said.

Dodge reached for his waistline where his Glock 9mm normally rested, but all he grabbed was a handful of shirt.

"It's in the trunk."

"That was probably a mistake on my part," Brown said. "Can you fight?"

"I feel like we're about to find out."

As Dodge stepped out of the car, he plucked a medium-sized rock from the ground and cupped it in his hand. The tattooed man and his accomplices were not through the gate yet, giving him a tactical advantage over the lone man driving the fork truck.

Dodge and Brown moved toward the open gate. Then Dodge broke off and charged at the fork truck driver. When he was within ten feet, he reared back and threw the rock with all his weight as leverage. The stone found its target, hitting the man in the fork truck on the bridge of the nose. Blood ran down his face, and he tipped over and fell to the ground, unconscious.

One down. Three to go.

"Nice throw!" Brown yelled, as they picked up speed and closed the gap between them and the three men.

The move must have caught the attackers off guard, because all three slowed for just a second. Dodge noticed the hesitation and quickened his pace to a sprint. The tattooed man positioned himself in the center, flanked on either side by the two men. The middleman's position, a step ahead of his partners, didn't allow him to see what happened next.

The man on the right must have decided this was not his fight, and turned and ran in the other direction. Dodge was upon the tattooed man in a matter of seconds. The man drew back his massive arm and swung a haymaker at where he thought his adversary's head would be. Dodge saw the man's muscles flex, starting the labor-intensive process of getting arms the size of tree trunks to move, and the parole agent decided to go low to avoid the falling branches. The tattooed arm hit nothing but air. Leading with his shoulder, Dodge dove and slammed into the man's knee with the crest of his shoulder and a full head of steam—a brutal hit, by pro football standards. He heard the cartilage crack and tendons snap as the knee joint pushed back and sideways in an unnatural movement. Hinge joints only move in one direction—that's their weakness.

The large man crumpled to the ground, grabbing his knee. The parole agent finished the job with a massive boot to the face, smashing the tattooed man's nose and breaking his jaw. Two teeth fell to the ground next to his limp body.

Brown's man saw what happened to the much larger man and turned tail, bolting to getaway. Brown gave chase for a few feet, then decided best they leave while they were ahead.

Dodge reached into the tattooed man's pocket and pulled the white envelope free. He opened it and took two hundred-dollar bills before handing the rest back to Brown.

"That covers my room for last night. Let's get the hell out of here."

Brown leaped onto the fork truck and backed it up enough for the car to pass. At the same time, Dodge pulled the driver by his ankles, over next to the tattooed man. The two men then drove the remaining distance to the road and made a righthand turn. Brown didn't bother with side streets this time. It was highways and populated areas all the way back to the embassy.

As Brown showed his credentials to the US Marine guarding the front gate, Dodge's phone buzzed. The prefix was 340, a US Virgin Islands area code. It was 11:30 in the morning.

CHAPTER 26

THE PHONE BUZZED TWICE before Dodge could pull it out from his front pants pocket.

He flipped open the device. "This is Dodge."

"Dodge, it's Agent Williams. First, let me say, I'm glad you're alive. You'll have to explain to me someday, over a beer, how you managed that. Your friend Brown filled me in last night on your situation. I gotta say, making deals with drug dealers is not the direction I would've gone, but I can appreciate you were in a tight spot."

"Thanks for the approval," Dodge said.

"Anyway, I have some ne—"

Dodge said, "I know who put Maria Delgado in that crate. I know who is responsible. José Melendez, the guy you have right now. I spoke to a guy here in Bogotá, and he let the name *José* slip. It's José, not Juan. Someone other than Maria Delgado carved that name into the lid of her crate. Juan was a soldier. He didn't have the clout to plan this, and no low-level drug dealer would go to the boss's hitman and request help to dispose of the boss's daughter. It had to be someone higher in the food chain. Someone with higher aspirations. Delgado gave me two names after he shot Juan in the head. He felt pretty confident Melendez would never betray him, and instructed me to find out who was responsible. If I did, he would give me information on the whereabouts of the pilot who flew me in the country. Naturally, I accepted the offer with Juan's brains puddled at my feet."

"Murder is an excellent motivator," Williams said.

"You're telling me!"

"Well, I hate to burst your bubble," Williams said, "but I already know all of that."

"You already know? Why did you let me go on if you knew what I was going to say?"

"You seemed so proud of yourself. I didn't want to hurt your feelings."

"Like I have feelings." Dodge's laugh echoed through the car's cabin. "So, tell me who told you."

"I'm a pretty talented investigator, too, you know."

"If you say so."

"It started yesterday," Williams said, "when I got the full coroner's report. The findings stated Maria's fingernails were removed by pulling and rocking side to side. The same way torturers have been doing it for centuries. If her nails came off because of the scratching inside the crate, the removal would've been front to back, not side to side. There also would've been abrasions to the skin at the tip of the finger, caused when her nails peeled away, exposing the end of the finger to the crate's surface."

"That makes sense," Dodge said. "But how did you know about Melendez?"

"He was trying too hard. He gave me two bodies, which turned out to be three, on a fishing charter in the bay. I had his cell bugged, and he received a call from someone, during which he found out Juan was dead. If Juan had been responsible for Maria Delgado, it was over. Why give me the bodies on the boat?" Agent Williams paused. "He was trying to frame his boss. Same with Agent McCaffrey's murder. I figure Melendez recruited Juan in on the plot. As soon as Delgado was put away or dead, Melendez would take over. His first move would be to install Juan as his number two. The incentive of going from a pay-by-job position to a ridiculous salary was too much to pass up. Melendez used his connections at the airport and on the island to move young Maria in secret. Too bad for him, a storm hit, killing her before she could be moved again. Once news of her death was out, he couldn't stop Delgado from coming to Saint Thomas for revenge. So, he planted the idea into his boss's head that the Trey-Deuces were likely involved, leading to the slaughter fire at the clubhouse. In the end, this was what these things are always about—money and power. It was all a play at leadership of the organization."

"All right, then," Dodge said. "I'll give the drug lord José Melendez's name, and throw in the guy I kicked in the face at the airport today. Then I figure out how to get my pilot back."

"Um, yeah, that's what I called to tell you. Melendez is dead."

Dodge ran his hand through his hair. "Aren't you just full of good news? What happened?"

"While I was out with the Coast Guard, the remaining members of the Trey-Deuces found out we were holding the man responsible for killing their brothers and torching the clubhouse."

"Did they breach the building and take him?" Dodge said.

"No. These guys were pure amateurs. They never got past the parking lot. I'm pretty sure if there were any brains in that outfit, they crisped up in the fire the other day."

"So how did he die?"

"During the attempted siege, my deputy followed SOP and herded the prisoner and civilian employees into the armory for safety. Melendez tackled one agent and tried to take his weapon. Poor bastard never got it out of the holster. The second agent emptied his duty weapon into the only available target—José's head. There isn't enough left for his own mother to recognize."

"Messy," Dodge said. "That causes a problem for me, though."

"Bad guys are dead, and we know how the girl died. Sounds like a win to me. I'm gonna get a beer, and maybe see if my wife wants to mess around later."

"You might want to hold off on the wife front for a bit."

Williams sighed. "What did you do?"

Dodge thought for a minute, trying to ease into the promise

he had made to Delgado. He decided on the tried-and-true Band-Aid approach. Just get to it fast.

"The thing is, Delgado had his heart set on personally dealing with whoever hurt his daughter."

"Most of them are dead," Williams said. "Just give him your guy at the airport and be done with it."

"Yeah, that isn't going to work. In fact, Martinez-Delgado made it pretty clear that if he didn't get what he wanted, he would kill me, you, your wife in her little white get-up, and even a girl I spent a few nights with on the island. He even said something about digging up my dead relatives and shooting them, for Christ's sake."

"I could see where that could be a bit of a hassle for you," Williams said. "How did you leave it with the informant today?"

"I hit his buddy in the head with a rock and busted the big guy's knee. But I don't think he would get me close enough to Delgado to take him out. I'll definitely need more to offer before our kingpin friend sets up another meeting."

"Well, we better think of something. My wife wants to have you over for dinner, and I can't tell her you aren't able to make it because some drug dealer chopped your head off."

"I'm gonna work with Brown here and see if we can come up with anything. I just need enough time to get the pilot back. After that, he can chase me all the way back to the States if he chooses. At least there, I would be on my turf."

Agent Williams said he would try to find a solution not ending with Dodge getting killed or left surviving on rainwater and tree grubs in the jungles of Colombia.

"Thanks. I appreciate that," Dodge replied. "Besides, I am more of a nut-and-berry guy in survival situations."

He hung up the phone and told Brown he wanted to take a walk around the block to clear his head. What he really wanted was a smoke. He always concentrated better when he had a cigarette.

"Just keep the embassy in site," Brown said. "If you can see us, we can see you."

Dodge exited the front gate after asking the marine standing guard where the closest shop he could buy a pack of smokes was. The marine reached into his front pants pocket and pulled out a half-empty pack of cigarettes.

"I have a friend at the embassy store. She gives them to me for free." The marine smiled as he handed over the pack.

"Is she cute?"

"Cute enough for free smokes."

After thanking the marine, Dodge exited the main gate and turned left. He walked the embassy's perimeter three times, finishing a smoke right around each pass by the main entrance. The more he walked, the more his doubts grew about how things had turned out. Discovering Melendez was involved in Maria Delgado's death seemed too clean. Too obvious. Both he and Delgado were smart men and used people every day to further their personal agendas. Dodge had no doubts Melendez and Juan were both involved, but both men being dead put Dodge at a disadvantage. Dead guys don't talk.

If Melendez was going to make Juan his second-in-charge, why put his name in that container? Maybe it was as simple as he didn't trust Juan, and Melendez needed to cover his tracks.

That was a risky proposition. Juan would talk sooner or later if Delgado tortured him enough. And the young man at the compound, El Jefe's cousin. Something stuck in Dodge's craw about him. He couldn't put his finger on it just yet.

His walk around the embassy raised more questions than it answered. The frustration was building. He decided he needed more time.

Dodge pulled the cell phone from his pocket and pushed send to the only contact saved in memory. The phone rang.

"Agent Dodge, I have been waiting for your call. Did you find out who murdered my daughter? Do you have a name for me?"

Dodge paused, still thinking about what to tell the man on the other end of the line.

"I am getting close. I need another day or two. People are hard for me to find, not knowing the city and all."

"You have until dark, tomorrow. If I do not hear from you by the sunset, those around you will suffer. Starting with the bank girl. Her name is Nikki, I believe?"

Delgado clicked off the line.

They needed to find the tattooed man from the airport again. He was the only person still alive who had a hand in Delgado's daughter's kidnapping, and he was the only bargaining chip Dodge had. Morally, he knew he could be sending a man to his death by turning him over to Delgado. But the tattooed man had made his choices. Those choices would get him killed, not the actions of Dodge or his new friends. Besides, this wasn't a case that would ever see the inside of a courtroom.

As he turned the last corner and re-entered the embassy grounds, Dodge snuffed out his smoke and placed the butt in his pocket. He took the elevator to the third floor and told the receptionist to let Brown know he was back from his walk.

Brown appeared from an office at the end of the hall, waiving him in. Dodge entered and sat in a chair across from Brown, who was holding a file while talking on his cell phone.

"Well, did you come up with any ideas?"

"The beginnings of one," Dodge said. "First rule in forming a plan, take no options off the table."

"You get that from a fortune cookie?"

Dodge nodded. "We need to talk to the tattoo guy again. He knows more, and we need to know what he knows."

Brown smiled. "I don't think he'll be too excited about another chat. You know, after you kicking out his teeth and all."

"He'll like the alternative even less. My guess is, the word has already gotten out that he helped a couple gringos. Delgado will sweep him up and get the information without me."

"And the pilot?" Brown said.

"I can't see any use for him being alive once Delgado has what he wants."

"I thought Delgado told you he didn't have the pilot?"

"I would bet dollars to doughnuts that he's the one holding our pilot. When I was in his armory, before he released me, I saw two shoulder-mounted rocket launchers. Perfect for shooting down a low-flying aircraft."

"If you are right," Brown said, "and he is the one who shot down your plane, why not just kill you when he had the chance?"

"He still wants his daughter's body, and I'm guessing he wants to make sure he knows everyone that was involved in taking her. If he tried to question people, or sent a guy like Juan, the guilty ones would run into the jungle and disappear. He would eventually find them, but his bloodlust is ripe now, and guys like Delgado run on pure emotion when challenged."

Brown leaned back in his chair, interlocking his fingers behind his head.

"Reminds me of a case in Afghanistan, where a tribal leader was taking money from the army, then turning around and trading the money for heroin, which he would hide in rival villages."

Dodge shrugged. "How is that relatable?"

"Well, let me finish. After hiding the drugs in or near the enemy's villages, this warlord would call the US Army and tell them he had suspicions of his neighbors selling heroin for al-Qaeda. They would then sweep in with Blackhawks and armored vehicles. What the Army didn't know was, he also told the Taliban about the drugs. They knew the US Army would come, and they waited to ambush them. It was a bloodbath. When the smoke cleared, every man in the village over age fifteen was cuffed and taken in for questioning. When the Americans left, the warlord would assume the role of an elder of that village and expand his empire."

"I still don't see the similarities," Dodge said.

"It was classic Hitchcock, man. *Criss Cross.* Only, this guy threw in a double-cross in the end. He used our money to kill all his enemies, including Americans. The kicker is, most of his drugs went stateside to feed our addiction. The US government paid for the drugs to poison its own citizens."

"I suppose there are some similarities." Dodge stood and walked to the window, which provided a spectacular view of the surrounding mountains. "Do you think Delgado is playing me?"

"I think Delgado is a stone-cold killer. He doesn't just let people walk away from his compound. In fact, I know of no one, outside of cartel members, who has been there and ever been seen again."

"Can you find the tattoo guy again?"

"Shouldn't be too difficult. When not working, he hangs out at a local strip club."

"Of course he does," Dodge said.

"Yeah, it's a real classy place. There's a two-scar minimum, and that's just for the dancers."

"What do you say we pay him another visit?" Dodge said.

Brown stood and grabbed his ID and a small pistol from the top desk drawer.

"Let me fill the boss in. Then we can go."

State Department, my ass.

After a quick elevator ride to the parking garage, Dodge and Brown headed across town to the strip club where they hoped to find the tattooed man. When they arrived, their target was sitting on a chair outside, talking to a girl who, based on her lack of shirt sleeves, and shorts that showed more than they covered, was a dancer at the club.

Brown didn't even try to be discreet this time. He parked the US government vehicle with diplomat plates, right in front of where the man was sitting. The two men got out and approached the tattooed man, whose real name Brown said was *Benicio*, but everyone called him Benny.

Benny moved to stand up, but Brown tugged up on the corner of his shirt, revealing the grip of his gun, causing Benny to return to his chair. Having seen two gringos, one of which had a gun, the dancer decided she wasn't interested in her large, tattooed friend anymore, and turned and went back into the club.

"First, I want to be clear," Brown said. "There will be no money now, or ever again. I'm still a little pissed you tried to jump us at the airport. But you can make amends by telling us everything you know about the girl in the container."

The man tensed up, and Dodge clenched his fists, readying for the impending fight. But the tattooed man relaxed, sighed, and dropped his head.

"What do you want to know? I'm dead anyway."

Brown said, "Actions have consequences, but I can help you. If you help us."

After repositioning his chair and glancing around to see if anyone was watching, Benny told a horrifying story about young Maria's last days. It turned out, José and Benny were family. Not first cousins, or even second cousins. More like fourth cousins twice removed. The kind of family that only shows up at weddings and funerals for the free food. But family, nonetheless.

He said José called one evening and said he needed to quietly get something out of the country. Tattooed man figured it was drugs, which was fine for him because he always took a little of the top for himself when smuggling drugs onto airplanes. But when José showed up, he was with one of Delgado's henchmen, and they brought with them an unconscious girl in the back of José's car. She looked to be a teenager, and she had a bloody bandage wrapped around one of her legs. The three men spent the next two hours preparing a shipping crate, drilling a hole in its side for fresh air. They packed the container with shipping material and stuffed the girl's body inside, then sealed the lid over her. Next, the men decided it would be safer to load the container on a truck and drive to Cartagena rather than trying to place it on a private flight. Private pilots cost money and created another loose end, and there were too many people that knew already. The container could then be loaded on a ship and sent to its eventual destination.

The truck took two days to reach the port at Cartagena, and the tattooed man rode along to make sure the driver didn't decide to tell anyone about his cargo. When they had to stop for gas, the driver would pass small pieces of bread through the hole, and using a spray bottle, he would squirt water into the girl's mouth. He didn't know who the girl was, and he didn't know where she was going once on the docks in Cartagena.

"What happened to the driver?" Dodge said.

"He's dead. An accident on the drive back."

"An accident? Brown said.

"His truck went off the side of a mountain road near Bucaramanga. The roads can be dangerous at night."

"That's everything?" Dodge said. "Who else is alive that knows what was in that container?"

The tattooed man shook his head. "No one. Just me."

Dodge turned to Brown. "We need to get to Cartagena."

Brown looked back at the man. "What about him?"

"If he's smart, he'll go hide in the mountains," Dodge said. "Or better yet, leave the country. But I don't care either way, to be honest." He turned back to the man on the stool. "You reap what you sow."

With that, the two men left the tattooed man sitting on his stool, pondering his future, which would likely be shorter than he had planned when he woke up that morning.

"How quick can you get us to Cartagena?" Dodge asked Brown, once back inside the car.

"Well, I would use my pilot, but since you went and got him captured...I might know another guy who can help." Brown made a U-turn and drove away from the city center, toward the mountains.

After traveling through retail areas and two barrios on the outskirts of town, Dodge noticed a small hangar about a half-mile ahead.

"State Department, huh?"

Brown said nothing, but a slight smile formed along the corners of his mouth.

The airport didn't appear to be used much, as the runway was just a field of grass. No cement or pavement, with only a tattered windsock marking the start of the runway.

Brown parked his car inside the hangar, next to a small twin-turboprop airplane. The two men got out, and Brown opened the door to the plane and pulled down the small ladder leading to the passenger area.

"Throw your gear inside and pack plenty of ammo," he said. "We might need it."

"How long until the pilot gets here?"

Brown gave a full smile this time.

"*You're* the pilot," Dodge said. "Why the hell didn't you just fly me to Colombia?"

"I don't leave the country much. Plus, you got shot down. I don't need to be hiding in the jungle, eating worms and drinking my piss for hydration."

"Worms aren't that bad," Dodge said. "It's those big tree grubs that are the worst. When those things pop in your mouth, it's like biting into a pus-filled boil that tastes like decomposing leaves. Ants, on the other hand...if you can get their head off without getting bit, they kinda taste citrusy."

Brown shook his head. "I never understood you ex-military types. Eating bugs for thirty-five thousand a year. How sad is that?"

Dodge shook his head and loaded the gear into the plane while Brown completed his preflight check. The small aircraft was in the air in less than a half-hour, and on its way to Cartagena. Dodge closed his eyes and faded off to sleep.

CHAPTER 27

THE JOLT FROM THE PLANE'S TIRES touching down on the grassy runway woke Dodge from his slumber. He wiped the sleep from his eyes, stretched, and yawned as the plane taxied to a small hanger identical to the one at the little airfield in Bogotá. Brown eased back on the throttle, and the aircraft came to a stop. He unbuckled from the pilot's seat and opened the cabin door.

"Leave the bags on the plane but bring your gun."

Dodge shoved the Glock semi-auto into his waistline and added an extra magazine to his rear pocket. A late-model four-by-four pickup sat in the hangar, half-covered by a tarp, and the engine roared to life when Brown turned the key in the ignition.

The airstrip sat five miles outside of town. It took fifteen minutes to reach the city limits, and another half-hour to traverse the busy streets before arriving at the docks.

The security setup was like the airport in Bogotá. A steel fence topped with razor wire, surrounded on three sides, and the fourth was bordered by the open waters of the Caribbean Sea. This time, Brown didn't follow the fence line. He drove straight for the main gate, showed his ID, and handed the gate attendant a twenty. The attendant hit a button inside the guard shack, and the barrier blocking the two men's path collapsed to the ground. Brown drove to a small building at the front of the complex, parking right in front of the door. A sign that hung above the entrance read, *Oficina Principal*.

The office was small and dirty, and contained only one desk

and no file cabinets. Behind the desk, typing on a computer, sat a gray-bearded man who stood when Brown entered the room.

"Brown, didn't know you were coming," the man said in a southern drawl. "The boss doesn't like surprises."

"It wasn't a planned kind of trip."

"Who is your friend?" The man gestured toward Dodge.

"This is Paul Dodge. We're helping each other out with a little problem."

Dodge nodded. "American?"

"Texas, born and raised."

"How did a guy from Texas get to Cartagena?"

"He asks a lot of questions," the man said to Brown.

"Call it a poor personality trait," Dodge said.

The Texan transplant stood silently for a minute, sizing up the two men confronting him, before sitting back at his desk and typing on his computer again. After a few minutes, the man behind the desk pointed at the only other door in the room.

"Go on in."

Brown opened the door, and the two men stepped inside. Dodge got the feeling they were entering a room not many people had been allowed into. The woo-woo hairs on the back of his neck stood at full attention. He tapped the grip on the gun in his waistband as he thought about his favorite rule: *Better to be prepared than dead.*

On the other side of the door was a tall, leggy blonde with red-painted nails and pouty lips painted deep red. She wore a fitted black dress which stopped at a classy two inches above the top of the knees. Dodge caught himself staring. His cheeks flush with embarrassment.

Brown said, "Don't worry about it. She's used to that reaction."

The woman stepped closer and held out her manicured hand.

"I am Miss White. So, you are the infamous Paul Dodge?"

He took her hand in his and applied just enough pressure

to show respect, but also a primitive desire to show his strength and virility.

"Miss White and Mister Brown? Not a lot of creativity at State, I see."

"Who said I work for the State Department?" She winked.

Brown said, "You know why we're here?"

"You didn't call ahead, and you brought Mister Dodge, who specializes in sex crimes. So, I'm guessing this is something you're working on off the books. The dead girl in Saint Thomas, perhaps?"

"You know who I am?" Dodge said.

That she knew he was in Colombia meant his secret mission had not been so secret.

"There is little that happens in Colombia that I am not aware of, Mister Dodge."

"That's good to know. You'll have to give me your number in case I ever come back to visit," Dodge said. "The dead girl was the daughter of Delgado, and she was drugged, then stuffed into a container before passing through this port on the way to Saint Thomas."

"I am well-aware of who the girl's father is," White snapped.

The tone of her voice carried a warning.

Dodge decided on a fresh approach. "How much do you know about what's currently going on in his organization?"

"There have been rumblings down here for a little over a year, about someone in the organization, someone close to Delgado, wanting to take over the role of El Jefe. We know it's someone with considerable pull among the dealers in the local villages and towns. He has even paid off a few politicians in Bogotá and Medellín to persuade local police to go after Delgado's supply chain."

"Why not just go after the man himself?" Brown said.

"From what I hear," said White, "you have been to his compound, Agent Dodge. So, you have seen firsthand the lengths he goes through to protect his empire and his own ass.

Oh, and remind me to make sure you tell me how you convinced our friend to allow you to leave his compound alive. A feat, I assure you, does not happen often."

"Never, I heard," Brown said.

"He is well-armed," Dodge said, knowing that was an understatement. "But so is every gang banger back in Los Angeles."

Ms. White chuckled, followed by a glare directed at Dodge that made his skin crawl. He watched as she reached for a black cloth shoulder bag that had been sitting on the desk behind her and pulled out a Sig-Sauer P226. She held the semi-auto up, rotating it to show both sides.

"I love this gun. I never leave the house without it. But this is no match for the fully auto assault rifles and rocket launchers he possesses. Not even in my hands. And I am an excellent shot. I believe you have had some experience with those."

White was a killer. She had the same look in her eyes that the veteran parole agent had seen a thousand times, staring back at him in the mirror every morning. It was like a dealer knowing an addict, or a pedophile knowing which child to approach and groom. It was ingrained in your DNA. And he hoped White saw it in him as well.

Ms. White continued. "Cutting off the head of a snake doesn't kill the snake. It just makes room for the other heads to grow. But if you cut the flow of cash, that will sow chaos. Chaos breeds fear, and fear leads to mutiny."

Dodge grew impatient. "What about the girl, Maria Delgado? How the hell did a bunch of low-level drug dealers smuggle a teenage girl past port security, through inspections, and onto a cargo ship without you or anyone else noticing? I mean, it seems you may want to give the locals a raise. Their loyalty appears to be questionable. This plan took a lot of money changing hands—most of it right here under your nose. Noticeable amounts of money to nominally paid workers. I mean, who runs the show down here? Because it doesn't appear to be you."

Brown touched his arm for the second time.

White stood and covered the short distance to the men in three steps, the clack of her heels echoing off the metal walls of the container-turned-office. Dodge stood his ground, never flinching. He knew it was an attempt to intimidate him. He couldn't win, but a stalemate would earn him respect, and if he was lucky, some valuable intel. He also noticed the P226 was not in her hand, increasing his confidence.

Ms. White stood with her face three inches from Dodge's. He could smell the odor of onions lingering on her breath from lunch. The two locked in a staring contest, waiting to see who blinked first. After a few minutes, he noticed a slight smile form in the corners of her mouth. She took a step back and looked down to see the barrel of a Glock pointing at her midsection.

"Not many people talk to me that way, Agent Dodge. And *no one* pulls a gun on me."

"Life's full of disappointment." He slid the pistol back into his waistline. "I just want to know who was involved in the girl's death. For God's sake, it can also help save one of your own."

White looked over at Brown.

"The pilot," he said to her.

White shook her head and leaned back against the edge of her desk.

"She didn't get past us."

"I don't understand," Dodge said.

He understood her. He just wanted to hear White say it out loud.

"We knew about the plan. My men on the ground had been tracking the girl the entire time. It wasn't until later that we discovered she was still alive when the container passed through here. We thought she was already dead."

"You agency people are cold. Maria Delgado didn't die until the storm killed her on Saint Thomas. Meaning, she was alive when she passed through here. That poor girl suffered from an assault, a broken leg, and died in a pool of her own feces after a thousand-pound container crushed her like a bug. You could've prevented it, and you chose not to."

"In hindsight, not my best moment," White said.

"No shit, lady," said Dodge.

White turned toward a file cabinet in the corner of the room and pulled out a manila envelope.

"How much do you know about Delgado, Agent Dodge?"

"I know enough to know he doesn't play games. Which means he'll come for me one day, too. No matter if I give him what he wants or not."

White nodded, and Brown agreed. Then she handed Dodge the envelope. It had the words *TOP SECRET* stamped on the front.

"I haven't been cleared for almost a decade," Dodge said. "Are you sure I should see what's in here?" He held the folder out like a toxic piece of trash.

And knowing too much about Delgado could be harmful. The man's life was an enigma because *he* wanted it that way, and he possessed the firepower and money to keep it all secret. Truth be told, Dodge wasn't sure if he wanted to have that much knowledge about one of the world's most dangerous men. But when in doubt, refer to the rules: *Know more about your opponent than they know about you.*

Dodge opened the envelope and scanned the documents. He looked at the photos of a young drug lord, maybe in his late teens or early twenties, flanked by numerous women in bikinis, in a place that looked like Miami Beach but was more likely Rio. But there were only two pictures of Delgado with a single woman. The date on the photos was decades ago, which Dodge could only assume had been taken by some clandestine CIA agent who had successfully infiltrated the compound twenty years ago.

The wheels began turning in the elite investigator's mind. All the information he had crammed into the deep recesses of his memory, things that seemed unimportant, came rushing forward. The pieces floated around in his brain like jigsaw puzzle pieces in a gravity-free environment, and he started to put them together as Ms. White told the story of a man's rise from nothing to the king of the drug world.

"As you can see by the pictures, he always thought of himself as a ladies' man. There were lavish parties with supermodels, cocaine of course, and rumors of affairs with some of Colombia's most famous women."

"I hear a *but* coming." Dodge kept his eyes on the photos.

White then told the story of a man who found his one true love. But this was no Romeo-and-Juliet tale. It played out more like that movie about a cop who falls for the rich murder suspect. Only, this rich murder suspect was the head of a major drug cartel.

The cop worked for the Colombia Special Police, and her name was Maria Fuentes. Maria had the looks of a supermodel, and a dancer's body, which other officers claimed helped boost her career in the police force, eventually landing her a spot on the Grupo de Trabajo Especial del Cartel, or the special cartel task force. But Maria Fuentes was a damn good cop. She had more drug collars than most of the men in the unit, and would have been a firearms instructor at the academy if women could do that sort of thing. Colombia was still a culture steeped in sexism and traditional gender roles, and there was no way a woman was going to teach a man to shoot. It seemed to young Fuentes that her career had hit its ceiling.

Then one day, her *capitán* came to her with an assignment. The work would be dangerous and include extended hours. He couldn't guarantee her any extra pay, but told her the target would be one of the most dangerous men in Colombia. Fuentes, being a good soldier, didn't hesitate and agreed to take on the assignment. Besides, bringing down a major cartel player would undoubtedly get her the respect from her colleagues that she so desired. People got to meet the president for such accomplishments, and she would be the first woman to reach those heights. So, Maria Fuentes went to work as an undercover agent for the Colombia Special Police, as a dancer in a strip club.

"It seems her body had something to do with her being assigned to the special task force, after all," Dodge said.

"It seems that way," White said, and continued telling the story.

But young Fuentes took the role seriously, and soon was the main event on stage, where troves of sweaty, drunk men tossed money on the stage for a closeup look at her topless body. It wasn't long before she caught the eye of her target, and just like a spider, she used a thin web to reel him in and wrap him up. Delgado instantly fell in love with the stunning young cop. Soon, the two were flying around Colombia in his personal plane, playing on the beaches of Tasajeras, and drinking wine at vineyards outside of Bogotá.

And it wasn't long before rumors swelled at Colombia Special Police headquarters. Stories of drug use and sex. Fuentes had told her commanders she was in control, and that the rumors were false. But that was a lie. She had used cocaine to keep her cover and was so high that when Delgado made a move, she let it happen. She only sank deeper into the lifestyle from that point on. She stopped checking in with her command staff, and would disappear for weeks at a time. The senior leaders at police headquarters had no choice but to call her in. And in she came, with her badge and gun in hand. She quit the force and moved in with Jesús Martinez Delgado and became pregnant within a month.

Dodge continued to look at the picture of Maria Fuentes with Delgado.

"This photo is too old to be of a fifteen-year-old's mom. There is no way this is our dead Maria's mother."

"That's right, Agent Dodge," said White. "Maria Fuentes was the mother of his firstborn son. The true heir to his empire. You see, he eventually found out about Maria's earlier betrayal, and murdered her right after the baby was born. Rumor has it, he buried her on his compound—a sign of his unending love for her. But I think he buried her there to remind him that those closest to him are his real weakness, and betrayal is always nearby."

"So, who knows about this son of his?" Dodge said. "Do we have a name?"

"We aren't sure anyone is left alive that might know the truth," Brown said. "Many of those around back then were killed in the drug wars over the past ten years. I'll tell you one thing, if people know, they will not talk about it. That's for sure."

"Not if they want to stay alive," White said.

"If Maria Fuentes had a son, where does Maria Delgado come in? Who is her mother?"

"That is a sad story as well," White said. "During a cocaine- and alcohol-fueled binge about sixteen years ago, Delgado slept with a prostitute."

Dodge said, "Who became pregnant with our young Maria."

"Exactly," White said. "Young Maria was not the product of love, but that of lust and sin. She was an embarrassment to him, both personally and socially. His indiscretion was the worst-kept secret in Bogotá. And to set things right, he killed the girl's mother and sent his daughter away with a family who lived in Buenaventura, a small fishing town on the west coast of Colombia."

"Doesn't exactly pay to be romantically involved with this guy," Dodge said. "So how did Maria, the young Maria, get dead on that dock in Charlotte Amalie? And I don't understand how the stories of the son and daughter got all mixed up?"

"That's for you to find out," White said. "You can keep the file. Brown will dispose of it once you finish with it."

"Roger that," Brown said.

"Now, if you'll excuse me, I need to attend to some things involving my sources."

The two men turned to leave but didn't make it to the door before Ms. White asked them to wait for a minute. She walked over to her desk and opened the top drawer. Pulled out a piece of paper, scribbled something on it and folded it in half before handing it to Dodge.

"Don't open it unless absolutely necessary."

"How will I know if it's necessary?"

"You'll know. Now get out of here before I shoot you both in the head and toss your bodies in the bay, just for annoying me."

The two men left and rode in silence the entire trip back to the airstrip. Once on the plane, Dodge collapsed into the captain's chair at the rear of the plane and stared out the window, into the coming darkness, trying to piece the recent revelations together with what he thought he knew. It was like someone tossing a new jigsaw puzzle on top of the one he was working on and telling him to make it all fit. He needed to find the edge pieces again and start building inward.

Two of the four corner pieces had changed. Before today, the corners were Maria, Delgado, Melendez, and Juan. Dodge now knew those corners to be Delgado, Maria, Delgado's newly discovered son, and the last corner piece was himself.

His mind began to wander back to *Kelly's Dream,* and he decided it was time to close his eyes. He dreamed again, but this time, not about Kelly or Anna or Nikki. This time, it was dark and cold and wet. He dreamed about young Maria in that container, alone, knowing she was going to die.

His eyes didn't open until the tires bounced as they touched the grass runway at the tiny airport outside of Bogotá.

CHAPTER 28

THE SILENCE CONTINUED for most of the drive to the embassy. Brown broke the silence as they turned into the main gate at the embassy.

"What are you planning on doing about all this?"

He flashed his ID to the Marine before crossing over the collapsed barrier and parking next to a door marked *employee entrance*.

Dodge replied, "Well, I was going to give up Melendez, tattooed guy, and maybe even you, before that plan got ruined with the information dump White handed me today. Now, I'm not sure what to do. Melendez is dead. I can't bluff my way around that for very long. Even if I could keep that secret, I don't think Delgado ever planned to give me the pilot, anyway. His plan from the get-go always centered on me being dead once I was of no use to him."

Brown said nothing.

"It would've been nice to have known all of this two days ago." Dodge said. "I have been chasing my goddamn tail since I got here. I should've shot the son of a bitch in the head, right there in his study. Painted the walls with his brains and ruined his precious book collection. Like that guy ever read anything that didn't begin with the name Delgado."

"You would've been dead inside a minute," Brown said. "His men would've put you down. And if you were lucky, you might've died before the dogs started on you."

"Maybe," Dodge said. "But he would be dead, and I would've

taken a few of his boys with me. That's a hell of a lot more than I have right now."

He kicked at a rock sitting by his feet, and missed, almost losing his balance, but caught himself as his momentum turned him in a complete circle.

"Why don't you have a smoke," Brown said. "I know I've seen the Marine over at the gate getting cigarettes from the embassy commissary."

"He gets them from a girl that works there," Dodge said.

"For free? I've seen the women that work in that place. Not sure I would diddle any of them for a carton of smokes, let alone a few packs a week."

"Marine standards are a little lower than most people's," Dodge said. "But all the services do the same thing. They have a girlfriend inside the embassy for things they can't get outside US property, like alcohol in Muslim countries. And they have a girl on the outside, a local, to get them free things they can't get on post, like bootleg DVDs and weed. It's part of an unofficial training manual passed by word of mouth amongst soldiers. Always have someone on the inside for..."

"You OK?" Brown said. Always have someone on the inside for what?"

Dodge said nothing. He walked over to the Marine guard, bummed a cigarette, and made a circle gesture to let Brown know he needed to take another walk. *Move and think.*

Following rules was important. He exited the main gate, looked right, but decided to walk left, against his nature. It was a trait of right-handed people. They see their left side as a weakness and will almost always favor anything on the right side when faced with a choice. Left was different. As long as the puzzle pieces refused to fit together, mixing things up might not be a bad idea, like how a chess player will turn the playing board one hundred eighty degrees to get his opponent's view of the board.

Turning left ended up saving his life.

Dodge dropped his cigarette to the ground. Carrying the

pistol and extra magazine prevented him from placing the butt in his pants pocket. He didn't want to get ash and tobacco into the firing mechanisms or inside the magazine and risk causing a jam if he needed to use the weapon. Not having flipped a butt on the ground in over a decade, he watched the trash roll in the breeze before resting in a gutter about twenty feet in front of him, next to a rusted-out Japanese four-door sedan. He initially paid little attention to the car, as it resembled many of the old beat-up vehicles on Bogotá's roads. It was dusk, but the lights attached to the embassy wall bathed the street in light, and Dodge could see the driver and passenger sitting in the vehicle. The passenger was in the back seat, behind the driver. Not uncommon if the car was a taxi, but this rusted-out shell of a car didn't pass the smell test for a commercial vehicle. Not even the lowliest city residents would pay hard-earned money to ride in that beat-up piece of shit. No. The two men were waiting for someone to come from around the corner in front of them.

The goosebumps rose to the surface of his arms as he drew closer to the car with the two men inside. At fifteen feet, he could make out the numbers on the rear license plate. He could see the driver's face at ten feet, in the reflection on the driver's door mirror. Both men were staring straight ahead. Neither seemed concerned about what might approach from behind.

Amateurs.

At five feet, the woo-woo hairs on his neck stood straight up. He could feel the wind blowing across each one—a heightened sensitivity from increased blood flow to the head and extremities, triggered by the fight-or-flight instinct.

At two feet, he saw the gun.

Dodge shoved his hand into his right front pocket, wrapped his fingers around the rugged plastic grip of the Glock, with his trigger finger resting on the frame. He had the pistol out in less than two seconds. Front sight alignment in less than three.

"Front sight in a fight," he said to no one.

Dodge would take out the passenger first. He was the most significant threat since he had the gun.

Just as Dodge's finger slid toward the trigger, the driver glanced in the rearview mirror and saw a man with a gun pointed right at his partner's head. Dodge guessed the driver would slam the shifter in drive and floor the accelerator, which would throw road debris at their attacker and cause a miss.

But he didn't put the car in drive. Instead, he put it in reverse and punched the accelerator. The car hesitated for a fraction of a second before it lurched toward Dodge, which gave him enough time to react. He dove to his right, and the sleep-deprived agent was slow. The rear fender caught Dodge's left foot and spun him around, forcing him to land hard on his side, away from his target. He swung his arm over his body to help him flip and reorientate to the threat. As Dodge rolled his gun, he brought the Glock up to eye level and placed the driver's head in line with the glowing green dot on the front sight post and squeezed the trigger.

The nine-millimeter round shattered the passenger side glass just above the doorframe. His aim was low. The round penetrated the driver's neck and exited the other side before ricocheting off the white cement wall that surrounded the embassy. Blood pumped out of the hole in his neck as he used his hands to stop the bleeding. An exercise in futility.

The alarm from the embassy sounded, and then the lights went out. A solitary streetlamp illuminated the rusted-out car, which became hung up after its rear tire popped, having slammed into the curb. The passenger appeared to be in shock. He just stared at his partner as the life drained out of him.

Dodge had seen that same look on the face of every man right before he killed them. It didn't matter if it was in war or on the streets. Everyone was surprised when death came for them.

Dodge swung his weapon and placed the man's head behind the green dot. Then he raised it a fraction of an inch and squeezed the trigger. There would be no slow bleed-out this time. His round found its target. Because Dodge was on the ground, and the man was sitting two feet above him, the bullet entered just above his ear and exited the other side at an upward angle. The compression popped the top of his head like a soda bottle shaken too much before opening.

The adrenaline-filled agent lay back and reached for his ankle. It throbbed as his heart beat, and he could feel blood filling the space between his foot and his shoe, which meant his sock was soaked, which meant he was bleeding a lot. His eyes became heavy. He tried to fight the coming darkness, but the wound in his leg was preventing blood from getting back to his brain, causing his system to shut down the things it deemed as non-essential. Sight and hearing were the first to go. Followed by manual dexterity, which caused his grip to loosen on the weapon, and it dropped to the ground just as everything went quiet. before succumbing to the darkness, he wondered if this was how it would end for him.

———

The light flickered—bright, then dim. Bright, dim. He didn't want to open his eyes, half-afraid of what he might see on the other side. Dodge was not a religious man, but kept open the possibility that there may be something on the other side of death. Not a bearded man in a white robe, or a minotaur with horns and a pitchfork. But some kind of different consciousness. Or an alternate universe, like in the famous comic book movies. Truth was, he didn't know. But as his hearing crept back to full strength, he knew he would not find out today.

His eyes opened and shut just as quick as the bright light passed over. The muscles in his face weren't responding to commands from his brain to open his eyes. It made him think about the Academy, and how pepper spray causes the same reaction. A sprayed person must use their fingers to pry their eyelids open to let air in, as air was the only thing that would kill the effects of capsaicin, the ingredient in pepper spray that irritated the eyes.

He needed to get upright. But stinging pain shot up his leg and through his spine when he tried to sit up, eyes still closed.

"Easy there, Dodge," a voice said. "You lost a decent amount of blood, but we got you all stitched up, and have some juice going into you."

Concentrating hard, and by sheer will, the injured parole agent forced his eyes open. He rubbed them with the palms of his hands and looked up at the four faces staring back at him: Brown, the Marine guard, another employee he had never seen before, and standing behind the other tree was a man in what Dodge thought was a thousand-dollar suit. The man said nothing while Brown and the Marine pushed on Dodge's shoulders, trying to force him to lay back on the floor.

Dodge pushed back with every ounce of energy he had, which was the equivalent of a five-year-old child. The third man, the employee he didn't know, was helping Brown by placing most of his weight on Dodge's shoulder, while Brown held his other one. The Marine was holding a tube and wrapping medical tape around Dodge's arm, preventing his elbow from bending. After the Marine finished his work, the other two men released their grip on Dodge's shoulders and backed away.

"There," the Marine said. "If you want to sit up, now you can without ripping the IV out of your arm. You are one stubborn son of a bitch, man."

Exhausted from his struggle, which was made worse by the blood loss and whatever pain meds they had pumped into his arm, Dodge forgot the struggle to sit up, and instead laid back. He concentrated on his breathing, stared at the ceiling, coming to terms with the extension of his life.

His next attempt to pull himself into a sitting position failed, and again he fell back to the floor. His gaze met Brown's, who had moved in and tried to catch him before his head cracked against the marble tile.

"Thanks."

Brown cradled Dodge's head in his arms, with his hands positioned down each side of Dodge's spine.

"You want some help to get upright?"

"Yeah, but take it slow. I'm still a little woozy."

"You just lean back into me and relax your waist. I'll do the heavy lifting." Brown used his legs to push, and then rose behind as he hunched forward, changing his center of gravity. "Now, place your hands on the ground, palms down, behind you. Like a kickstand on a bicycle."

Dodge did as he was told, and after a few minutes, could hold himself upright with little trouble. He shook off the effects of his blackout and noticed the IV had red liquid flowing from a bag the Marine was holding high, letting gravity do the work.

"How many bags so far?" Dodge said.

"This is the second," the Marine replied. "You lost a liter on the street before we could get to you. The second liter came out when we removed the rusty piece of steel from your leg. You are damn lucky, buddy. That hunk of Japanese steel nicked an artery. Five more minutes, and we'd have been forced to stick coins over your eyes to pay the boatman."

A scan of the room told Dodge he was not in a hospital or a medical office. There were circular tables with chairs stacked on top. Four chairs to a table, repeated six times, he counted. Vending machines for snacks and soda stood at the far end, next to a set of double doors. It was a break room or cafeteria, he guessed.

He asked the three men to help him to his feet. Two of the men each hooked an arm under each of Dodge's armpits, and the third lifted him by the waist. Once on his feet, he could feel his energy coming back. His legs tingled as the blood rushed back to his feet. He could stand under his own power.

"Can you get this thing out of my arm?"

The Marine looked at Brown and the other man, who nodded his approval, before pulling the tape loose and freeing the IV from its vein. A drop of blood trickled down Dodge's arm and dripped on the floor before he could apply a Band-Aid over the small hole.

Dodge turned to Brown. "What the hell happened out there?"

"You don't remember?"

Dodge ran his hands through his hair. He hadn't had a

haircut in two months, and his fingers slowed as they fought against tangles and knots that had formed from lack of proper combing. He closed his eyes and tried to picture the events from earlier in the evening.

"There was a car outside the south wall, facing west. Its engine was running." He paused and opened his eyes. "There were two men inside. A driver, and a passenger in the back seat."

The man in the suit said, "Any reason you put two rounds into the security wall of my embassy? You could've hit someone inside."

It was the US Ambassador. Dodge should've known. A shooting outside the US Embassy was reason to get the head man back to the office.

"Dodge, this is Ambassador Contreras." Brown pointed at the man in the suit.

Dodge raised his hand in acknowledgment.

"Does somebody want to tell me what the hell is going on here?" Contreras said. "I got two dead locals parked outside my embassy, in a car that looks like someone stuck a pig and locked it inside while it bled to death."

A little dizzy, and his head pounding, Dodge ran through the entire story, from young Maria in that container in St. Thomas, to his run-in with Delgado, and the meeting with Ms. White in Cartagena. Brown interjected to add details Dodge either didn't know, or had planned on leaving out, resulting in glares in Brown's direction.

The ambassador instructed the Marine to resume his duties at the main gate, and told the employee Dodge had never seen before today to go home. Both men complied immediately.

Ambassador Contreras pulled a chair off a nearby table, spun it around backward, and sat with his arms crossed over the top of the chair back. He locked eyes with Dodge.

"So, what you are telling me, is you are running an off-the-books operation against one of the world's most powerful drug lords. They have killed an FBI agent. You were captured and forced to make a deal to secure your release, just so you can save a pilot that shouldn't have been involved in the first place." His gaze turned to Brown, who averted the laser stare by looking down at the ground. "And to make things worse, the man you made a deal with tried to assassinate you right outside my embassy. Does that sound about right?"

Dodge agreed with the ambassador, but the recent events had left a bad taste in his mouth and ornery from the pain in his leg. A smartass answer was all he could muster.

"You left out the part about the dead girl, sir."

The ambassador's head snapped back, his eyes shooting darts at their target.

"I think we all know this stopped being about a dead girl a long time ago. Don't you, Agent Dodge?"

The accusation enraged Dodge. He could feel his face and neck flush as the blood rushed to his head. How dare anyone accuse him of forgetting about a victim? He had fought for people like Maria Delgado his entire life. Who was this guy to question his ethics and commitment to finding the truth?

He opened his mouth, ready to unleash a sharp tongue to defend himself, but he was cut off.

"Now calm down," Contreras said. "I didn't say I wasn't on board. But I believe, in moving forward, we all need to be on the same page and honest about our motivations. We need to put some lipstick on this pig if this becomes public, like if an American law enforcement officer got himself killed outside the US Embassy. Does that make sense?"

The other two men agreed.

"Good. First, Agent Dodge—"

"Just call me Dodge."

"Okay, Dodge. I don't know if you have noticed, but you are being used. Being used by Brown here, Delgado, the FBI, and Miss White, who I feel I need to warn you, is no one to be trifled with. She might be the one person responsible for more deaths in Colombia than Delgado. You know what she is, right?"

Dodge said, "I made an educated guess."

"Then you know she has an agenda, same as Brown." The

ambassador pointed at Brown.

"As do you, I assume," Dodge said.

Ambassador Contreras laughed. It was the first time he had cracked a smile.

"You learn fast," he said. "Yes, even I have an agenda. But I am also the only one with the top cover of the White House. If this whole thing explodes into an international incident, I'll have no choice but to clean it up. Do you understand what I'm saying?"

Both men nodded and said they understood.

Brown pulled a chair off the table and sat. Dodge, his leg still hurting and his shoulder sore from the hard landing in the road, struggled to get his chair off of the table. Brown stood and helped move it to the floor. Dodge nodded and sat, letting out a heavy breath as he sank into the seat.

Brown said, "I have a few ideas about how we can—"

"I think we should let Agent Dodge tell us what he thinks we should do," said the ambassador. "He is the puppet in this little operation. Not to mention, he is the only one Delgado has tried to exterminate. I think he's earned it, don't you? I mean, he has made more inroads in under a week than you people have in the last five years."

Dodge thought the ambassador's comment directed at Brown was condescending, meant to injure his pride. And it worked. Brown tensed up, but he guessed Brown knew better than to respond.

As a soldier, Dodge had spent some time posted at an embassy in the Middle East when he was in the Air Force. He understood how embassy postings worked. Brown was still a guest. Spook or no spook, the ambassador had the final say in what agencies and which employees were stationed in his compound. If Brown had been overseas before, he would've been aware of the ambassador's authority in matters concerning embassy personnel.

"Agent Dodge, what have you got in mind?" the ambassador said.

Dodge thought for a minute, before sliding the chair out from under him.

"I need a good night's sleep to let the drugs wear off and rest my leg for a bit. Why don't we meet back here tomorrow, after breakfast?"

Even though the next day was a Saturday, embassies never closed.

Contreras agreed, and said Dodge should stay at the ambassador's residence for the night.

"They already took a shot at you. No reason to give them another chance. Delgado isn't dumb enough to go after you at the residence. This isn't Benghazi."

The three men left the embassy through the front gate—Brown in his government-issued diplomat's car. Dodge and the ambassador rode in a black, armored SUV with diplomatic security in the front seats, and a chaser car behind.

They arrived at the mansion ten minutes later. The ambassador said the Colombian government had seized it from a drug lord and gifted it to the United States as a thank you for their continued cooperation in assisting Colombia in the war on drugs. It was a payoff for the use of aircraft and military advisors in carrying out the drug raids. Whatever means the US had used to gain the property, it was well-fortified. A six-foot-tall stone wall surrounded the entire property, topped with razor wire and dual cameras facing inside and outside, every twenty feet, providing a full video feed of the whole property and the surrounding neighborhood.

Once inside the residence, the ambassador showed his guest to the spare quarters. He poured a drink from a bottle sitting on the bar, and offered one to Dodge, who declined.

"Probably shouldn't with the drugs in my system."

"Suit yourself." The ambassador swallowed his drink in one gulp, then turned back to Dodge. "You should be careful. It's not just Delgado that should concern you. There are others in Colombia with a vested interest in the drug trade and the windfall of cash it produces."

Contreras placed his glass on the counter and closed the door behind him as he left.

Dodge thought about both what the ambassador had said earlier, about him being a puppet, and just now, about who he could trust. His rule was, *When in doubt, trust no one.* It was time to cut the strings and move on his own. Starting with Delgado. The drug lord had reneged on his deal and made a move against Dodge's life, but failed, which switched the axis of power. Delgado would learn of the failed attempt and assume his prey would go into hiding. If the roles were reversed, Dodge would believe the same thing. It was time to go on the offensive. Time to use the one piece of information that was important to Delgado, to turn the tables against him.

Dodge undressed and took a long, hot shower. Then he shaved and found a pair of scissors and trimmed his hair short. He washed his clothes in the sink and hung them over the shower door to dry.

Feeling in charge of one's own destiny was relaxing. He laid on the bed and kicked the covers off. Closed his eyes and formulated the beginnings of a plan before drifting off to sleep.

He didn't dream tonight.

CHAPTER 29

THE SMELL OF BACON WAFTED through the air and tripped a switch in Dodge's brain. His eyes opened before he was completely awakened, and his stomach growled at the prospect of food. It had been over sixteen hours since he had last eaten a meal, which made him a little woozy when he stood up from his bed.

First things first: time to try out the ankle. He sat back on the bed and pulled his left foot up to rest it on his thigh. The wrap was clean. No extra bleeding had occurred during his sleep. He caressed the gauze the Marine had placed over the stitches, but felt no excessive pain. The thought of tearing off the bandage crossed his mind. However, he decided against it. The wound wasn't bleeding, and it didn't cause him much discomfort. If it isn't broke, don't fix it.

After retrieving his clothes hanging from the shower curtain rod in the bathroom, Dodge dressed, brushed his teeth, and tried to find where the smell of cooking bacon was coming from. He wandered the halls for five minutes, stopping to look in every room he passed, before finding the kitchen in the main house. The place was even more prominent in the daylight. The hungry guest stood in the kitchen's doorway, watching a staff of three cook eggs and bacon, butter toast, and pour a cup of coffee. One servant noticed him standing there and ushered him to the dining room, where a place was set for him. The woman poured a cup of coffee, looked at the condition of his hair and the stained shirt he wore, then added a shot of espresso to his cup.

Dodge tried to thank her, but she hustled out of the room and back to the kitchen, passing another servant carrying a plate of food. The man set the plate on the table in front of the house guest. He then pulled an envelope from a pocket and handed it over before scurrying back through the entryway to the kitchen.

Dodge took a large forkful of scrambled eggs and shoved them into his mouth. They were the best eggs he had ever eaten. He would make sure to tell the cook before he left for the embassy.

The envelope contained a piece of paper with one sentence written by Ambassador Contreras: *Enjoy your breakfast—AC.*

He did just that. Once finished, Dodge carried his plate into the kitchen to compliment the chef, but the butler said she had gone to the store to purchase supplies for that night's dinner. He asked the butler to let her know how much he enjoyed the meal, but that he would not be returning.

The butler made a call over the intercom, ordering the chauffeur to bring a car around. He was to take Agent Dodge to the embassy. No stops. Dodge nodded and looked around the room. The butler pointed at a door on the far side of the kitchen. Dodge thanked the man before leaving, and followed a hallway to the front door, where the driver was waiting outside with the rear passenger door open. Once at the embassy, he signed in, then took the elevator to the third floor, which was where the receptionist said Ambassador Contreras was waiting for him.

The ambassador was sitting at a desk in front of a stained-glass window. On the window was a flag of the United States and the Colombian flag, their flagpoles crossed to form an X, with the words *United 'til Death* printed at the bottom.

Contreras didn't see Dodge approach his office, so the agent knocked on the doorframe.

"Good morning, Agent Dodge. I hope you enjoyed breakfast."

"I've got to find out how she makes eggs so fluffy," Dodge said.

"She uses fresh goat cream instead of milk."

"Hmm, goat cream. Not sure 1 can buy that at the corner store back home."

"Not likely. The chef will be the one thing 1 miss about this place once 1 am gone."

A presidential election was scheduled in eighteen months, and the new leader would get to choose his ambassadors.

"Maybe the new guy will let you stay on," Dodge said.

"Honestly, I'm not sure 1 want to. 1 work fourteen hours a day, seven days a week. You think you're the first person to come down here on a revenge mission? Believe me, you aren't. You're just the first one to get into a shootout at the embassy."

"Yeah, about that," Dodge said. "How's that going—with the locals and all?"

"It'll stay quiet enough. The cops don't know about you, and 1 don't have to tell them anything. So, you're safe for now. Just a couple dead drug runners. They see it every day here." Contreras closed his computer. "Did you come up with a plan on how to handle this mess?"

Dodge bit hard on his bottom lip. "The beginnings of one. Though, 1 don't know how feasible it is. 1 still have to work out the details."

"Which details are you still working out?"

"The ones that won't get me killed."

Brown had entered the room, unbeknownst to Dodge.

"That sounds promising," he said.

"Well, 1 hope you can figure it out within the embassy walls," Contreras said. "Because you're not going for another walk. Why don't you share with us what you *have* figured out."

Dodge stood and paced the length of the room, a slight limp still noticeable. But with so many more pressing matters, like the pilot and the attempt on his life, he pushed the pain aside, burying it deep in his animal brain.

He told the men about the kid at the compound, and the

resemblance to Delgado. Still, when Delgado said the boy was his cousin, he didn't think about it again until the conversation with White.

"So, some kid looked like him," Brown said. "That's far from proof it was his son. I mean, nobody claims to have seen the kid. Not a relative, no members of the cartel. Hell, not even Melendez."

"No one alive," Contreras said.

"That may be true," Dodge said. "But I know one thing: six men and that kid were with me when we arrived at the compound. The kid is the only one still alive. I don't like coincidences. And if it is one, it's the white whale of coincidences."

Brown looked at Ambassador Contreras and shrugged.

"If the kid is his," said Brown, "that is a weakness we may be able to exploit."

"Maybe," the ambassador said. "But how do we use this information against him?"

Dodge stopped pacing. He placed his hands on the back of his chair and shook his head.

"It was all there right in front of me the whole time. When I was a *guest* at his compound, he fed me some cockamamie story about how the boy belonged to a cousin in the city. Same old story—a drug addict gets pregnant and has a child. The girl can't afford to feed a child and her drug habit, so she turns to the street for money. In the world of prostitution and drugs, you can meet some unsavory characters, including those in the business of selling children."

"We know this already, Dodge. It's in this file here." Brown waived it in the air. "Except, the son the hooker had was a daughter, and Delgado was the father."

"That's right," Dodge said. "But I got to thinking. White said that Delgado was so embarrassed by the result of the one-night stand, he executed her, then dismembered the body and sent the child off to live with a family in a remote fishing village on the coast."

Brown had a look of confusion on his face, but Contreras shook his finger at Dodge.

"Why not kill the child here?" the ambassador said. "It's not like this guy has any form of a moral compass."

"Exactly." Dodge's voice rose an octave in excitement. "He didn't kill her because he needed the kid."

Brown was scratching his head, not grasping any of the concepts. Dodge slid his chair over in front of him and sat.

"When we were in Cartagena, and Miss White gave me that file you have in your hand, I started working on a puzzle in my head, with the information I knew about Delgado, Maria, Melendez, and what the tattooed guy told us. Then I looked in that file on the plane, and it was like White had just pushed my half-assembled puzzle to the floor and dumped a new puzzle on top of the pile. But it wasn't a new puzzle at all. It was the same puzzle. I had just been working with half the pieces."

Brown still looked confused.

Dodge said, "Don't you see it?"

"See what!" Brown yelled.

"Why would he keep the girl alive if she was such an embarrassment to him?" Dodge said.

Brown shrugged.

"Because he needed her!" Ambassador Contreras shouted.

"Yes. He needed her alive."

"But why?" Brown said.

Dodge looked at Contreras, who then looked at Brown.

"Because the mother is still alive," Dodge said.

In the excitement of the moment, he shook his head too hard and became dizzy. He had to catch his breath before speaking again.

"She is alive. Not only is she alive, but she is the one feeding information to his enemies. Think about it. Who else would have all that knowledge about him, his son, and Maria Fuentes? He needed the girl to bring her mother out of hiding. First, he kept Maria around, but the mother never came for her. So, he sent her away. But to a place he could have ears to the ground if anyone came looking for her. No one ever did, though. But secrets can only be kept for so long. Then rumblings formed in the organization about his leadership and weakness in letting the prostitute live, and people began conspiring to carry out a coup. Who would take over? When he was ready, Delgado wanted it to be his son. But people like Melendez saw the girl as a weakness, a vulnerability. He hadn't killed her, so she must be important to him. Maybe they install her as the heir apparent to the empire. A shadow figure they can easily manipulate and toss away when no longer useful. A good way to screw over Delgado and his son."

"But this is all just speculation," Brown said. "Why wouldn't Miss White just tell us all this?"

"Because the girl's mother is her source," Contreras said.

Dodge snatched Brown's folder and dumped it in the garbage.

"Misinformation to lead me away from her source. She is protecting her informant. I called Agent Williams this morning, and he is going to check with an old academy buddy who now works counterterrorism at the Agency. I'll bet you my boat, he confirms my theory."

"When is he supposed to call you back?" Contreras said.

"Tonight."

The ambassador looked at his watch. "It's lunchtime, boys. Why don't we get some food and go home? If Agent Williams calls Dodge, he can let us know, and we can meet back here tonight. Dodge, you want to come back to the residence and wait?"

There was jealousy in Brown's face, and part of Dodge wanted to say yes just to rub it in, but he said he would be fine at the embassy, if it was all right with Contreras, who agreed but warned him not to wander too far from the gate. As long as the Marines could maintain a visual on him, his safety was assured.

Brown and the ambassador left, and Dodge ventured down to the cafeteria. There was still a small bloodstain on the floor where he had lain last night. He bought aspirin for the pain in his leg, along with a sandwich, chips, and coffee for lunch. Then he handed the register girl some cash, but she refused and said the ambassador gave orders not to accept money from guests of the embassy. With his headache getting worse, he convinced the girl to take money for the aspirin because pain pills were not a food item, and he didn't want to get her in trouble.

Dodge grabbed his tray and turned to walk away. He glanced back at the girl and noticed she wasn't attractive—a little heavy in the midsection, with large breasts that fit her body type. Her teeth were crooked, and she smelled like she had bathed in a perfume bottle.

He stepped back to the counter and asked her name.

She said, "Connie," with a smile.

"Connie, do you know the Marine standing post at the front gate?"

She blushed. "Yeah, he's kind of my boyfriend."

"Kind of?" Dodge said.

"Well, no one is supposed to know. He could get in trouble for seeing me. It's against Marine rules or something. He said, when he leaves this posting, he'll take me with him."

"Where will you go?"

She thought for a second, trying to find a memory stuck in the recesses of her brain.

Finally, she said, "I don't know. He never said where he lived."

A sense of sadness came over Dodge. She wasn't pretty, but he hated the way soldiers treated girls on post, using them and then running off as soon as their posting was over, leaving emotional wrecks for someone else to deal with.

He decided to help her.

"Do me a favor. When your boyfriend comes in and asks for something—say, cigarettes for free—tell him you can't do that anymore. Tell him your boss found out someone is stealing, and they will fire the responsible party."

Connie gave the worst look of surprise he had ever seen.

"I would never steal, sir."

The poor girl couldn't even lie well.

"I know that, Connie. But if he asks, just tell him what I said. Can you do that?"

She pawed at the register, picking up items for sale and placing them back on the counter. After a few uncomfortable moments, she agreed.

His work here done, Dodge smiled and walked away.

———

Delgado sat in his study, a cigar burning in the ashtray as he spoke on his cell phone.

"What news do you have for me?"

The person on the other end of the call hesitated, not wanting to be the bearer of bad news. People that relayed news of failure to El Jefe, many times took their last breath not long after. The man felt a little relief because he would be providing the information over the phone and not face-to-face.

"The American is still alive," he replied.

"And the men?"

"They are dead. The American shot them both. The local police have the car and the bodies."

"Are the men and the car clean? I don't need this coming back to me."

"They are clean. I saw to it personally, sir."

Delgado took a long pull off his cigar and rolled it between his fingers as he exhaled a thick pillow of smoke.

"You have failed me once. If you disappoint me again, you are aware of the consequences."

The man's voice cracked with fear. "I won't fail you again."

Delgado ended the call and took another long drag of the cigar before snuffing it out in the ashtray. He thought about the decision he had made to eliminate Agent Dodge. He would have kept his word under normal circumstances, but the last two weeks have been anything but ordinary. He was under attack from inside his organization, and outside forces were closing in on him. He needed to send a powerful message that he was not weak or vulnerable. And killing a US citizen, a law enforcement figure, would have sent that message. Now, he wondered how his adversary would react. Would he come for him?

Delgado pondered the possibilities, running ideas through his mind. Everything he knew about Paul Dodge said the man would come for him. He was not the sort of man to just let things go, as far as he could tell. If he was coming, Delgado figured the best place to be was on the compound. He had enough food and water and weapons to hold off an army for days. He would hunker down in his mansion and wait for the coming fight. His eyes and ears on the streets would tell him if she returned.

—⁓—

Agent Williams finished a call with a friend who worked for the Agency. The friend told him what Dodge had expected. Maria Delgado's mother was, in fact, not dead. He would not divulge where the woman was, other than to say she had been in witness protection for the better part of the last decade. The friend said he could neither confirm or deny any HUMINT gathered by the Agency, concerning Delgado and his criminal empire. His standard answer affirmed Agent Williams's belief that Maria's mother was the source for most of the information coming in about Delgado.

Agent Williams flipped through the Rolodex on his desk, where he kept the names and phone numbers of contacts for which he didn't want an electronic record. When he got to the S's, he pulled out the first card, punched the number into his personal cell phone, and waited. The phone rang four times before a woman on the other end answered.

"This is Smythe."

"This is Williams."

"Is this line secure?" the woman said.

"It is my personal cell, so no one should be listening in."

The woman was silent for a moment.

"What can I do for you, Williams?"

"I need to know the location of a protectee."

"We go to great lengths to hide people in plain sight, and I am not inclined to place any of my charges in jeopardy without first knowing why."

Agent Williams went through the story for the second time that day. He told the woman about Agent McCaffrey's murder. The plan he and Dodge hatched to get the drug lord, and the additional information revealed to him concerning the dead girl's mother and Delgado's son. When he finished, the line was silent.

"I'm sorry, but I can't allow you to use this woman as bait in your trap. She is too valuable of an asset to us. The intel she has provided on cartels all over South America has been invaluable."

The denial of assistance put Agent Williams off. But he had groomed and hidden confidential informants during his career, so he understood the reluctance to help him.

The woman he spoke to was with the US Marshals Service. She oversaw the safety and security of witnesses in counter-drug operations in South America. So, Maria's mother was somewhere in South America.

He called Dodge back and left a message. He told his man in Columbia about the US Marshal's unwillingness to help, and his idea that the elder Maria was somewhere in South America, likely in Colombia or a bordering country where she could be easily accessed if needed.

The senior FBI agent hoped the new information would help get the man responsible for Agent McCaffrey's murder. He leaned back in his chair and smiled for the first time in days.

CHAPTER 30

BY THE TIME BROWN AND AMBASSADOR CONTRERAS returned to the embassy, Dodge had put the finishing touches on his plan. He told the men his idea, down to the most minor details, including a list of the supplies he would need.

Brown voiced his reservations about the part of the plan that involved using Ms. White. Dodge knew she frightened Brown, but the veteran parole agent wasn't scared of her. He carried healthy respect for her abilities and the callousness at how she motivated others to do her bidding. She was ruthless, and he knew if White found out she was being used, there would be hell to pay.

Ambassador Contreras appeared to be more concerned with any part of the plan that could come back and embarrass him or the president. That was his job, and Dodge had grown to respect him and his opinions. The plan wasn't perfect, but it gave the best chance of providing justice for Agent McCaffery and getting the pilot back.

Brown said, "I think using White for anything is a bad idea. Dodge, you met her. She is crazy. If she faked the file, she gave you just to mislead us, then she might do anything to keep her source a secret, including burying us in a shallow grave. I hear it wouldn't be the first time."

Dodge replied, "But protecting her source means she'll have to contact her source. As you just said, White is highly trained. So, she won't make contact over the phone if she believes they have compromised her source. You will follow her wherever she goes, and call me when the two are face-to-face. All I need is a picture of the meet. That's it. And then you come right back here to the embassy."

Brown nodded.

"What do you need from me?" the ambassador said.

"Cover, and as much time as you can buy me. I need you to keep the locals off my back. Oh, and I need another car."

Brown shook his head and laughed. "The last car I gave him is probably being used for target practice on Delgado's compound as we speak. So, I wouldn't give him anything traceable, or that you ever want to see again."

"Anything I can give you from here will have diplomatic plates, so that's not an option."

Dodge thought for a moment. "How about petty cash? I met guy a who can get a car that won't be traceable."

"Do I even want to know how you know a guy that deals in stolen vehicles?" the ambassador said.

"Probably not. But remind me to tell you if this works and I don't end up as dinner for Delgado's dogs."

The ambassador sat silent for a moment. "I can take the money out of my personal account so it can't be traced by the government accountants. Besides, a couple thousand won't raise any red flags. You will have it by this evening."

The three men went in separate directions as they left the building. Brown traveled to the airstrip outside of town. He needed to be on the ground in Cartagena, with eyes on Ms. White, before the plan could go into motion. Brown tracking White to Maria Delgado's birth mother was key to their plan. He was to call Dodge the moment he spotted White at the docks.

Ambassador Contreras headed for his residence and the safe hidden in the floor of the master bedroom closet. The remainder of the ambassador's duties were to do nothing out of the ordinary and bring no unwanted attention to himself. All three of them assumed Delgado would have men watching the embassy.

Dodge and Brown wanted to create the illusion of the drug

lord's prey being holed-up for his own protection until he could leave the country. So, Dodge would smoke a cigarette with the Marine guard to help move the façade forward, making himself visible to anyone recording his movements.

Once the ambassador returned to the embassy with the money for a car, the two men got into the second of three SUVs waiting to drive them back to the residence. On the way out, the lead vehicle hit a pedestrian crossing the street, just as the car carrying the two men pulled out of the main gate. Dodge had paid two hundred dollars to a Hispanic-looking Marine to play the part of an accident victim, allowing him to bail from the SUV and sneak back into the embassy compound.

After twenty minutes, and the local police's involvement, the ambassador's SUV left. The embassy's closed-circuit security cameras recorded the entire scene.

The first part of the plan went off without a hitch. Brown called, saying he had eyes on Ms. White. The accident in front of the embassy worked perfectly. Dodge was sure his escape went unnoticed, because a small red car with a *Taxi* sign on the top pulled out into the street directly behind the ambassador. *Pretty clever.* Using a fake taxi would allow the men to hide in plain sight. But there were two men sitting in the front seat as the car passed the front gate, and the taxi's vacancy light was off.

He should've been alone in the vehicle. *Amateurs.*

A five-minute wait after seeing the men in the taxi pass the main gate elapsed before Dodge left the embassy. Wearing a gray hooded sweatshirt and a black baseball cap, he walked to a small coffee shop down the street that the Marine had told him about. His in-town girlfriend worked at this shop.

Dodge ordered a café leche and pulled his phone from his pocket, along with the piece of paper Ms. White had told him not to look at. He dialed the number. The phone rang and rang and rang. The thought of hanging up entered his mind, and calling Brown to see if he still had eyes on White. But on the tenth ring, the phone clicked on.

"Who is this?"

Silence. He wanted her to keep her on edge. The more irritated she became, the more likely she would make a mistake.

"I said, who the fuck is this?"

It worked.

"It's Agent Dodge."

"Dodge? How did you get this number?"

"You gave it to me the other day, right before Brown and I left Cartagena."

"Oh…what do you want? I am swamped and don't have time for your or Brown's bullshit."

Another round of the silent treatment might cause White to hang upon him and not answer when he called back.

"You told me to call if I had some news. So, I'm calling."

"Hurry up, then."

"I found Maria Delgado's birth mom." Dodge paused for a response.

"Maria Delgado? The dead girl?"

"Maria Delgado, the girl who died in that crate shipped from your port in Cartagena. When Brown and I were with you the other day, you told me a story about Maria Delgado's mother. You said Jesús Delgado killed her after Maria was born."

"That's what I said. So, what of it?"

"Well, I found her."

"What do you mean, you found her? Like, her grave or DNA?"

"No. I mean, I found *her*. She is alive. I plan on going to see her as soon as I can pin down her address."

"So, you don't know where she is?" White said.

"Not at this moment. But I'll know in a day or two. My source tells me she's in Colombia or near the border regions in Brazil. I have a guy on the ground tracing her steps, and it shouldn't take him long to find her address. We already have a phone number associated with her, but I didn't want to send her deeper underground by calling. I figured we could tap the line and trace any calls she makes or receives to help pinpoint her location."

"Why are you telling me this information?" White said. "Why call me at all? I could not care less about some prostitute who may or may not be dead."

"I remembered; in that file you gave me. There was very little information on Maria's mother. In fact, all it really said was a prostitute had a baby, and the father—Jesús Delgado, in this case—killed her out of embarrassment. I thought you might want to update your file."

"I appreciate the information, Agent Dodge. I'll pass along what you told me, to my superiors. If they find your information credible, we will update the file and databases to reflect the intelligence. Now, if you don't mind, I have a briefing to give on another subject."

Ms. White hung up. Dodge immediately called Brown.

"She took the bait. Be ready to get the picture and get back here."

"I'm on it."

Dodge ordered a refill of his coffee. Then he stepped out onto the sidewalk and hailed a taxi. After checking the driver to make sure it wasn't the man that had been watching the embassy, he got in the back and gave the driver an address.

Fifteen minutes later and twenty bucks lighter, Dodge was standing in front of Pedro's garage. He banged on the door and stepped back for the camera. Just as the time before, the garage door rolled up, and a boy answered. Unlike the last time, the boy invited him in without hesitation. The parole agent found Pedro sitting behind his desk at the far end of the shop.

Pedro stood when he saw his friend walking toward him.

"Gringo! What a pleasure to see you again. Do you have something else to sell me this day?"

Dodge held out his hand, and Pedro shook it.

"Actually, I'm in the market for a car."

Pedro looked around the shop. "As you can see, I don't have much."

Dodge pulled out a wad of cash and flashed it, watching Pedro's eyes as he stared at the bills and the prospect of having more American money.

"Two grand." Dodge put the money in his hand.

As Pedro smiled, the crow's feet at the corner of his mouth pushed his cheeks up and made his eyes narrow.

"I have just the thing for you," he said.

"Is it reliable?"

"It has never let me down."

Pedro nodded at the boy, who ran out of the building and into the street. A few minutes later, the boy returned, driving a black pickup truck with oversized tires and a light bar attached to the roof.

Dodge shook his head. "I was thinking about something a little less conspicuous."

"Unfortunately, you have come to me when business is slow. This is all I have now."

Dodge thanked Pedro and told him he could find the truck parked on the street behind the US embassy in three days. The keys would be inside the fueling door.

"I'm keeping the money, even if I get my truck back."

"A deal is a deal. Keep the money. Leave the truck or pick it up at the embassy. That's completely up to you."

Once on the road, Dodge placed another call using the cell phone Delgado gave to him at the compound. He didn't know if the phone was being tracked in real-time, so he parked under an overpass to help shield his location from GPS b efore turning on the device.

Delgado picked up on the first ring.

"You sent men to take me out. That was a mistake."

"Agent Dodge. How nice to hear from you."

"Listen, dickhead, your guys are lying face up in the morgue. One's family will be able to identify the remains. The other, not so much. You shouldn't have killed Juan, because if that's the best you've got left, I feel pretty good. And you should be worried."

"What can I say? I'm an opportunist. I saw an opening and took it. And rest assured, what I lack in professional men, I make up for in sheer volume. I have plenty of men willing to shed their blood for me."

"Well, now I know your word is as useless as tits on a boar hog."

"You should not talk to me in such away. Think about Agent Williams and his lovely wife and kids before you disrespect me again."

"Yeah, yeah, yeah. Save the routine for somebody it might impress. Right now, you need to listen to what I have to say. I know all about your son—that young man with us at the compound the other day. I also know about Maria's mother, the prostitute you banged one night while high as a kite on your own supply."

"Neither of those things is a secret. As for my son...it's not that people don't know about him. It's just that over time, those with knowledge of his existence either died off, or forgot about him and his ties to me. Except for me, that is. That was not the case with Maria. Too many people knew, and I needed to make an example out of her mother."

"That's a nice story, and I'm sure it helps collect against lowlife debtors on the streets. But I know the truth. I know she is alive. I also know she has been singing like a canary ever since they turned her."

"Excellent. You have found my secrets. Unfortunately for you, those that know too much have a way of becoming food for my dogs."

Dodge sensed anger in his voice for the first time. But there was something else—fear. A hint desperation in the man's voice.

"Anyway, unlike a greasy dope pusher," Dodge said, "I keep my word. The men responsible for putting Maria Delgado into that crate are José Melendez, Juan, who you already dispatched, and a tattooed guy who works at Bogotá's airport cargo area. I didn't get his name, but a blind man could pick him out of a lineup."

Delgado was quiet for a moment. "You have given me what I asked of you, and I will keep my end of the bargain. I'll text you the house's address in the Bosa District, where your pilot is being held. But know this, Agent Dodge. You, nor your pilot, will make it out of Colombia alive."

The text with the address came through as Dodge flipped the phone shut. He knew the pilot was still alive. Delgado planned to make examples out the two of them by feeding both to his dogs. Dodge wondered if the entire event would be streamed online, or if Delgado would mail invitations for in-person viewing. Either way, he didn't plan on being puppy chow.

He took the battery out of the phone and put both in the glove box before leaving the overpass's security. He pulled up a map on his other phone and typed in the address Delgado had just given him. The computer inside the smartphone did its thing in a fraction of a second and produced a driving map. Turns out, Dodge was only five minutes from where the pilot was being held, giving him the advantage. Delgado's men would know he was coming, but he could get there before they expected.

He pulled the truck to the side of the road and reached behind the seat to grab the black duffel bag Brown had been holding for him. Unzipped the bag and removed one of the RPGs and the shotgun. Filled his pockets with rounds for the shotgun and Glock until he became concerned about the weight affecting his mobility.

Time to make some noise.

CHAPTER 31

IN MOST SITUATIONS, Dodge would visit a home in person before attempting an entry. At a minimum, he would drive the surrounding blocks to locate escape routes and get a sense of the neighborhood. But preparation was not a luxury he had this time. He couldn't afford to be seen, and any car driving past the house that night would be a target of opportunity for the men inside. Dodge's only option was to use the map function on his phone to get a satellite view of the area, zooming in to see if he could see potential hazards.

He studied the map and saw that the information for this neighborhood was last updated in 2018. Three years—not too bad.

As he scrolled the map, the clarity decreased with each spread of his fingers as he tried to zoom to a street-level view. A fence surrounded the backyard and a small shed-like structure next to the house. An alley ran behind the houses, and he didn't see any poles that might hold streetlights. That's where he would make his entry.

Dodge knelt beside the far wall of the house next to the home the pilot was being held in. He watched for twenty minutes, noting the number of times he saw people in the windows peering down the street, awaiting his arrival.

The house he was hiding behind appeared abandoned. The only sign of activity was the beer bottles and drug paraphernalia littered across the front porch. The door was open and using the house as cover to reach the back alley that ran behind

215

the houses lining the street was viable. Cover was good, and concealment was better.

He readied the rocket launcher, locating a car through the viewfinder on the side of the device, parked thirty feet beyond the house. He lined it up with the correct sightlines based on his distance from the target. Steadied himself by taking a deep breath and exhaling. Again, inhale, exhale.

The trigger didn't squeeze like that of a handgun. It clicked like the trigger of a plastic toy gun, then a slight pause. The click seemed loud, and Dodge worried someone might hear it. But the rocket roared to life and shot off the end, fire and smoke trailing in its wake.

Since being out of the military, he hadn't shot any type of anti-personnel weapon in over a decade, and his poor aim showed it. The rocket hit the street five feet in front of the target, and a loud clank echoed off the surrounding homes. Dodge winced, but the explosive head didn't detonate until it slammed into the front grill of the car after bouncing two feet up off the street.

The car shot up three feet and flipped over on its top, engulfed in bright orange flames. Dodge leaped onto the abandoned home's front porch and ran through the open door, into the blackness inside, where he dropped to one knee and waited for the sound of people running from the house next door to investigate. Instead, what he heard was the sound of a door opening and footsteps coming from behind him.

He ducked out of sight, behind a knee wall that separated the front room from the adjacent room, clinging to the Glock and sliding his finger closer to the trigger. A man appeared, walking toward the front door. He stopped on the porch to watch the commotion down the street. Dodge creeped to the back door and into the yard before reaching the alley. He peered over the fence and ducked back down after creating a mental picture of the backyard from his glimpse.

He saw no goons, but the building he saw on the map was not a shed. It was a doghouse. The lack of planning resulted in him not running more than a few scenarios. He was forced to prioritize and chose what he would do once in the house, and the best way to get out if things went south.

He picked up a small rock and tossed it over the fence. It bounced off the concrete path leading to the back door. The attempt was met with silence—no dog on a chain, barking and running toward him. And no movement from inside the house.

Dodge climbed over the fence, using his upper body strength to pull his chest to the top of the fence. Pain shot up his leg, but he continued on, each leg pushing up against the boards in the fence until he could swing one leg over, then the other. He landed square but facing the fence. He spun around and crouched, waiting for anyone who might have heard him pop out the back door, and try to take a shot at him.

No one came. The distraction on the street was still working.

Dodge closed the distance between himself and the back door in six long strides, about twenty feet. He peered in through the window. The house was built in a shotgun configuration—meaning, a person could see straight through to the other side by looking through the front or back doors.

He could make out three men, all of whom were standing on the front porch or in the doorway. He turned the doorknob, cautious not to move too fast and have the mechanism squeak and click. The door cracked open a few inches. After another quick peek through the window, he placed the Glock in his waistline, then pushed open the door with the barrel of a Remington Model 870 twelve-gauge shotgun. The door swung into the house and to the left, allowing Dodge to see the man standing in the doorway at the front of the house.

The house had two bedrooms, both at the back of the home. The doors were open, and Dodge glanced into both rooms. Empty.

There was no basement or second floor. Also, no pilot.

He placed the bead at the end of the shotgun's barrel, over the man's chest. As Dodge began to back away, toward the rear entrance of the house, the man in his sights swiveled and their eyes locked. Dodge held his finger up to his lips in a shushing gesture. The man's mouth opened, and a blast from the shotgun slammed him in the chest, knocking him through the door and into one of the other men standing on the front porch.

The third man on the porch spun around. He fired three shots toward Dodge, through the front window, covering the living room floor with pieces of broken glass and shards of wood from the window's framing. But none of the rounds found their intended target. Dodge had dropped to a prone position after firing the first shot, causing the rounds from the man on the porch to fly over him.

A second blast from the shotgun cleared the remaining window glass from the opening and forced blast debris and lead pellets into the neck and face of the man on the porch. If he wasn't dead, he would wish he was when the doctors plucked glass and metal from his head with tweezers.

The second guy, the one the man in the door fell into, rolled off the porch and ran down the street. *Smartest man in the world.*

But the veteran agent had forgotten how to do simple addition. Three people, plus the man he had encountered from the house next door, equaled four, not three.

Dodge felt the wood from the house siding embed into his neck and arm. The shot had missed him, barely.

Dodge dove from the porch, his shotgun tucked into his body, and rolled into the yard. He flipped until he was on his stomach, facing the house next door. He didn't aim. Just pointed the barrel toward the neighboring porch and squeezed off a round. Then he pumped in another shell and pulled the trigger again, repeating the process until the magazine was empty— four shots in all. At least two of the rounds found their target as the man leaped back into the house. He made it inside, but with a backside full of buckshot. He wouldn't be coming back out anytime soon.

Dodge rose to his feet and pulled a splinter of wood from his neck, then turned back to the wounded man on the porch. He was still alive, his hand raised, reaching out for help.

"Tell me about the pilot," Dodge said. "Where is he?"

The man stared up, blood running down his cheeks, pieces of the window frame embedded in every inch of his head.

"Help me."

"Tell me about the pilot, and I'll take pity on you."

The injured man hesitated for a moment, took a deep breath, and preceded to tell Dodge everything. When the would-be captors came upon the wreckage, the pilot had put three rounds into the first man dumb enough to approach the cockpit. The other men in the group unleashed a hail of lead into the wreckage, much ending up in the pilot's chest and head. A round ricocheted, hitting the fuel tank, and the plane exploded. Everything, including the pilot, turned into a pile of ash in a matter of minutes.

It was all a trap, from the moment Dodge boarded the plane for Colombia, to the events unfolding at that moment. And he had fallen for all of it, forcing him to play his opponent's game and break another rule: play offense, not defense when in trouble.

"Is that everything?"

The man nodded. Dodge put a shotgun round into his face.

He could hear the sirens closing in. They had the European sound to them—a short woo-woo, not the long wail of US sirens—and were only blocks away by the time he reached his truck.

He pushed the accelerator all the way to the floor, and the truck leaped forward, its tires breaking free from the pavement. He maneuvered the truck between cars that lined both sides of the street, barely missing a few onlookers who had come out to get a better view of the chaos unfolding on their block. The truck slid sideways as he made a left turn at the end of the block, his rear tires climbing the curb and onto the sidewalk before he could straighten back out, leaving a mailbox flipped on its side in the vehicle's wake.

He slowed when he saw the approaching red flashing lights, and even pulled to the side of the road to make sure the emergency vehicles could pass. The driver of the fire engine tipped his hat. Once the convoy of three fire trucks, two ambulances, and four police cars passed, Dodge pulled back out into the street and headed toward the embassy.

Once out of the barrio, he pulled over in a parking lot filled with people and picnic tables. Food trucks and pushcarts selling local fare and alcohol lined the edges of the lot. Dodge was hungry and thirsty, and needed to get his bearings before driving back to the embassy. He needed to call Brown to tell him the pilot was not at the house and was likely dead. Leaving anyone behind was hard. But in reality, if the pilot was alive— and Dodge doubted that very much—he wouldn't be for much longer. Dodge could do little to save him without knowing his location, and time had run out.

Brown answered on the first ring. "You will not believe this! The woman, the girl's mother, she is alive, and she is not in Brazil. She is right here in Bogotá."

Brown explained how White had booked a charter plane for Bogotá after Dodge had called her. She was in a panic. Brown said he had never seen her this worked up before. At one point, at the airport, he thought she was going to punch the ticket counter lady over an overbooked flight status. White ended up having to wait for the next flight, which left two hours later.

"She was furious," he said.

Brown drove to the tiny airstrip, and instead of flying to the secret airfield in Bogotá, he risked landing at the main airport. If he arrived before her, he could tail her from there. And that is what he did, following her across town and into the mountains. When she turned onto the road that led to Delgado's compound, Brown drove back down the road, stopped when it met the highway, and waited for Dodge to call him.

"Why would White be meeting with Delgado?" Brown said.

Dodge thought about the question for a second, then answered with the only explanation he could come up with.

"She's selling out her informant."

"Why the hell would she want to do that? She is at the top

of the list for a slot at headquarters. Why would she throw that all away?"

"Because she's on the take. We know that smuggling drugs through seaports and airports happens every day, all over the world. Multiple smugglers use the same exit points to get their products to market, and all require people on the inside to get the job done. Tell me, Brown, was she a part of any busts at the port in the last five years?"

"Of course she was. That was her job."

"Did any of the busts involve Delgado's product?"

"A few. But most were rival cartels." Brown paused. "Come to think of it, some of the largest busts came from rival gangs. The ones that involved Delgado were small, and not harmful to his bottom line."

"There you have it," Dodge said. "She isn't smuggling for him. She's beating down the competition. My guess is, it pays well and gives her a feeling of moral superiority, pretending her actions keep dangerous drugs off the street back in the States."

"While she profits off the chaos and death," Brown sneered.

"I guess we don't need that picture of White with her source anymore," Dodge said.

"Well, I got a shot of her driving onto El Jefe's compound. Clear as a bell, right through the passenger side window. Her big stupid face with that smirk. I got to tell you; I never liked that bitch."

"That may be useful," Dodge said. "Can you send the picture to my phone?"

"Sure. It's on its way. What are you planning to do?"

"I'm going to make the two of them find a new target. One that poses more of a threat than Maria Delgado's mother. At least, for the immediate future. I need you to get back to the embassy and tell Ambassador Contreras everything that has happened. Tell him I'll be back after I handle a few things. Let the Marine at the gate know he might have to be fast on that barrier when I get back. I don't know how much heat I may bring with me."

"But you don't know where she is," Brown said.

"I don't have to. She'll come to us."

Dodge hung up the phone, ate his empanada and finished his beer while sitting in the cab of his truck. The food was excellent. The beer, not so much.

Dodge tossed the trash behind the seat and started the truck, which rumbled to life. It was now close to midnight. He hoped Delgado had not yet made a move on White's informant. Only one way to find out. But first, he needed to make a call to Agent Williams to let him know the FBI was looking for Maria's mother in the wrong place. They needed to focus their efforts in Bogotá, emphasizing barrios or small villages just outside the city limits.

Agent Williams had an idea on how to draw out Maria's mother, whose name turned out to be Carmen Montenegro. He would have the local news put out a news blast about Maria Delgado's death. It would say the FBI is looking for tips in finding an unknown girl's family and is offering a reward to any credible leads. For good measure, the Bureau would purchase a front-page ad in the local paper, with her picture at the center of the ad. Agent Williams said he could have it out tomorrow. He had some contacts in the local island press willing to help with their Colombian counterparts.

Dodge said, "The only problem I see is, how do we get White and Delgado not to move on her until tomorrow?"

"Do you listen to the news at all?" Agent Williams said. "Mother nature has already taken care of that for us."

"I don't speak Spanish. I have no clue what they're babbling about on the radio."

"You should try one of those language programs. I bet your department might even pay for it."

"So, they can stick me with another caseload. No thanks."

"Well, the Bureau just put out a message to all its offices in Colombia and the surrounding countries. The mountains are getting pounded with rain. Flash floods. Washed out roads. The whole nine yards. Miss White will be stuck up there until morning. And she won't tell him where the woman is and give up her only leverage until she is off that mountain, with the money in her hand."

"He could just torture her and drag the information out of her," Dodge said.

"I thought about that."

"And?"

"Delgado is a smart guy who does his homework. He would know all about Miss White and her reputation. Meaning, he knows she would die before she gives up anything. He might choose to kill her later. But for now, he needs her."

The theory seemed right. A dead White was of no use to Delgado. He needed to know what she knew.

"All right, do it," Dodge said.

"What are you going to do?"

"See if I can't push her over the edge."

"Be careful, Dodge." Agent Williams disconnected.

Before leaving, the parole agent checked the battery on his phone. He had two bars left, about twenty-five percent. He hit the recent calls button and scrolled to White's number. Used his thumb to press the Send button.

CHAPTER 32

WHITE FELT HER PHONE VIBRATE in the purse she had clutched in her hands. But the phone wasn't the reason the bag was close to her. She was protecting the Kimber Micro 9mm tucked into a tearaway pocket.

She reached for the phone, looking at the number on the screen.

"It's him," she sneered.

"Answer it," Delgado said. "And put it on speakerphone."

White hit the Accept Call button and placed the phone on the corner of an antique cherry desk in Delgado's office.

"Hello, Agent Dodge," she said, her voice calm and harsh.

"Miss White. I assume El Jefe is there. You know, it's not polite to place someone on speakerphone without first asking."

"What makes you think I would be in the company of such a man?"

Delgado's phone made a *ding* sound—the alert he used to notify of a new message. She watched as he pressed the screen and retrieved it. Delgado squinted as he stared at his phone. Then he turned his phone around and held it out at so White could see the message. Her face became flush, and her ears burned.

"Where did you get that picture?" she said.

"Turns out," Dodge said, "sitting behind a desk has softened you up a little. You need to get back into the field and learn how to spot a tail."

"Brown!" she said. "I should've known the little prick would turn on me one day. He is weak. He never could do the hard jobs, which is why he works at the embassy. No blood to wash off your hands behind the secure walls."

Dodge chuckled. "He was good enough to get you."

"He'll be dead soon enough, and so will you." Her voice shook with anger.

And just as fast, it returned to calm.

"Why don't you and the traitor come on up for a visit. Mister Delgado is a gracious host."

He glared at White.

She rolled her eyes at him. "For God's sake, they have a picture of me driving onto your property. He knows I'm here with you. Say hello to Agent Dodge."

"Let's dispense with the pleasantries," Dodge said. "I know everything. For instance, I know the pilot is dead. Don't worry. I'll find the person responsible, and they will pay for it. I know all about your two's little drug smuggling ring at the docks in Cartagena. White, you would turn a blind eye to his shipments and make sure any competitors didn't make it to market. Sure, you would hit one of his small shipments so as not to arouse suspicion. But nothing larger than a few kilos. I'm guessing El Jefe hardly knew it was missing."

White tried to talk, but Dodge left no gap in the conversation.

"I also know about Maria Delgado's mother, Carmen Montenegro."

"She is dead." A ball of spit formed in the corner of Delgado's mouth.

"There is no need for the lies anymore," Dodge said. "I think we have come too far to revert to that phase in our relationship. Anyway, I know about her. And as I'm sure you already know from Miss White, your old lover is alive and well."

"That is a business problem I plan to remedy, soon," White said. "You and Brown, I'll do for pleasure."

"How's the weather up there in the mountains? I heard a heavy rainstorm could wash out a mountain road, making it unpassable at night. Cars just fall off the side of the road and get swallowed up by the jungle, never to be seen from again. My guess is, you already know this. Or you would be back in town already, meeting with your informant."

"Agent Dodge, I'll be out of here soon. I'll find you and Brown and the whore. You will find out what it's like when I'm in the field. There won't be enough of you left to feed to Delgado's dogs."

"Looking forward to your arrival." Dodge hung up.

White looked at her host. "Is it true about the mountain roads?"

He nodded. "Many people go missing every year on mountain roads in Colombia. Even I don't drive them at night. It would be best if you waited until morning."

White was as furious as she had ever been. Dodge had ruined everything. There was no need to give Carmen Montenegro to Delgado now. She had zero bargaining chips left. She would leave this place at first light and get her revenge—starting with Dodge.

Dodge spent the rest of the night in his truck, driving around town. His mind was all over the place, and he needed to calm it so he could think straight.

He knew White would come for him. But he didn't know if Delgado would send his goons to kill him as well. The one thing he was sure about was that the drug lord himself would not make an appearance.

Agent Williams called and said the local radio and TV stations were already airing Maria Delgado's story. The newspaper was less inclined to plant the story in that day's edition. They would run it tomorrow.

Dodge guessed Delgado had seen the coverage. And if not, someone in his organization would soon call to let him know.

After finding a quiet spot to pull off the road, Dodge slept for two hours in his truck, and the alarm on his phone woke him at

5:00 a.m. The rock-face side had a natural indentation covered overhead with branches from a tree that had sprouted in a crack in the stone. The indentation was directly after a hairpin turn in the road, so anyone coming from atop the mountain would have to come to almost a complete stop to maneuver the sharp turn. He could see any headlights bouncing off the side of the trees before they reached his location.

The rain had stopped during the night, worrying Dodge that White may have left the compound the second the rain stopped, causing him to miss her. He didn't pass another vehicle along the way and assumed she would leave first thing in the morning.

He didn't have to wait long.

The headlights lit the side of the mountain, showing the bare rock face and the few plants that clung to its side. The roar of the engine echoed as its soundwaves bounced around the curve toward Dodge. He heard the engine whine slowly, and within a few seconds, the vehicle had made the turn, its lights now focused on his truck. The car stopped; its headlights extinguished.

With a flick of a switch, the lights of the truck flashed on. Then a small toggle switch mounted on the dash engaged the fog lights, each one like a mini sun. Dodge could see White with ease as she tried to shade her eyes from the onslaught of manufactured light.

He heard the first shot ricochet off the side of the surrounding rocks. The second hit the metal of his driver's side fender. Shots three and four slammed into the grill, putting a hole in the radiator and knocking out one headlight.

Dodge remained motionless. She had no chance of seeing him. He watched as White opened the car door and swung her arm over the top of the doorframe, pistol pointing at the truck. She used the door for cover and fired two more rounds into the windshield where he should've been.

Six shots. None of them hit the intended target.

Brown had told him she liked to carry a small semi-auto pistol in her purse, with a single stack magazine—six rounds.

White approached the truck, the barrel of her gun focused on the driver's side of the windshield. She grabbed the door handle and slung it open. A single shot echoed through the cabin, but no one was home.

Seven shots. *She must have had a round in the pipe with a full magazine.*

She needed to reload. Dodge listened for the sound of a magazine being ripped from its home in the gun's grip, and when he heard it, he stepped out of his hiding spot behind the truck, his Glock raised and finger on the trigger, breaking a cardinal sin in weapons training: *never put your finger on the trigger until you're ready to fire.* But he didn't know how good White was, and fractions of seconds could be the difference between who gets off the mountain and who stayed behind, dead.

"Drop your weapon," he said, as White spun in his direction, her weapon in one hand, and an empty mag in the other. "Don't do it. I'll kill you right here."

The two faced off like two gunfighters from the old West. A Louis L'Amour novel come to life. Their eyes locked, waiting for the other to make a move. The two stood still and silent for a minute.

Then Dodge saw something. A tell. White's gaze darted toward her gun hand for just a fraction of a second. Had he blinked, he would have missed the cue. But he saw it, and he shot her in the head. The bullet entered the bridge of her nose, carving a path through her skull cavity, and exited on the opposite side. Her body fell back through a red mist of blood and gray matter. The CIA agent was dead before she hit the ground.

Dodge didn't have time to rest. He needed to get rid of the body before anyone else came driving down the mountain road, looking for him.

He grabbed the weapon and magazine from White's hand, disassembled it, and threw its pieces in three different directions over the edge, into the jungle below. Then he carried her body to her car, shoved her into the driver's seat, and fastened the seatbelt to hold in in place. Next, he turned the headlights back on so that if anyone found the car, they would believe the driver lost control and careened over the cliff at night.

Dodge removed the grenade from the RPG and jammed the end containing the propellant into the front grill. He turned the steering wheel toward the cliff and put the transmission in drive. The car lurched forward and picked up speed before sliding over the edge of the mountain and out of sight. The sound of metal crunching and bending echoed as the car bounced off the rock face on its way to the bottom. It landed in the jungle and exploded on impact. Next, he took a little dirt and spread it over the area to hide the blood, then made a quick sweep of his footprints with a leafy tree branch.

He still had to deal with the hole in the truck's radiator and add enough water to make it back to town.

A small stick with some tree sap plugged the spot. And thanks to the rain, there were puddles of water everywhere. He topped off the radiator with fluid, spun the truck around, and headed for town. Once back in the city, he placed one last call to Delgado, who answered on the first ring.

"White is gone. They may never find her body. And even if they do, there won't be enough to identify her."

"Saves me the trouble of killing her myself. I should thank you."

"I was a little disappointed that you weren't in that car with her. I really wanted to put a bullet in that stupid face of yours."

"You'll never get the chance again. But don't worry, I'll get you. You'll never see me coming. I'll hire doctors to keep you alive while I torture everyone you know right in front of you. See you around, Agent Dodge."

The phone went dead. Dodge didn't doubt the words Delgado had spoken, and he wasn't excited about the idea of looking over his shoulder for the foreseeable future.

He had to get back to the embassy. He needed to get back to St. Thomas for Agent Williams and his family. For Nikki, too.

CHAPTER 33

DODGE ARRIVED BACK at Cyril E. King Airport in Charlotte Amalie at 10:00 a.m. the next day. Brown and the ambassador had escorted him to the airport in Bogotá. They said it was for his safety, but he believed they just wanted him out of their hair and out of Colombia.

On the ride to the airport, the exhausted agent filled the two men in on the previous night's events. He told them his plan was to lie in wait for White on the road back to town and bring her back alive. But it was still dark, and the road was wet when she made the hairpin turn. Dodge had flipped on the truck's high beams to blind her and force her to stop, but she hit the accelerator. He could only guess that she meant to hit the brake but got confused, or her foot slipped off the brake and onto the gas pedal. Either way, she lost control of the vehicle and drove over the side of the mountain. He assured the men that the explosion when the car hit the ground killed her, if she wasn't already dead, and burned any evidence away.

Dodge felt the two men didn't buy his story, but they had no vested interest in proving him a liar. They both wanted this to go away with as little attention as possible. A car accident for a US citizen in Colombia's mountains was a perfect whitewash.

As he walked off the jetway, he saw Agent Williams waiting next to the departure and arrival counter. He waved.

"What, you just couldn't go another day without seeing me?" Dodge said.

"Thought you might need a ride."

The two men shook hands.

"Let's get out of here," Dodge said. "I miss my boat."

The two men got into a sedan parked in the law enforcement spot reserved for officers responding to calls for help at the airport.

"New ride?" Dodge said.

"I had a minor accident while you were playing soldier in Colombia."

"Under control now? Or do you need my help again?"

Agent Williams bellowed a laugh. "I hope I never need your help again. No offense."

Dodge smiled. "I get that a lot."

"Seriously, though. Thank you. You got those responsible for McCaffrey's and Maria Delgado's deaths. I never could've done it without you. Unfortunately, no one will ever know the truth about what you did."

"I didn't get all of them." Dodge looked out the passenger side window, at the bay on the other side of the access road.

Agent Williams put the car in gear and backed out of the parking spot. Then he placed the transmission in drive and paused, looking at Dodge.

"By the way...about your boat."

"What about my boat? The only thing you had to do was not let anything happen to it. I would take care of the bad guys, and you take care of *Kelly's Dream!*"

Agent Williams smiled. "*Kelly's Dream* is fine. Your friend down at the docks, that Sebastian fellow, saw someone in a small raft milling around your boat one evening. He contacted the Coast Guard, who sent a patrol boat to check it out. The men in the dinghy hit land and disappeared before the Coasties arrived. Still, after checking several boats in the harbor, including yours, they found a small explosive attached to the hull of *Kelly's Dream*. They removed the device. It was amateur hour, and the Coast Guard's explosives diver said he wasn't sure if the device would have worked or not. It seems that in their haste to make the bomb, their efforts to make it watertight had failed. Eventually, the device would have been waterlogged and detached from your hull and sank to the bottom of the bay."

"That son of a bitch tried to blow up my boat. I thought he might let well enough alone."

"Who? Delgado? He isn't the let-things-go type."

"I should've killed him. I should've driven to his compound and shot an RPG right through the front door of his house. Then went inside and shot him in the head. His dogs could've finished the job from there."

"Jesus, Dodge. He really got under your skin. Don't worry. I doubt he'll follow you to the mainland when you leave Saint Thomas. You are leaving, right?"

"Maybe in a week or two. To be honest, I don't work as hard at my job as I did on this vacation."

Agent Williams pulled an envelope out from his shirt pocket and handed it to Dodge.

"What's this?"

"A little extra to cover your...expenses. I hope you don't mind. It's a check. Thought you might need to go to the bank."

With that, the two men rode in silence to the pier, shook hands, and patted each other on the shoulder—the kind soldiers leaving the battlefield give each other.

Dodge turned and walked to the end of the pier, where Sebastian waited in his yellow plastic chair. He stood as soon as he saw his friend coming.

"Welcome back, my friend. I fueled 'er up this morning."

"Thanks for looking after her. They told me what you did, and I appreciate it."

He held out his hand for Sebastian to shake, slipping the rest of the cash he had left over from what he'd taken off his adversaries in Colombia. Sebastian tried to refuse the money, but Dodge was having none of it. He ignored the pleas to take the money back, jumped in his dinghy, fired up the motor, and pushed away from the pier, heading out to *Kelly's Dream*. He wondered if he should change the name of his boat. Kelly had wanted him to use the boat to get away from his work. To relax and get straight with the world. All he had done since he owned her was more work and cause more death and destruction. *Kelly would be pissed.*

He tied the dinghy off, climbed the ladder to the board, and fired up the generator. It was hot in the cabin. Once it cooled down, he stripped off his clothes, tossed them in the waste can, and climbed into a hot shower to wash the grime, along with the memories from the last week, down the drain. When finished, he put on clean clothes for a trip to cash his check at the bank and see an old friend.

The sound of a small electric motor moving away in the distance wrestled the parole agent from his slumber. He grabbed his weapon and climbed the steps from the cabin to the deck. After scanning the deck first, then the water, he saw nothing but the ripples left behind from a small watercraft.

Then he noticed a brown envelope sitting on the captain's chair. He felt a hand run down his back, and her soft lips on his shoulder.

"What is it?" Nikki said.

"I thought I heard something."

Nikki looked around. "Come back to bed." She brushed her hand across the front of his shorts. "I'd say you're ready for another go."

Dodge turned and kissed her. "I'll be down in a second. Let me just make sure everything is where I left it."

Nikki pinched his butt and disappeared into the cabin's darkness.

There were no identifying markings on the envelope's face. He untied the string used to close the top and dumped its contents onto the chair. A cell phone.

Dodge looked back at the cabin entrance to see if Nikki was lingering about, before powering on the device. After a few seconds, the screen lit up and a video popped up. The caption said, *Play me.* He took one more look around, then pushed the little sideways triangle.

The video was in black and white and grainy, but he recognized what he was seeing. In the Air Force, he had watched a video taken from the nose cone of fixed-wing fighters and drones. Then the video switched to night scope. He could make out the shape of an extensive structure. There were heat signatures, human-shaped and moving, at each corner of the building. Two men stood next to a vehicle that Dodge could tell was running because of the heat plumes escaping from the exhaust at the vehicle's rear. Thirty seconds passed, and one man by the running car got in the driver's side and drove away from the building. The vehicle disappeared as the screen flashed white. Next, the camera zoomed in on the second man. Dodge could see him running toward the house. The camera zoomed out, showing the area from a higher altitude. Then another flash of white light, filling the entire screen, and the feed ended. Seven words flashed on the screen—*Justice for Maria. Sleep well, my friend. —B.*

Dodge smiled. He could now stop looking over his shoulder. Well, less than usual, anyway.

He turned the device off, pried the back cover off, removed the battery, and tossed the phone over one side of the boat, the battery over the other. He let out a low laugh and stepped back into the cabin. After climbing into bed, he lay his head on Nikki's chest as she ran her fingers through his hair.

They had set the world right. He could finally relax.